JOURNEY

Part III of III

VOLUME I

WITH ANY JOURNEY OF SIGNIFICANCE...

WISE TRAVELERS KNOW

UNEXPECTED EVENTS SHAPE THE FUTURE.

CONCLUDING...

THE LOVE STORY OF THE CENTURY

Never stop believing in the magic^{tm}

For more information about Journey, to order bulk copies, or to have comments directed to the author, send an email to: catlansamuels@gmail.com

About our books, visit: www.treborarthurpublishing.com

Paperback: 978-0-9884957-6-0

Kindle: 978-0-9884957-7-7

Edited by Denise Semion, Peggy Schaefer

Front cover art and design by Erin Maureen Wirth

Book photos, are by the author, in various places around the world

Google Search,   **Journey Catlan Samuels**

Facebook: **Catlan Samuels**

Search for the Journey trilogy
on the internet using the words:

Journey Catlan Samuels

Part I

Tis not so much the path we take that counts,
What counts, is how we choose to travel the
path…

352 pages

https://www.amazon.com/Journey-Part-I-III-
1/dp/0988495716

Part II

When you step on it, sometimes, it pushes
back…

374 pages

https://www.amazon.com/Journey-Part-II-III-
Continuing/dp/0988495724

Part III

With any journey of significance, wise travelers
know unexpected events shape the future.

300 pages

For

Peg

No one else

has made exploring the world

such a blessing;

you have brought joy, laughter and love to my journey!

And our journey is just starting to unfold…

Dear Journey Traveler,

Part III picks up where our friends left us in Part II.

Part III concludes our tale for Torrin, Dessa and friends, however, as you will experience, you may feel you are part of the story. And, you will realize, this journey has followed you to where you are and will never leave you alone.

Catlan Samuels

Journey's Three Parts:

In Journey, Part I, you meet Torrin, Dessa and the people of the north. For some unexplained reason, both Torrin and Dessa have been chosen for a purpose that is bigger than themselves, or anyone around them. They must endure fate to discover their true purpose.

The purpose? People will fall in love, suffer and die along the way for the true purpose to be understood. And in the end, we find evil stands in the way of true love. Love that is the purpose. A love that is bigger than love itself.

In Journey Part II, all must be lost and then evil must be conquered, with a twist of fate, of course. And the power of true love, for others, becomes evident, even amid tragedy.

The purpose is complex, involving love, suffering, mortality and more. Throughout their journey, characters encounter challenges revealing the presence of evil as an impediment and an opportunity to grow. Ultimately, it becomes evident the purpose revolves around a profound concept - one surpassing conventional understanding.

Journey Part III, invites you to tread deeper into the fabric of the amazing world of these people, exploring the edges of not only what they know, but what they will change. Every twist and turn is laden with meaning. Every chapter unfurls as a tapestry, woven with threads of love, loss, and triumph. The characters, who have captured hearts from the beginning, now face their ultimate reckoning. Every word, every step impacts the future where choices are not merely personal, they are universal in impact. Through joy and despair, fates intertwine in ways both unexpected and inevitable, beckoning you to reflect on your own journey, as never before.

And by the way, this ends right in the middle of your heart.

Imagination is everything.

It is the preview of life's

coming attractions.

Albert Einstein

Growth...

I love those who can **smile** in trouble,

who can gather **strength** from distress,

and **grow** brave by reflection.

Tis the business of **little minds** to shrink,

but they whose **heart** is firm,

and whose **conscience approves** their conduct,

will **pursue** their **principles**

unto death.

Leonardo da Vinci

Prologue

Ambling is over.

The easy part is over.

Truth is dawning its hard rasp
like nails on dry cracked skin.

For anything to become clean,
something else must become dirty.

For anything to become dirty,
it must be seen as a weed.
strong and supple.
Yet ultimately, unwanted.

When ambling turns into purpose,

purpose creates energy,

energy enables momentum!

The momentum of nature is what propels us to a future of blessings.

First, foremost, last and always,

Mháthair Nature will have the last word.

Background and Origins of the JOURNEY trilogy...

So very often readers, friends and family (who are very supportive – for which I am grateful) ask me to tell the story about the origins of Journey. And after having repeated the tale below numerous times, many told me (and they were quite frank about it), that the origin of this trilogy should be told to you, faithful reader. These friends have implored to me that this little background adds something because the underpinnings of Journey come from real life experience and drama. Yes, mixed with more than a little anguish, but nonetheless, 'tis real.

So here it is for you if you are interested in a bit of real life romantic drama. (deep breath on my part)…

…At an exceedingly difficult, yet telling time in my life, I was in a new and intensely dynamic (very passionate) relationship with an extremely energetic, smart and incredibly beautiful lady. Things were quite exciting as they often are early in relationships, but there was something nagging at me. The nag was deep in my head, and it was not a good one. But of course, I was blinded as many men are, by the passionate events taking place. Anyway, it was, I would find much later, a tiny yet very accurate little voice that was giving me a warning – and it was quite some time before I really learned to listen to that voice (foolish me).

OK, back to this rather exotic (oh my, VERY exotic) and compelling relationship – as I had said, things were very exciting and I had sat down to compose a "love letter" to this lady (yes, I am a bit of a romantic). This letter would tell her from the bottom of my happily beating heart how I felt about her, and about our connection. It was important for her to know how she made me sparkle; how special she was and how much her meaningful friendship mattered to me. Please understand, it was a deep and personal letter, and my plan was to write it as a short adventure/romance story – it was to be something different. In my head the plan was to read it aloud over candles and wine with all sorts of flourish and panache to truly express the depth of the feelings I had at the time.

Alas, it did not work out. The letter (a.k.a. story) was about half written when she told me, and quite nicely too, that our relationship was over. It was not working for her, and she needed to move on. At least she had the strength of character to do it in person and with real tears.

To be honest with you, I was devastated.

So, that night, while rain soaked the world outside and grief poured from my heart, I was but one small step away from turning that love letter into a forever gone, shredded pile of worthless trash. Most likely destined as blown-in brown recycled insulation for some cold northern attic with nothing left but the memory and a little dust.

Instead, I decided to bid her and rather hot memories of our lost relationship a final farewell. This small act was to reread what I had written and see if after the "fall" I still felt the same way about her and us as I had when I started this little adventuresome love letter.

The rest, as they say, "is now history."

That night, after I read the story, I did not sleep. Instead, as the rain pounded and the lightning blasted the sky, I sat and wrote. I wrote with my head, my heart and through my tears. That night Dessa, Quillan, Torrin and all the characters were born of love and loss, of fear and courage; of anger and justice – all of what we face in life. The whole thing just poured out and continues to do so.

You see, Journey is not just a story – it's real... And so with a little research, a long grasp back to my ancestors (thanks to some thoughtful digging on the part of my cousin Herb in Paris) from the old northland and a dash of faith, I let the characters go, and go they do, on their Journey.

Take your time as you read, pay attention to the details and embrace the story. You see, as you will find, you are living this story every day.

Welcome to the Love Story of the Century.

Words

The language you encounter as you make your way through Journey is an eclectic mix of (very or verra) old and new. In addition to distinct local vernaculars and dialects, many of the more interesting words come from ancient Gaelic and Celtic cultures, as well as some very colorful, yet old-fashioned street slang. The more obscure words are listed below. When a word is used for the first time, it is translated for you, such as, athair (father).

Word	Description
antikythera	Ancient Greek orrery (mechanical model of the solar system, used to represent relative positions and motions of stars and heavenly bodies), considered the oldest known example of an analog computer. Device also used to predict astronomical positions and positions of ships on the oceans and seas. Often used with an Astrolabe
astrolabe	Used by mariners to determine latitude by measuring the angle between the horizon and Polaris, also called the North Star, the Pole Star, or Stella Maris (Star of the Sea).
athair mháthair	Father, mother in formal terms. Children often use a form of 'daddy or mommy.' We stick to the formal here to easily differentiate. See also seanathair, seanmháthair.
beòir	Beer – feminine form in Gaelic. See also 'leann'
borgmästare	Mayor or highest ranking government official in a town, usually serves at the behest of the federal government and at the pleasure of the nearest

	garrison commander.
bràmair	Affectionate word for girlfriend or boyfriend. Can be used in the feminine or masculine sense.
braw	'Very good,' common Scottish meaning: fantastic, great, brilliant… essentially all that's positive and wonderful.
buidheach	Drambuie like mix for whiskey, sweetens a drink or drink alone, aromatic. Means, 'The Drink that Satisfies.' Generally, a mix of fennel seeds, honey, fresh rosemary leaves and scotch.
buntàta	Gaelic for potato, also termed at tattie in modern times.
chac	Shit. Uttered often by folks as an angry slang term. Favorite term used by my grandmother in its English form. Excreted from cows and horses in large piles, often referred to as 'Road Apples.'
chéile	The Irish Gaelic term for wife.
chinking	Material between logs of a cabin to keep wind, snow, rain and small animals out. Most often clay, sometimes mixed with straw or moss. Historians have found evidence of crude concrete and mortar in the chinking of ancient dwellings.
chippering & twerping	Words of my own creation. When you have a forest full of animals, they make noise. This was the noise I could hear. Consider it the music of nature as heard by Catlan.
clach	A man's balls or scrotum, whichever you prefer.
convictive	Describes a low down, dirty, cheating miserable scoundrel.
crenels, merlons	Alternating pattern of walls and gaps in a fortress wall. Enables a defender to hide behind raised solid portion, known as merlons, then quickly move in front of the gap (crenels or embrasures).
curmudgeon	See muigean
damnú	Damn – see also mac an donais!

deamhan	The 'devil.' Derived from the Latin daemon (demon), refers to an evil spirit or a wicked person in norse mythology and folklore.
deartháir	The Irish Gaelic term for brother
deirfiúr	The Irish Gaelic term for sister
dòigh nàdair	"The Way of Nature." Can also refer to following a specific practice of being or being in a positive state.
dubisary	Odd foreign material that might cling to your face, like a wood chip or a bit of your supper.
fesker mah	Good evening.
galla	Gaelic street slang term for bitch.
go n-éirí leat	Good luck to you (Gaelic)
gnèitheach diabhail	Gaelic word said to indicate 'you are a sexy lady.' Gnèitheach diabhail, for sexy devil
helvete	A term generally used to tell someone to "go to hell," however is of very strong language and is more along the lines of, "Go to join the suffering of the damned."
Hnefatafl	Hnefatafl, family of ancient Northern European strategy board games (also known as Tafl) played on checkered or latticed gameboard with two armies of uneven numbers.
kauppasaksa	A form of master traveling salesperson selling finer goods (sakas is a term for "master"). A name given to early Norse traders. Also, a peddler.
knarfing	Not really a word, it's made up. Went to see Katie's horse, listened carefully to his eating grass; needed to describe horse chewing to honor Samoot who eats like I wish I could. The sound was amazing, the best way to describe it was "knarfing."
kuk, crann	Penis.
leann (beer), masc. form	Leann searbh - bitter (ale), leann trèicil - treacle/beastie beer (made w/ dark sweet syrup),

	leann nam biast - dregs/beastie beer
mac an donais!	Damn it! – see also damnú.
machicolation	Opening between the supporting corbels of a projecting parapet or vault of a gate through which defenders can drop stones or burning objects onto attackers. Fortress architecture.
math-ghamhainn (mathan)	Reduced form – mathan, Gaelic word for large brown bear. Celts venerated the mathan goddess, Artio, like a mother mathan they believed she offered protection. Brown mathans of the north are normally very gentle creatures, however can become VERY large.
merlons	See crenels
mháthair athair	Mother, father. Formal terms, children often use a form of 'daddy or mommy.' We stick to the formal here to easily differentiate.
muigean	Gaelic for curmudgeon; a disagreeable person.
neeps & tatties	Combination of potatoes and turnips, cooked together to resemble mashed potatoes. Other vegetables may be added as you like. A good way to use up produce before it goes bad.
nighean ponach	Gaelic for "girl" or "young female," child or adolescent. Gaelic for "boy" or "lad."
ò dhìol	Galic for 'oh my goodness' or if you want to add a sense of deity, it could mean 'oh my God.'
plucsh	After having spent years in the woods listening to the leaves fall in autumn, this is the best I could come up with to describe the sound of millions of leaves landing all around.
ponach nighean	Gaelic for "boy" or "lad." Gaelic for "girl" or "young female," child or adolescent.

refectory	In an institution where communal meals are taken; Latin, "reficere" meaning "to restore" or "remake." A 'dining room.'
rowan	Trees, like mountain ash, are a thicker shrub. Native throughout cool temperate regions of Northern Hemisphere, with highest species diversity in mountains. Some are fruit bearing.
seanathair seanmháthair	Grandfather, grandmother. Formal expressions of grandparents; children tend to choose a more informal name.
seidr	Ritual magic performed to convey messages from spiritual to mortal realm. Ceremonial actions used by Ipi (see also Völva).
sgiot	To scatter. In the context used, to go away.
silver penningar	We would regard it as a penny. Was the only coin in ancient northern culture, would be cut into pieces when a penny was too much. Gold was measured in bullion weight and given a value (was tremendously valuable).
slàinte mhath	"Cheers" in many countries over the world, (pronounced Slanj-a-va) is actually both Irish and Scots Gaelic.
scruvuling	A derogatory term to describe a person or group who are of a lower position and overall intelligence than yourself – such as "a scruvuling lot."
snappling	The sound a fire makes when it's just a quiet fire. Not loud crackling. Just snappling.
snèap	Swedish turnip. In Scottish it's 'neep.'
snèap is buntàta	Gaelic for Neeps and Tatties, traditional Scottish side of mashed potatoes and swede (rutabaga), goes with haggis or beef roast.
sporran	A type of purse used mostly by men since pockets were not available in most pantaloons or on a kilt.
spryte	Somewhat akin to a forest fairy but carry responsibilities. Unlike fairies; sprytes are playful,

	perform magic, are shapeshifters and tend to drink a lot.
tábhairne	Bartender, barkeep, mixologist.
tattie	Modern term for a potato. Gaelic is buntàta.
tuilli	A bastard.
tiadhan	Man's testicle. Times to use such a word are painful or filled with negative emotion.
uisgebeatha uisge	Aqua vitae is Latin for 'water of life,' which in Scots Gaelic translates as uisge beatha. At some point, possibly over centuries, uis ge became the modern word 'whiskey.'
verra	Very
Völva	A seeress, a mystic. Generally, a woman, with ability to foretell future events, "wise woman." Ipi is a Völva. See also seidr.

The Time...
- And -
The Land...

The story of Journey begins, as Part I states, *"a long time ago, before the mountains were fully tall and the seas very salty."* The place is actually a northern hemisphere environment with a very ancient Celtic/Gaelic flavor to it. Imagine a place not too distant from the Arctic Circle.

The time? Well, it will become more evident as you read; just suffice to say it was an extremely long time ago (before mathematics, before writing, before clocks, before lots of things...) with the origins of our main characters being in the far north. They were not privy to modern technology or practice (until now).

This tale is built on what is currently a commonly held truth, or could be myth (but the author feels, after considerable research and conjecture, the story is of probable reality). It is a story of such vast proportions and long-term dire consequences that the very roots of our cultural ideologies, as we know them would change if it became common knowledge.

As the story is told, a great civilization grew up in the far north of what we now know as Europe; one that built and held dear, many centuries before, the kind of culture and freedoms we enjoy as leading free societies of today. The people lived and protected some of the same ideologies practiced by hard-working, honest people of today. These folks held the same passions we hold for our natural right to the 'Pursuit of Happiness in a free society.'

For these northern folks though, their story ends on a sad note. These smart and advanced people did everything right except develop the written word. So, in the end, they could never really spread their ideas, save or archive history for the future and share their ideology, other than through the sharing of their stories. They are, as is the common thought amongst historians on much of a worldwide basis, "lost." Their whole way of thinking was lost with the demise of their society when they were conquered sometime during the dark ages.

Well maybe that's true, and maybe, just maybe, they had some other way to spread their political theories, passion for life, freedom and their version of truth?

There are some who say their ideas and way of life were crushed and lost. There are others who feel differently. You may find the truth lies here in this marvelous tale of love and deceit.

Or, maybe something else happened?

And it may cause you to rethink history as you believe you know it.

Most definitely, you should rethink the future, because there might be forces in charge whom you have not considered.

The JOURNEY Inn,
Characters
&
Places

For early readers of Journey manuscripts, a character synopsis was added and folks loved it; so here is a quick overview of each of our friends. You may want to read the descriptions now or wait until you run into them. It's your choice, really – it's your Journey now and you are in control! The little table to the right of each character is meant to give you a quick review should you need to come back and remind yourself of some details.

If you are new to Journey, this will put some perspective on the folk you are about to meet (I do suggest you read Parts I and II; our friends got into and out of so much trouble, you'll really want their background to understand true feelings and perspectives). For those of you who have ventured this far after reading Parts I and II, what follows may put to rest some of the mystery surrounding our friends. For others, well, it deepens...

The Journey Inn:

The original Journey Inn was a large robust, log cabin style inn located in the middle of the northern forest.

The place itself was monstrously old. In some places, Journey was two stories tall with a few special rooms upstairs.

The horses and animals appreciated the large, attached stables that sported sturdy stalls, a wide variety of solidly crafted tack and plenty of food.

An enormous woodshed full of dried timber to heat Journey during the angry winters that befall the area was attached.

During those days of captivity due to the weather flexing its might, the Great Room is where much of the life of the Journey Inn took place. The Great Room sports a huge stone hearth and fireplace (part of the lore of Journey in Part I) for heat and the constant drying of wet clothes. The room is full of large tables and many folks sleep there in the winter on top of the tables to stay off the cold floor.

To one side was the very innovative kitchen that produced enormous quantities of food and treats. The kitchen was adorned with a fruit cellar, running water, a large stove and baking hearth as well as a cooking fireplace.

The Journey Inn was the center of the world for all the people of the valley. They met there, had their festivals there in its broad clearings and found refuge from life's storms amongst their friends who live there.

Higher up in the valley are small fields where various crops are grown, these were used in the great kitchen of the Journey Inn. It's a short growing season, and all efforts were expended to bring in a good crop.

Alas, at the end of Part II, the original Journey Inn succumbed to a raging inferno. However, as you would expect from sturdy, hardworking people who love their land, the people of the valley and from Garwen's kingdom had already begun rebuilding before Torrin and Dessa left on the trail to head south and spread the idea that everyone should live as a free person.

Will you get to visit the new Journey Inn? We'll see. And if you get there, it may take on a whole new meaning!

Some Characters...

As you travel along the mystical paths of Journey, please consider, that this takes place a long time ago, when kings ruled and religious supremacy was growing. Everyday people, enjoying freedom of will and pursuing their own higher purpose was not a thing yet. Having these vital concepts become normal in the order of life will be an adventure, could get a bit bloody and doubtless will require a lot of trial and error.

You will meet countless transient characters along the way. Many of them bring learning, ideas or trouble to Torrin and Dessa. What you will find below are some of the more poignant folks either in Part III or they influenced the story from Parts I & II.

Some people we meet and then they go away, and we are sorry to see them leave. Some we usher out, some we, well, we play with, because they need to be played with (not always in nice ways you see...).

Yes, you will meet some children. In a child, there is often a truth or a purity of thought that matters to the world. As you meet these children, whether they are annoying or not, I ask you to do this: 'See what the child sees, and what they see may be of pure heart.'

With Journey, Part III you get to come along and experience what can happen. What can happen when you follow your heart and embrace your true purpose in life. Nobody said it would be easy.

Now on to the people and at the end, a few of the animals. The character's name appears in **bold print**, *quick facts in italics* after that, and then a short bit about each of them:

* * *

Ancropolis - *Partner to Chrisholm. Runs most of Eskil.*

Hard working, nice guy. Powerfully built, a little fast to anger, and the anger is told to be pretty destructive, especially if he is protecting Chrisholm. A pretty good thinker, but mostly a bit of a caveman. Runs the bar and oversees the kitchen work at Eskil. Big man, strong and capable, there is a soft side to him as he cares for Chrisholm.

* * *

Anton & Alvinia - *Previous kind and caring owners of Eskil.*

Anton is now a widower, having lost the gentle and loving Alvina to disease. His grey eyes are sad for his loss, yet he is kind and caring. He passed Eskil to Ancropolis and Chrisholm, the details are later in the book. Alvina was a classic Nordic blond; kind and tough at the same time, like a grandmother would be to children. In her eyes, everyone was her grandchild.

* * *

Bourdicca - *Captain of the garrison stationed at Kalmar. Upstanding soldier, takes orders without question. Caring man.*

Bourdicca, captain of the garrison stationed at Kalmar. Second in command, cares deeply for his commanding officer, Gustav. In Gaelic, Bourdicca' s name would be translated as Búadach, which means "victorious" or "successful," derived from the Celtic word "boudā,", meaning "victory". It's essentially the Gaelic equivalent of the name Victoria. He is the perfect soldier, follows orders, and has a soft side that somehow endears us to him.

* * *

Chrisholom - *Partner to Ancropolis. Connection with nature.*

Chrisholm is the significant other to Ancropolis and helps run Eskil, the local tavern in Kalmar (port city, a few days ride south of Journey). She runs the kitchen and is the main server for the evening, especially with the soldiers about. There is a connection with nature for Chrisholm that we have yet to understand. She is a is a tall blond, with green eyes.

* * *

Dessa - *Daughter of King Tarmon and Queen Gersemi. Grandfather (seanathair) is Gale. Blue eyes change to turquoise at danger, flaming red hair. Talks with and has an interesting relationship with the animals of the forest, dead on shot with bow and arrow.*

A princess, daughter of King Tarmon and Queen Gersemi (sister to the late Prince Kael). Tall young woman in her late teens with flowing waves of sturdy red hair, deep blue eyes and a 'dead on shot' with a bow and arrow (even atop a moving horse!); smart, nimble and bold (sometimes a little too bold?).

Dessa married a real miserable and nasty crumb by the name of Darius at the start of Part I. Darius had the bad manners of falling out of bed the third night of their short and miserable marriage, impaling himself on his knife (although he was such a rotten sod, no one really missed him). Though not clear at this time, the writer expects there might have been foul play involved. Dessa, although fast asleep when he fell, was charged with his murder and sentenced to be burned at the stake (ouch!). It is an old law in Tarmon's kingdom that anyone convicted of murder be burned at the stake – it helps to keep the peace. And in Tarmon's kingdom, no one is above the law (even the daughter of the king).

With the help of Sanura, (Dessa's personal maid) and her father (King Tarmon), Dessa was able to pull off a very spectacular and sneaky escape. The residents of Tarmon's kingdom thought she had burned; instead it was a miserable leach named Valdemar who had tried to rape her while she was under house arrest. And, when you consider it, at a very sensitive time of her incredibly young life. The escape meant she had to go far away, final destination, the Journey Inn. Dessa was outfitted at the kingdom's hunting lodge by the head stable master, Gale, for the trip. While at the lodge, although she received orders never to return, she was told to let them know she was OK. Dessa also discovered that Gale was her biological grandfather, since her named Grandfather Keegan was unable to sire children. Quite the triangle of lovers and carrying on preceding her birth.

Dessa learned much about herself on her way to the Journey Inn. She discovered her inner strength. She called upon this strength when she had to kill Haphethus, the twin brother of Darius. He had beat her with intent to rape in the deep forest. Fortunately, she had been tutored in the ways of self-defense by the wicked teacher Tallon, who in the end turned out to be a pretty good guy (and is brother to her half-brother Quillan, so he is her half-brother too).

Dessa arrived at the Journey Inn perched upon her horse (Uta) almost dead. In fact, she fell off Uta in a dead faint, neatly into the arms of Quillan (who at the time was quite taken by this ravishing, yet very filthy girl). He had no idea who she was until a bit later.

In time, Dessa found she was very attracted to the affable and kind young prince Torrin (it was a slow burn though, both were pretty unsure for a while). Her other suitor for a while was Quillan – until they discovered they were half brother and sister. Maybe the red hair on both should have been an early clue?

It seems Torrin and Dessa were meant for each other from a higher order. Once they found their love, strange and wonderful things began to happen to both of them. Dessa can talk to animals and many of them serve her needs in times of trouble (although there are some wicked animals of the wood who want her dead – as in the case of the old gray wolf Ahriman whose brother died trying to kill her at shepherd Phlial's cottage. He almost succeeded and she has the scars to prove it.).

Dessa's green eyes turn turquoise when she senses danger. She is very lethal when she needs to be that kind of person.

The other wonderful thing is, when she and Torrin kiss each other, blue sparks of fire erupt in wild abandon, and they create tremendous amounts of heat. It's quite entertaining, but also very dangerous.

Of note, Dessa and Torrin have been blessed with eternal life as long as they love each other. And, together,, they can heal most any injury with the use of their jointly clasped hands over an injury.

* * *

Gustav - *Commander of the Kalmar garrison.*

Commander of the garrison at Kalmar in the huge fort, tough guy, gets his way. Very politically aligned. His dark hair, beady eyes and challenging demeanor put most people ill at ease. There is something bothering him. Stay tuned.

* * *

Harold and Karina - *Harold: Could sense danger and threats when present, for self and people he cares about. Karina: Saw the future and knows what people want, a Seer of sorts. No known children.*

Harold and Karina were the second set of caretakers for the Journey Inn for many winters. Truly a perfect match in every way for each other. Harold was kind, hardworking and honest. Karina ran the kitchen. Both Harold and Karina had been waiting for a new couple to arrive who are blessed with the "gift" to take over, so they could retire. As to the question of how long they have been at Journey, as was revealed in Part II, it was close to 3,000 years. After Dessa and Torrin arrived and settled in, Harold and Karina walked off into the woods, hand in hand, never to be seen again. And both were smiling.

* * *

Ipi - *World traveler, wise in every way, lover to Ol' Dogger from many years ago.*

This woman is pure knowledge, curiosity and wisdom. She is an age where her hair is very gray, yet her large mischievous eyes are full of curiosity and spirit. Although slight of frame, she is incredibly nimble and full of energy. Ipi has traveled the world and explored for a long, long time. She introduced math, writing, medicinal compounds, and more to the folks of Journey. Ipi is Ol' Dogger's lover from way back. She fled the relationship because she was afraid of her feelings and of getting hurt. Ipi is kind and you may get to know her much better. Her big brother is Zachariah.

* * *

King Gaerwn - *Father to Darius, Haphethus (twins), and Chadus. Dead. He was evil.*

To define evil with one word, Gaerwn. He was the father of twins Darius and Haphethus and the evil leech Chadus. All three sons are now dead (and for most intents and purposes, rightly so), by the direct or indirect hand of Dessa. Gaerwn raped Ethelda and she bore Accalon who is now ruling the deposed Garwen's kingdom.

* * *

King Tarmon and Queen Gersemi - *Son Kael (dead), daughter is Dessa.*

Tarmon's mother was Saoirse. Saoirse needed a fertile man to create an heir; she utilized the young Gale to produce Tarmon. Tarmon made Gale stable master to be close to his granddaughter Dessa.

A wise man, King Tarmon is the father of Dessa. Tarmon inherited the throne from his father, Keegan. In Part I, Dessa discovers Keegan was sterile, so Tarmon is really the son of Gale. To keep Gale around, he was appointed the stable master of the kingdom and tutored Dessa in riding and hunting. Seems Dessa's grandmother (Tarmon's mother) Saoirse was not going to move on to the next life without leaving an heir.

Tarmon's wife Queen Gersemi was killed by a pack of wolves early in Tarmon's rein; we don't know much about her. He was devastated, but through the urging and understanding of Gale and Sanura, he recovered to lead his people through a time of peace and relative prosperity.

Tarmon is fair, he is aging; the issues with Dessa and Darius seemed to sap his strength. Quillan was appointed king as Tarmon recedes in health.

* * *

King Trebor and Queen Ethelda - *Torrin's Family*

Torrin's mother and father. They lived high in the hills, was a small kingdom.

Garwen's army destroyed the kingdom and killed Trebor. Ethelda was captured. When Garwen was killed she stayed at Garwen's castle to be next to her son Accalon, who ascended the throne.

* * *

Marjie - *Spryte with magical powers. Tends to be incredibly positive, is never a pushover. Nature's agent for the future.*

A forest spryte, with flowing blond hair, perfect skin and her face turns bright green when angry (she is never frightened). She is tightly aligned with the true essence of the natural world. She can take any form, not always physical, she might appear as sound, fog or what seems supernatural. Marjie possesses magical powers, and her guidance comes from nature. Marjie has a gentle, yet persistent sense of humor, however, she is not a pushover. Note, Marjie is not a fairy. Fairy's tend to have a not so gentle side, especially when confronted; Marjie is more refined when faced with issues. Sprytes struggle with evil, however, their approach to conquering evil is always surprising, and they are the ultimate team players. Marjie loves a good scotch; it helps her think clearly in the face of adversity and trial.

* * *

Normadia - *Bright, friendly and helpful and industrious. Tall young woman, long brown hair.*

A quiet hardworking lass who had been Karina's ever faithful assistant for oh so many a winter in the bustling kitchen of the Journey Inn. She arrived to be by the side of Quillan when he took the throne in Tarmon's kingdom.

* * *

Ol' Dogger - *A fixture of a character at Journey. Old guy, one good eye. Very funny.*

A fixture character at the Journey Inn, very old, and sometimes shows his age. However, he often acts as if he is just a young man. Kind, friendly, funny with a selfless sense of humor, he often has a sense of wisdom that is not understood by many. Ol' Dogger has one good eye and one that wanders (makes for great fun for everyone about halfway through a barrel of strong brew!). He has enjoyed a long, long romantic relationship with Ipi. Only son of Kaitlyn and Valterra.

* * *

Quillan (full name Quillan GianFrachesco) - *Big man. Red hair. Son of Sanura and Tarmon. Half-brother to Dessa.*

A big man with red flaming hair. Quiet and steely deep down, he was sent by forces of nature to the Journey Inn to guide Dessa and Torrin. We did get a glimpse of Quillan's wild side early on in Part I as he is quite the romantic party animal with the young lasses.

Quillan is crowned King of Tarmon's kingdom when we find out that Tarmon is his father. Normadia arrives to be with Quillan, they are madly in love and very much meant for each other.

* * *

Rebecca and Bartoly - *Bartoly is a smithy. Rebecca a potter. Very much in love. Live in the woods. Son MacGowan.*

Are intensely in love, make for a picture-perfect romantic and creative couple. They live in a well-crafted bungalow deep in the woods, hidden from most other living creatures   Gave birth to their first child, MacGowan during Part II.

* * *

Sanura - *Mother to Quillan and Tallon. Father is Tarmon. Personal maid to Dessa.*

Wise woman from a distant land; of Greek descent and is part of the family of the Greek hero Odysseus who is purported to have developed the idea of the Trojan Horse.

* * *

Torrin - *Prince, son of Trebor and Ethelda. Long thick black hair, good with hands, tends to be an explorer of things. His hair stands on end and head hurts when danger is about, akin to Harold's gift.*

A vibrant young man in his mid-teens, he is kind, but a little headstrong (imagine that of a teenage boy?). Part I starts with Torrin escaping from the inside of a dragon.

Unfortunately for Torrin, being a little headstrong, he had to learn the hard way to believe and accept his destiny. Readers of Part I may remember Gwendolyn. The very surprising and violent end to her life was a truly hard lesson for Torrin.

Torrin has a special gift that erupts when danger is around. His head hurts in direct proportion to the level of danger and the hair on the back of his neck stands up in attention.

* * *

Valterra & Kaitlyn - *Valterra: Big man. Silver sword. Redhead like Quillan. Kaitlyn: Sturdy Nordic blond. Coronado: Valterra's horse, 18 hand tall (typical is 14 – 16). Ol Dogger, only son.*

These two passionate lovers built the original Journey Inn exceptionally long ago. They were special in their own land.

You see, Valterra and Kaitlyn were of the city of Troy. Their flaming power was the secret weapon that kept the Greeks at bay for ten long years of war. Just as Torrin and Dessa throw off sparks and heat when they are intimate, so did Valterra and Kaitlyn. Not until the Greeks used the Trojan Horse to sneak into the city was anyone in real danger. When the great city was overrun, Valterra and Kaitlyn escaped via a secret water tunnel to a ship and sailed north with as many of their fellow Trojans as possible. The story is, the Trojans were not only mostly blond and redheaded, but were by nature extremely fierce warriors, great engineers and a people of profound passion for justice. As the legend goes, they predated the Vikings (and very likely were their predecessors) and built that adventuresome if somewhat brutal culture, so many years later.

Readers of Part II met these two lovers through Ol' Dogger's story. Alas, they will not show up in Part III, however their story lives on through Torrin, Dessa and, well, you shall see.

A juicy tidbit brought forth toward the end of Part II was about our friend Old Dogger (Ol' Dogger). He is the only son of Kaitlyn and

Valterra which is news almost of dramatic proportions to the folks of the valley that a person lives on from their union.

⁕ ⁕ ⁕

Zachariah - *Takes care of the Center in the forest.*

Massive man, strong as three horses, huge hands, dark eyes, dark hair. Is an accomplished smithy and fine woodworker. Does what he needs to do to get things done. Big brother to Ipi.

* * *

The Animals

The animals in the story play a significant role in many areas. Is good to remember that Dessa can communicate with the animals in a sixth sense sort of way.

Uta	Dessa's best horse, a stallion, is the alpha horse of the group.
Calandra	Uta's sister. Somewhat quiet, but firm in her ways. Keeps Uta in line (as many sisters do for their brothers). Acts as the pack horse.
Samoot	The horse Torrin rides from the Journey stables. Strong, dependable, does not spook easily.
Praritor	The good alpha wolf of all alpha wolves. Tasked to watch over the fates of Dessa.
Ailis the Fergal	Large, good cougar who watches over Dessa.

**You will no doubt meet
some other interesting characters
in the pages ahead.**

And now

Journey Part III

The Love Story of the Century

Holding on tight will do you no good,,,

0. Where We Left Off...

From the very end of Journey Part II of III...

~~Tough~~ Pure Love

A brief introduction... The Journey Inn has burned to the ground. Cause unknown.

And from the depths and mysteries of the deep and broad forest, to the ruins of the Journey Inn, the people of the valley returned.

They all returned.

Just as flowers emerge in the spring from what was frozen winter ground, they all emerged from the forest.

As leaves fill the trees of the forest when warmth and daylight conquer the cold black of winter; they filled the fields around the ruins of the Journey Inn just a short time after the fire.

Many more people in number than the crowds attending and playing in the summer festival arrived to help. Even more than the celebration that had just brought such happiness. More in number than the good folk that seemed to wander to and away from the Journey Inn all during the warm days of summer, did they appear.

Hammers, saws, axes, pitchforks and shovels were their choice of weapons. Small forges upon carts full of tools and raw stock, pulled by strong steeds were already fired in the morning sunlight, ready to build, bend and create.

Together with eager faces and strong arms, prepared to work did they stand. They stood side by side, ready to beat back the evil that had taken what they loved.

And they would take it back together.

*   *   *

Torrin clambered up and stood tall on the large rock that not long ago had been the center of the great party. His eyes scanned the crowd. The sheer magnitude of the number of people astounded him. He was instantly humbled that so many folk would drop their work, put their home, put their very life on hold, and come to help.

Unbidden.

Unasked.

Unpaid.

Dessa reached up a hand and he held it. He held it for just a moment and then brought her up to stand beside him. It was clear to him now, more than ever, that she was with him.

They stood together.

Never ever really alone.

They were one!

His gaze turned over his shoulder at the black ruins of the Journey Inn. Hot flashes of the memory of their narrow escape were still seared in his mind.

The door that exploded out at him in the hall had saved him. Saved him from being cooked by the flashback of flames that shot out of the stairwell and for an instant covered the space and ceiling above him. If he had been standing in the hallway, he would have been gone in that violent moment of explosive flame and scalding heat.

After the terrifying flashback subsided, Dessa dragged him back to their room, knocking on doors along the hallway. She made doubly sure everyone on the second floor was following them. One by one, they quickly escaped a fiery death via one of the large windows in that special room Torrin and Dessa shared. Safety was but a quick run across the roof of the stables and a short jump to the ground.

Some twisted ankles and one broken arm resulted from this second story escape. No one was terribly injured though and all were entirely grateful.

The same could not be said for many other poor souls. Poor souls who had been sleeping in the dark of night in the Great Room downstairs.

That big room that had been their safe haven, until it turned to turmoil and death.

Journey had escape windows. But as with any fire, for anyone in it, their world was dark, smoky and turbulent. These escape windows were hard to find in the ensuing panic and confusion. Yes, these windows had been a savior for some. For others, a goal never achieved.

Two other doors had been built for just this sort of event. But unfortunately, as is often the case, some people had stood up as they ran from the room. These unlucky folks were instantly suffocated by the heat and smoke. They fell in the doorways, blocking others' escape.

For the rest of the dark night, Dessa and Torrin had used their healing powers on as many as they could. They saved many. Cured many wounds. Brought life back from death, stopped blood and pain in its tracks and brought restoration to the horrific damage of burned flesh.

There were limitations. They could not rush the process. And it consumed them rapidly of their own energy.

As the sun rose to illuminate the devastation, their eyes saw their worst fears. And then Dessa became very sick. She retreated to the forest for a while to let the nausea calm down. She knew the nasty feelings would pass, as they had done for a few days now. She and Rebecca had talked about and even shared a bit of a laugh at the cross they had to sometimes bear. A cross that gave them but the greatest gift of all. If it was that gift, or some dreaded disease.

Torrin was worried for her, but she assured him she would be fine, after a fashion. She hugged him gently and told him that she was the least of his worries right now. And unfortunately for this day, and many more, that was too true, almost too true to comprehend.

*   *   *

Standing on the rock, Torrin shook these memories away and returned to look at the crowd. Just as this crowd had looked for guidance and assurance when they heard the news of Garwen's intent. They wanted now the next step to bring back normalcy to their valley.

But they looked for more. More that they could not have, and he would not promise. For what they needed, was much deeper than what they wanted.

Torrin and Dessa had discussed this at the waterfall the day after the fire. Many people were gathered there. Washing what they could. Nursing wounds. Supporting each other.

Mourning.

Resetting.

The talk around the water had been of rebuilding. Of creating the new Journey Inn. Of a bigger, better, safer and longer-lasting building. One that would last for more eternities than the original.

This talk engendered back the spirit of these damaged people. This talking was what they needed right now. They needed to build some hope.

He and Dessa had together, quietly disagreed with the talk. They agreed between the two of them that something more was needed. Simply rebuilding the structure was not what was needed deep in the hearts and souls of the people here in the valley.

After consideration, they took counsel with Ipi. They knew they needed her deep thinking.

They found Ipi seated on the ground, her back against a wagon wheel. She was cradling Ol' Dogger's head in her lap. Dogger had lost a hand saving Alexia from the inferno. Dessa and Torrin had been able to heal the wound, but his hand was gone.

Dogger looked haggard and old.

Ipi looked haggard and old.

Dessa and Torrin explained their feelings to Ipi. Their feeling that simply rebuilding the Journey Inn was not what was needed. That there was a larger opportunity. An opportunity to deliver the destiny that had been worked on and so carefully preserved for so long.

Ipi sat with lips pressed together for a while. She was deep in thought as she gently stroked the singed hair on Ol' Dogger's head.

Then after a time, Ipi agreed with them. Yes, there was something more, and something less that was needed. She spoke just a few words, that solidified Dessa and Torrin's decision, "Yes, in times of loss, people strive to go back to da way they knew. The old way. They see it as the safe way. But to do so is not really possible, because it's never really the same again. To truly beat a loss, one must grow and create something bigger and new."

And with those words, Ipi fell into a much-needed sleep from which there would be no disturbing.

      *   *   *

Now, perched upon the rock, facing the people and after a long deep breath, Torrin began to speak. He tried his best to choose words carefully and he held tight to the hand of Dessa. "We have suffered a great and mighty loss. We must mourn and honor those whom we lost and what we lost."

His eyes scanned the wide array of upturned faces. Hardly an eye blinked in the bright sunshine. Not a sound could be heard from the assembled community.

"We are all sad. I am sad. I canno put into words just now how I really feel. It is too difficult. But what I feel about the loss, is nothing compared to how I feel about this." And he waved his hand across the crowd, indicating the assembled group.

He continued, "Look around you. Look at what you are. You are bigger than the loss of the Journey Inn and you know it. You always have been and it's time that the Journey Inn became as big as you!"

The crowd murmured their agreement, but it was a murmur of some confusion. They dinna know clearly of what he meant.

Torrin continued, "You must rebuild the Journey Inn. You must make it better and stronger and a place for the future and of the future. A place where you will teach. A place where you will love. A place where the very souls of every traveler and searcher of truth is welcomed with open arms. Just as you have done in service for eons before."

Loud applause and cheers rose up from the crowd. And then quickly died out as the very subtle nature of the words Torrin had uttered sank in.

Questioning murmurs now emanated from the group. People glanced around, inquisitive looks dawning on their faces.

And Torrin removed the subtly of the message.

"To truly love something is to build it and use it in service to others. We have accomplished that over many winters here at Journey." He paused to let the words sink in for a moment and then said, "But we have only accomplished that here."

Torrin breathed deeply and bared his soul with these words, "For us to spread the truth of the promise, to let others experience what we know as good and right, we must take it to the rest of the world. And when we do that, the rest of the world will prosper as never before. You and I both know, in our hearts, in our dreams, and in our verra souls; the only way to build a better world for our children, our families and our neighbors, is to live in a world that is free for all people."

A stunned silence descended over the crowd. The true power and uniqueness of what they had here in the valley had never really occurred to them as a group before. They were simply used to living this way. The pain and suffering of those who lived under the rule of a king, benevolent or not was not truly known to them.

But sure! Why not let others live free? Why not even out the power so that not only the kings and queens lived well, but all people? It worked here! It could work anywhere.

But to take it to the world? They all knew that keeping the valley free had been work and dangerous at times.

Wow!

Torrin concluded, "We leave you in the verra good hands of Larenzque to guide the rebuilding down at the waterfall. A place where running water will keep the new Journey Inn as fresh as the promise of this valley." Torrin nodded to Larenzque and was greeted with a confirming nod.

Someone shouted, "What if others won't listen? What if you fail?"

Torrin replied, "Then too many will suffer needlessly. Which is what will happen, if we do not take the chance to do what Valterra, Kaitlyn, Harold and Karina strived so hard to save. What you all have committed to and saved for so long, for yourselves, your families, your future and your grandchildren!"

"How will you do it?" another shouted.

Torrin smiled at Dessa and said, "Of that, you may be rest assured, we have no idea."

* * *

Since the fire at Journey they all had been living in the wagons fashioned for the sneak attack on Gaerwn. It had not been easy living but was not terrible. They had stayed dry and off the ground. But of course, sleeping with four others close around you every night did get old.

Torrin and Dessa agreed that some quiet time alone was sorely needed. They both concluded having a quiet and unhurried time to repeat the intimacy they had shared on the rock above Phlial's cabin was in order and overdue.

It was late summer before Dessa and Torrin were ready to make their way south toward the great port city of Kalmar. Actually, the light of the days had worn short, and many would see this as the season of fall. Leaves were turning brown, colors abounded, and chill, dry, autumn evenings were met with sweaters and blankets that had been stored away for the warm summer.

This trek would begin their journey of taking the promise that had departed from the sacked city of Troy thousands of years ago back to the populations of the world. And in doing so, they would face all the power hungry 'Garwens' of their time.

They packed their meager possessions, some recovered from the fire, but really did not want for anything vital. The people of the valley had been very generous in resupplying their needs for their journey. And from what they had been told, it was only three days by a good trail.

Over the summer days, the new Journey Inn was rising in good stead above the pool near the falls. More and more massive timbers cut straight and clean greeted each day. It was construction of incredible proportions and great engineering.

When the designer's heart links to their spirit, nothing stands in the way. It also helped that folks working on the new Journey Inn had their hearts set on creating both masterpiece and opus of their spirit.

The people of the valley had sent word to Gaerwn's old kingdom; they were looking for ideas on how to rebuild. Smart and practical engineers, craftsmen and artists of all kinds appeared to help. It was amazing how creative and innovative these folks were in the art of putting together a large structure. These people were joyful to be able to share ideas and innovations. Such as an ice cellar for the storage of fresh foods as the valley people had never seen before.

All of it, coming together; verra (very) massive and verra exciting!

Torrin and Dessa were sorry to know they would miss the completion of this new and special place, as well as the multi-day celebration that would ensue.

The two promised to return and report on whatever transpired of their quest.

They also promised to fill everyone in on their plans before leaving for any long period. If they decided to travel off the port to distant lands on one of the huge ships with the billowing sails (as told by the late Etworth of Kalmar), they would return for goodbyes. And, both Dessa and Torrin had some verra important farewells to make to friends and relatives scattered about the vagaries of the beautiful lands of the north before going far.

In both their minds, they felt that the immensity of what they were embarking on was not yet clear. So, they had decided, just maybe, this first foray was to see what the world had to offer. And to offer the world some new ideas around freedom, and gauge reactions to these radical thinkings.

As they trotted off down the trail, the sun was early in the day, with a promise of warmth. Dessa sat tall upon Uta, she was still comfortable in the saddle, even though there were moments when she felt a bit full for no particular reason. Although she felt sure those days were not many, but worry wormed its way into her thinking that something might be amiss in her body. Memories of a large Rebecca on the horse with her after the rescue on the trail wandered through her mind. Dessa was already feeling a little full and somehow blossoming. It felt good, as long as it was what she hoped.

Torrin rode Samoot as was usual. The mare had grown fond of his riding style, and she always behaved. They paired well.

Calandra took again the role of pack horse. It suited her and she trundled along at whatever pace was set by the others.

Dessa said to no one in particular, but loud enough for Torrin to hear, "I do declare, these horses still smell like a smoky fire."

And then surprisingly, she heard, "Maybe we need a bit of a bath."

Dessa was stunned to have again heard Uta's voice in her head. All she could muster in reply was, "Really?"

Uta said in a verra matter of fact way, "Seems you are going to need our 'elp."

1. Altered?

The trail continued south. It is a well-worn trail, obvious even to the untrained eye. Worn from constant use during the passable seasons. Wagon ruts appear occasionally on the soft sides where the forest meets the pathway. This is where the moss green of the forest ends and the brown dirt of the trail may never see green again, due to use. These ruts occur where two wagons pass, hauling their contents and passengers north and south.

Every rut, every footprint represented a growing commerce to the north. The wagons heading south are mostly empty.

The lack of horse dung on the trail was apparent, and not a surprise. With all these horses, and Torrin and Dessa encountered many, there was not a pile of the sticky muck to be found anywhere. Most travelers, especially those lucky enough to, or willing, to travel by wagon would scoop up all they could find. As a family or team wandered forward on their trek, anyone riding would take the time to roll the fresh dung into elongated spheres, about the length of a hand, from wrist to fingertip, and let these spheres dry for a few days. Once dry, they made for free fuel. Free fuel for the cooking fire and if dried well, these rolled spheres burned as hot as good charcoal (although the smell was a bit horrible if not well dried).

Travelling along this well-worn, mostly clear trail, Torrin and Dessa were comfortable in the saddle. For Uta, Samoot and the pack horse Calandra, the pace was steady. The first day out, was so far, uneventful.

For Dessa however, everything had suddenly changed with the words from Uta. Everything all at once.

And.

Without so much as a sound.

The physical world seemed to simply, fall away.

Dessa was no longer thoroughly, or more accurately, physically aware of Uta's movements. The regular heavy breathing sounds of the horses vanished. The clop of hooves dissipated into thin air and left her ears.

She was also no longer aware of the normal passage of the forest's gentle breeze, that ever-present breath of the land. The forest made no sound that caught in her ears. Even the harsh scratching of squirrel feet on tree bark, the twittering of the birds, the swoosh of air through the leaves.

All gone.

As if in a trance, Dessa torpidly rode the big steed Uta.

No sounds.

No movements.

No experience.

A strange and utter hush enveloped her whole being. Ears, hands, skin, face. All devoid of any and all sensation.

It was like she wasn't there; the phenomenon was akin to a feeling of floating weightless. Yet she knew she was atop Uta. And at the same time, it was as if she were gone from the world. Or the world was gone from her. She was not anywhere.

Surreal and unsettling, and at the same time, she felt oddly peaceful. This magnificent trance-like state was the calmest Dessa had experienced since she had found herself safe within the hunting cabin so long ago with Gale, her seanathair (grandfather).

Safe with a friendly companion at that delightful cabin after a harrowing day of hard riding, fleeing from being burned at the stake. Recollections fresh in her mind of the trap Sanura and her athair (father), King Tarmon, had unleashed on that disgusting leech Valdemar.

Her memory was still burned vivid of the full-on terror of riding Uta at an unrelenting gallop through the dense forest. The thunderous beating sounds of horse's hooves pounding upon the dusty trail often resounded fresh in her mind. The sight of the great evil wolf Ahriman upon the hill straight ahead of her sizzled like a lightning bolt. And yet, even after all this time, it still made her jaws clench tight. She always felt as if the wolf was sizing her up, like a tasty lunch or something to toy with as he enjoyed his fresh kill.

And then Ahriman disappeared as if he was a whisp of smoke on a flurry of gray misted wind. She remembered the secure feeling of the arrow, notched and ready between her fingers, bowstring tightening as her muscles contracted. She had him dead in her aim! And then, poof, he was gone.

She had relaxed when alone, the following day, at the outer hunting lodge, only to be attacked by Sgail. The big cat's exit from the fight still intrigued her. Even though she had sported a knife on one hand and a long blade in the other, Sgail could have done fatal damage. She never knew why he just trotted away. And since he was dead, she had to accept what she may never know.

And now, as the trail passed beneath herself and the big steed Uta, Dessa's brain began to slowly, gingerly, catch up. Or was she reawaking? The only sensation of which she was aware was an oddly foreign buzzing in her ears. She could see but was not fully aware. She was simply not aware of anything. Just the buzzing. Maybe she should have been concerned? But she wasn't.

Awake? Asleep? Coming back? Not here? Where?

Before long, Dessa gained the sensation of her heart softly beating in her chest. A perfect rhythm. A perfect rhythm with the world around her, in a manner she had never experienced.

She became aware of the sounds of her breathing. Now just heart and breath. Nothing else, just yet.

Slowly, Dessa looked down at her hands. Her well-worn gloves held Uta's reigns. It all seemed normal, nothing was wrong, still, nothing was right.

Or was it?

Something had changed.

But what?

Something had changed!

As Dessa let her mind come back to her, come back to her surroundings, she began to ponder. Ponder an experience that was as elusive as sunshine on a rainy day.

Ponder? What a strange sensation! To ponder while lost in my mind? Lost in the world? Lost in...? What the deamhan (devil) just happened and moreover, why?

Or more importantly; what did it mean?

Did it mean anything? Goodness, she was talking with her horse again. Back with the sweet magic of being one with nature. A oneness she had so terribly missed. That wonderful and special gift of communing with nature had left all of them, and it had felt like such a loss.

When did it leave? She had no distinct memory of the loss. But she did remember Praritor and Ailis walking away without words.

But now, with those stunning words from Uta, the world seemed to have shifted. Had it shifted to better or worse?

Yes, it shifted. And, there was no obvious reason, however a shift like this did not happen without reason. Who made the shift? Or what had caused it to happen? Why did it appear before, why did it leave, why did it come back and who made that call?

That word, those words Uta had uttered. Did he know? He had said, 'You are going to need our help.'

What did he know?

Did the horse decide to come back into communication?

A wonder? A mystery?

And then as suddenly as it had all fallen away, the world was back. The clopping of horse hooves. Heavy wet breathing from the big steeds' nostrils. Wind in the leaves, the call of birds. Air passing over her cheeks.

Two squirrels, chattering loudly, chasing each other around a large old tree. Their tiny, pointed nails, sharp as pins loudly scratching on the bark. Dessa was amazed that even that loud fast scratching had gone away just moments ago.

Dessa pondered a bit more. Was anything really different? Has something changed in the world? Or was it just her? She thought, and said out loud, "Did I really hear Uta or was I just imagining it?"

"No, you did not imagine it," said Uta, quietly.

"Why? Why are you back, or what I mean, why can we talk again? What changed?" said Dessa, who was suddenly a bit out of breath. She had the same feeling as having been reunited with an old friend. One who had been lost for many winters. A friend who simply showed up at the door, and said, "Hello."

"Don't know," said the horse in a matter-of-fact way. "It just came on, like it did before. Also, we could use a drink soon."

Dessa smiled, she loved horse sense. It was so logical, and pragmatic.

"Torrin!" shouted the now excited Dessa, as she pointed at Uta's head, bobbing head, "Did you hear that?"

2. Start

The kitchen at the Eskil Tavern in Kalmar was always busy. Usually three or four people were cooking or cleaning or serving or washing. Like any kitchen in a popular tavern, there was always work to start, or finish or just do over again. But right now, the big stove was only partially hot. A small fire burned inside one corner under the big pot while the food was prepped. Everyone else had stepped out for a break. A break before the evening rush began.

So right now, Chrisholm was alone, working on the vegetables. She had some quiet time to just do the mindless task of prepping. As much as she liked and got along with everyone, she enjoyed a bit of peace and quiet.

A peace and quiet that would suddenly be interrupted in the most odd of ways.

With her piercing green eyes, Chrisholom looked down at the partially rotten, mostly gray buntàta (potato) she was holding firmly in her hand as she quartered a large pile of them for the tavern's supper. These buntàtas were bound for the big pot simmering on the huge cast iron stove. Bound to make many servings of mashed snèap is buntàta (Gaelic for Neeps and Tatties, traditional Scottish side of mashed potatoes and rutabaga), under braised beef for hungry sailors who would fill the town's favorite diner/watering hole for the evening. The snèap had been cut earlier, their hard interiors soaking all afternoon, softening up for the mashing.

A few moments ago, a tingle had spread from the buntàta to her fingers. The tingle worked its way up toward her shoulders, just as ice silently creeps up a slow-moving stream in winter. The gray molted tuber in her hand morphed into a sweet firm root, as if it had been harvested from fresh soil during the glorious summer days of fresh food. She knew this sordid pile had come from early fall's damp moldy ground. Yet in a flash, she saw with astonishment they were firm, white and fresh.

Looking across the table to the pile of beets, radishes and carrots she had been struggling to clean for the evening's always hungry and generally rowdy crowd, she watched. She watched withered vegetables together transform back to fresh. Fresh as the sun is warm on evenings during the too short summer.

She picked up a carrot and when she bent it in two, it cracked in half. Like it was fresh from the harvest. A freshness she longed for during these damp darker and ever colder, fall days.

Slowly, she put the tattie down on the big butcher block table next to her carving knife. As she let go, the tingle slowly faded from her fingers and dissolved in her arms and shoulders. However, the air in the big kitchen had cleared. The underlying fetid smell of rotting vegetables disappeared, and the fresh scent of clean air arrived. She stood and stretched her hands, arms and shoulders and twisted her neck to dissipate the built-up tension.

The stretching helped some, but not enough, the tightness in her muscles was painful and annoying. Slowly she tried to breathe normally, but the sudden stress and tension of a dire message she did not understand, was pounding on her verra being like a thunderstorm would pound the ground. She felt a bit suffocated, although she was not certain why.

Ancropolis walked into the warm kitchen, put his large strong hand gently on her shoulder and said cheerfully, "Looks like a full house tonight." He stopped in his tracks, looked at the love of his life, his dark hazel eyes suddenly cautious and said, "What? What is it, you look like you've been there in the daytime and ye is scaring me daylights dark."

Chrisholom could not speak, she could hardly still breathe, let alone give an answer to the sweet man with his hand warmly griping her shoulder. She gulped in lung-full, after lung-full of air trying to calm her entire self. Slowly she sat upon her stool, struggling to take the stress of the moment out of her body. Her entire being shuddered and she ultimately found the strength to relax. Finally, she was able to settle herself, her mind, her breathing and closed her eyes as tears cascaded down her cheeks.

Between long gasping breaths, she had looked up at Ancropolis and rested one trembling hand upon his. Finally, she was able to quietly mutter only these fateful words through choking sobs, "I think it has begun."

The big man just stood and looked at her. He knew she was different. He had accepted a fate of something bigger than himself when he had asked her to share his bed, his tavern, his life. And as big, tall, strong and courageous as he was, he felt absolutely weak at this moment.

Ancropolis had steeled himself for this moment. He had thought long and hard about what he would do when it came. Hours of washing mugs at the bar had given him much time to contemplate his response.

And for all the creative ideas that had emerged through countless iterations of thought, at this point, when the reality of the actual 'now' occurred, all he could do was grit his teeth and not speak. He did not know, for the life of him, what to say. He'd really never fully thought she would tell him it had begun. Even though he had tried to be ready. He always wanted to support her.

She'd tried to prepare him, and yet he was not prepared. He felt a bit foolish. Quietly he said, as he did many times, "We'll figure it out." And he meant it, with all his heart. He just was not sure how that might come about.

3. Interruption

"Huh? Hear what? I don' not hear nothin," said a confused, surprised and tired Torrin. He immediately drew his sword and looked alarmed. "Is there somethin' nasty about? I'll take good charge of the pesky rascal!"

Torrin had been lulled almost asleep in the saddle, however the word sleep did not aptly define the moment. The quiet clomping of the horse's hooves, the gentle chirping of the birds and scattered, almost noiseless rustlings of squirrels had lulled him into a tender trance-like slumber. A peaceful slumber bordering on hypnotic sleep.

You might think of this slumber as a self-induced, or environmentally induced state of restful hypnosis. Dessa, on Uta, behind him had experienced a transformation, one she did not yet understand. Torrin on the other hand, was simply in a wonderfully relaxed state of restful slumber.

Were the two verra different mind states related?

Torrin was enjoying the kind of slumber people in crowded cities and urban areas yearn for. Yet, they don't even know it. Oh yes, they know it, but not on the level of consciousness that makes day-to-day sense. This knowing lingers in their respective trans-ancestral being.

Many years later, after our two heroes were long gone from this dusty trail, psychiatrists would define a term. This term is known as the "collective unconscious," and innate in that term is an eternal yearning for a deep and awesome peace. Torrin had been experiencing that kind of peace.

This is a peacefulness scratching at the edge of transcendence (considered being beyond the limits of an ordinary experience). It's a kind of slumber you might enjoy while lying on warm grass, sun shining, in the early summer. Of course, after enduring the harshness of a cold and relentlessly long winter. The cold of winter is a just-lost memory that no longer haunts what were your very cold fingers and toes. This slumber is a lumber beyond the cool wet days of spring. Days that only promise summer; these being gone in the flash. This is a warm peacefulness encompassing not only your body, but your soul. A lumberance of cerebral delight where ears are empty of sound. Its true peace. A peace that is scant and scarce for most people to experience.

Once experienced though, it is often yearned for, sought and desired, deep within the human soul. The challenge though is, it is rarely recovered or found again. We will though, keep looking.

People, just a few, experience this peacefulness a few times in life, some never at all. Once known in the soul, its memory returns as a wanting. A wanting for a level of serenity that calms the heart, brings peace to the mind and a gentle feeling of hush to a person's entire body. A wanting that is somewhat out of touch with what is really known, albeit understood, in the conscious mind.

Anyone who has experienced this kind of peace, knows of it. Folks who meditate often find this peace in their soul after a lot of practice. That is why they continue to meditate.

And Dessa had just interrupted this level of peace in Torrin.

He would spend many winters looking to repeat this moment of true peace. The yearning desire to recreate this peace in and of itself creates a stress that makes the achievement of this restful experience hard to achieve.

Call it a Catch-22 of sorts. You want it, but it eludes you because in the wanting, is a stress to achieve. The stress to achieve must be abandoned.

Anyway, back to Torrin… Male breeding and instinct took over when he "awoke" riding comfortably upon Samoot. Torrin rose high in his stirrups to slay the oncoming dragon, the menace, whatever it was! For to be interrupted from such a wonderful peace must mean danger. This the instinctive response for a young man who plays the protector role, such as Torrin.

But no. No dragon was about, and the world, as he had come to accept it, was now different. He did not really know how it was different yet. The change would be coming over time. He would feel it long before he understood it. He would feel it in many ways.

Even Dessa did not know the details or the why, or the how. She knew something was up.

However, as is the truth, in their adventure of the long tale of what shall be, it would come to pass; they were the reason for all the change. Well, at least they were designated diplomats of more than they understood.

4. What

Ancropolis stepped back and took stock of the teary-eyed, distraught, wild-eyed lass in front of him. She was never, ever, ever out of sorts like this. She was never beside herself. She was always unflappable. She was always his calming force.

Until just now?

He loved her with his whole heart; he loved her beyond even himself. In his mind he flashed the life they shared together, the thoughts, experiences, realities and musings. These soared with searing speed, like lightning through his memory.

To say he had been taken off guard by all her emotions and turmoil would be the understatement of the gathering fall and coming winter. His head was spinning in surprise. And he would only admit to himself, he was just a bit scared. Yet, he wondered, was he scared for himself, for her, or for them?

Ancropolis knew in his heart and soul that Chrisholom was kind. Kind-hearted to a fault. If you were hungry, she would feed you. She kept a pile of cast-off clothes hung along a wall for anyone in need of something warm, dry or better. She took in stray cats (not all bad since this ensured the tavern suffered none of the nasty atrocities mice and rats would wreck upon them). Stray dogs arrived every evening along the dark back alley for food from the scrapings bucket.

Peculiar though he had just recently noticed the odd behaviors of the dogs. Some were obviously nasty wild animals. These dogs were living on the dirt roads, paths and trails of Kalmar. They were big, drooling buggers who could chew your arm off with one bite. They would look at you with large dark piercing eyes, and the feeling you had was they were just sizing you up as their next tasty meal.

However, when Chrisholom went to the alley with her scraps bucket, an entirely odd behavior took place and peace reigned. Instead of all the viciousness that could have occurred in what was a dark alley full of strays, all these dogs lined up, calmly waiting their turn. Not a yap or woof to be heard. Large and small, all behaved, serene and just gently panting, waiting.

The first time he noticed it he simply did not truly experience it. He moved on with what he was doing, not paying attention, since there was little to notice, no noise, no barking, nothing. A few moments later, his mind snapped to the stark realization that a herd of stray dogs, in the alley behind the tavern, should be unruly and viciously eager for food. Not standing quietly in a damnú line.

So, he wandered back and keenly watched the event in the alley unfolding before his unbelieving eyes. And this event, just as he was watching it now, quietly unfolded every evening after closing. There she was, handing out servings from the scraps bucket, each dog calmly took its portion and moved on. She seemed to be talking to each animal. Having a small bit of conversation.

No!

Yes?

He thought again, she was kind to a fault. But there was no fault. Ever. The unruliest of creatures, with two legs, or four, would suddenly turn calm in her presence.

People. Dogs. It did not matter who.

Yes, he was noticing it with people too!

Even the meanest of soldiers seemingly intent on delivering harm would suddenly turn chill and be kind. Customers unhappy with a meal would calm down and patiently wait for their plate, now fixed, to be brought from the kitchen. Screaming babies, red in the face and pounding their fists on their mháthair's (mother's) faces will lie back calm and serene. All smiles and giggles when Chrisholom held them in her arms.

Not really understanding yet what she truly meant about, "I think it has begun," he closed his eyes and thought carefully about how to better respond. She had taught him this tactic. Be still, think, take a moment, then respond, and things will go better.

The idea that what she had been seeing in her visions could become real began to enter his thoughts. But the business of the tavern with the evening fast approaching could not wait. The work of the day always reigned supreme!

However, he loved her. And she, her needs, their relationship came before the tavern. So, he said, gently, "How do you know?"

She pointed at the table of vegetables, and he still did not understand. Giving a bit of a sigh, she picked up a tattie, and with one graceful swing of her knife, split it in half. He looked at it, still wondering what was up.

Chrisholom had by now gathered her wits about her. She demurely smiled, knowing that this gentle man was confused, and said, "When I started cutting these this morning, they were all just a dull gray. Everything here was limp and old. It was a pile of vegetables suitable only for a well boiled soup."

She raised the bright white tattie up to her nose and smelled its freshness. She then handed it to her lover and told him, "Feel it, smell it! It is like it just came from good earth during the warm season. Not leftover from this summer's final crop and been sitting in damp moldy soil for the fall."

He felt the firm tattie, gave it a sniff and continued to look a bit puzzled.

"Ok, they happened to stay fresh. I'm not sure of what it means or why we are, or, errr, you are having a time about it?"

Having partly come to grips with all the emotions swirling around, Chrisholom now smiled and said softly, "Nature has decided to make things right. Something is going to happen, and it's going to be big. You and I, and all the soldiers, and all the armies of the world will not be able to stop it."

Getting excited, she clapped her hands and said, "It's finally going to start!"

He stopped breathing for a moment and then said, "Let's talk about this tonight, after the crowd is gone. You know we have more and more people every night! When I can think, and you can think. You can talk me through all this. I'm hopeful, if it's this big, it should wait until later?"

She bit her lip for a moment, looked down at her feet and quietly said, "OK. But!" She added, with a bit of a sly smile, "Tonight, I want you naked, holding me in your arms, because things could get crazier around here than we have ever seen, and tonight might be the last night we have, for a long while."

Before he left for the front room, he swept her lithe frame into his powerful arms. Slowly he brushed her wayward blond hair from her face, looked into her green eyes and said, "You scare me you know, I don' always understand ye, but ye make me feel safe in a convictive world." He kissed her deeply.

She held him tight for another moment and let go. As he walked from the kitchen, he did not see the tears running down her cheek. Nor did he hear her softly mutter, "I will miss ye so much, it just breaks me heart."

5. A Path To...

As they left the north behind, for Torrin, Dessa and the steeds, it was not a simple hiking path leading south to the port town of Kalmar. Trodding along during the day, you could even see the path as a road of sorts. Of course, the roots of ancient trees lifted up within the path. Rocks of assorted shapes, primeval colors and textures wrought long ago from volcanic fire littered the trail. The kauppasaksa (traveling salesperson) engaged young children to help walk ahead of their wagons and remove the most dangerous stones to avoid breaking a wheel, or the leg of an animal.

This dusty, rutted path was wide enough for a wagon pulled by one or even two animals. And of course, you needed to be observant for the periodic chac balls (road apples)! Large and small, excreted on a regular basis from the horses, mules, and donkeys working tirelessly, lay everywhere. The loud buzzing of flies in the midday warmth of the sun was almost like music. Mountains of flies feasted on the chac where travelers had not gathered them for fuel. The only respite from these bug's tireless hunger would be the cool darkness of the evening when the buzzing stopped and quiet edged like unseen vapors from the forest.

Newly traversing this route were fully loaded wagons pulled earnestly by plodding, sweating animals (and sometimes humans). Less fortunate kauppasaksa trudged along the dusty path hunched over, straining and sweating under a piled high backpack above their dirty hat. Packs full and heavy with what the casual observer might comment and say, 'Oh they are only the peddler's wares.'

This path. This route. It's not just a path in the woods. It is the route of dreams. More than dreams really. It's the fulfillment of dreams and hopes of a better future. Of a better life.

To the knowing observer, watching these determined kauppasaksa diligently place one foot in front of the other, the pack represents a fulfillment of desire. A quest of achieving a future of possibilities. A future of wealth, and life lived in prosperity.

Every hard-working and successful kauppasaksa starts somewhere, usually with a used backpack (they are never comfortable). The wise and strong of spirit, who never give up the hard work are the durable ones who arrive the following year with a wagon, having been successful enough to trade in the backpack. That first wagon is usually secondhand, patched together with twine and castoff wood. Each year, the hard workers, those who are intense in spirit, show up again. Always better equipped and ready to do more business.

Gain for these folks is progression, and they understand those concepts and ideals. It might just be a stronger horse or a larger wagon. For some, hiring a helper is a huge step forward. Engaging good help is not easy, so many people will steal your hard-earned wealth. But with two or three trusted helpers, so much more is accomplished. Kauppasaksa with two or three helpers were always happier. They no longer carried their pack or attended to their burdensome toil alone.

On this road to a better future the crowd was growing steadily. Every day the number of people, the variety of items and the curious mix of people increased just a wee bit, transporting goods and ideas north.

News of the demise of Garwen had spread. The threat of his tyranny no longer haunted travelers, traders, teachers, or even the simply curious explorer and traveler. Evil tyranny no longer troubled the adventurous souls who brought niceties such as salt, silk and knowledge to the hard-working people of the northern lands. The threat of tyranny no longer hindered the human spirit.

As they travelled south, Dessa and Torrin found bits of time for quick discussions with the kauppasaksa and travelers who passed by on their way north. They learned the ships of Kalmar were unloading wares for the kauppasaksa, now willing to venture to unknown areas north without the threat of evil upon their future. The Kalmar docks were full, bustling and bursting with all the goods the world had to offer, proposing a finer future for all.

As it always does, peace brings prosperity. Evil and tyranny crush the working spirit of the people. When a person is threatened, they basically go into survival mode. Survival mode is a focus on nothing more than right now, today and survive. Curiosity is not a consideration. The future beyond today is not part of someone's thinking. When people they are free to pursue purpose, they blossom.

Both Dessa and Torrin certainly had not witnessed such an array of goods and commodities before. Pots, pans, rugs, spices, cloth, medicinal healing, tools… the list seemed endless, and the assortment overwhelmed the brain. So many treasures, niceties, necessities and frivolities they had never seen, or even dreamt of passed before them, heading to the folks of the north.

Glass, that new marvel, dazzled in the sunshine. Glass bottles, of all sizes, colors and shapes. Some tall, some empty, some full of wonderful newness, invented and delivered from other worlds. Their tops sealed with a bit of tightly stretched leather, secured with wax covered twine to keep air and curious bugs away and the contents fresh for new customers.

And now, packed carefully, crystal-clear windows. The old Journey Inn had sported just a few glass windows. None at Journey as clear and

lacking the wild colorful prisms from every angle as these, they now witnessed along what was becoming almost a trail of magic. Glass panes, new wonders, as fine as any great work of art, each of them from a place called Espanola. Clear panes packed with straw between their fragile panes were in abundance. Torrin knew these would adorn the new

Journey Inn and a part of him wished he was there to share in the marvel of their installation.

On this dusty thoroughfare to the future, such a delightful array of goods and hard-working people passed before them. They commented often and were awestruck by the variety that abounded. In one wagon, knives, daggers, swords of all sizes and shapes overflowed the interior. These were as fine as any work Bartoly could produce. At once, Torrin was concerned about his friend's ability to compete, until he heard from a kauppasaksa about the need for more quality stock to refill his wagon. He was looking for a good smithy.

Ah, there is always a place for a good worker who is willing to expend the sweat and time it takes to be the master at their trade!

Torrin knew though, their larger agenda beckoned. He and Dessa were going to deliver to the world the message the people of the valley had held close for so many winters. The message held close and practiced in lives filled with joy. Of course, challenging work was a daily part of the joy. And yes, the sorrows of life did visit upon people. Those sorrows are the natural course of life.

However, the larger agenda seemed to be so much larger that it was hard to put into words. Their agenda was the message so dear to the ancient Greeks, they died for it. So dear to the heart of the human soul, it gives hope to the weary, life to the downtrodden and energy to the drained.

Freedom. So? What of it?

Here among the travelers, the hard working, sweaty kauppasaksa of the trail was the time for Torrin and Dessa to inquire and learn from strangers. Learn about people's reaction and attitude on whether this idea of living free mattered. Did it make sense? How do they react to the idea. The whole concept was new to people south of the valley?

Was a life of freedom and the ability to pursue one's own goals in life important, or was it just a thought that was as frivolous as too much alcohol at a party?

In the discussions they had, all of them too short to gain real depth the concepts of freedom was met with a lot of stares. Mostly, comments along the lines of 'tell me more.' Some people were afraid to even respond. One lad voiced his concern saying, "Are ye from the King's tax squad lookin for those tha want te skip payin?"

It seemed the concept was in and of itself a bit vague for folks to take up in a casual conversation.

One thing they did discover, the road to Kalmar might be a bit further than they had been told. This news was of little concern to them, they knew they could forage or hunt if needed.

But, along the trail, you need to be flexible!

Along the trail, when traveling, a surprise can come from even the strangest of places.

6. Arrivals

South from where our heroes were travelling, at the Eskil Tavern at Kalmar, Chrisholom stood and stretched a long bone tingling, joint popping stretch. The kind athletes yearn for after a hard workout. The stew was on the boil at the big kitchen stove. Tthe bread was rising and would be baking in just a while, and she needed a moment to draw a few satisfying and calming breaths.

She and Ancropolis had procured this tavern just a few winters past. The tavern, with a few rooms, was located near the long stout docks where the big ships with their huge billowing sails all secured, tied up. The ships being the key to how Kalmar links this long cold island to the world. The two of them had had no gold, no means, nothing to pay the previous owner. But they were fair, had much heart in the venture and loved the work.

So, the deal had been struck. The founder, and previous owner, Anton, had lost the love of his life, Alvinia. After a short illness, Alvinia had succumbed to a fever that lasted a fortnight. Now, Anton was tired and ready to stop the long daily toil of operating and managing Kalmar's most popular overnight inn and tavern. A prevalent gathering place for sailors to enjoy after having spent weeks on a ship. There were also regular soldiers and government officials who ran roughshod over the good people of the town. They ran roughshod in the streets, and in the tavern.

Now, with a handshake and a smile, Anton lived in the first room on the first floor. He ate, drank and enjoyed visiting with his old customers and he did not have to worry about coins changing hands. He came and went as he pleased, which brought him much joy and stress relief. He did not have the worry of running the business, dealing with a myriad of details that come daily with a busy establishment. Alvinia had taken care of so many of the daily tasks, Anton had found himself missing both her company and her talents.

Chrisholom and Ancropolis worked to procure and prepare both the food and drink. Hired hands cleaned the upstairs, always full rooms. The rooms were not big considering today's standards; however, they offered a clean room, fresh water, a good meal and most of all, good company in the tavern below.

As the business prospered, Anton was finally able to get his smile back and enjoy himself again.

Anton's loss of Alvina a few winters back had been harsh for him and the loss had crushed him almost beyond recovery. However, with her dying breath, Alvinia had reminded Anton to be true to the place where they had shared a life full of love and caring. The place, the tavern they had affectionately named Eskil.

The term Eskil has a warm meaning to the people of this remote town on the ocean. Eskil signifies a divine cauldron. Anton and Alvinia had thought the name to be very charismatic and endearing. So, people came to quench their thirst at the 'divine cauldron.' Anton and Alvinia felt they could add caring and love to what they offered and the regular visits by most people in the town proved they had been successful.

So, when Anton was looking for new proprietors, he carefully looked for not just a sense of business. He looked for caring. He looked for a love of serving others. Anton felt that true success in business was not only hard work. It seemed that Chrisholm and Ancropolis brought all the elements; love, caring and hard work. Not only to the tavern, but to all the patrons.

This evening, as were so many others, the busy time was approaching. Chrisholom finished up what she could and then left the kitchen. She walked into the main room and looked around. The place was slowly filling with customers looking to end their day with a good drink, a sturdy meal and a bit of news gathering. With a bit of a whimsical sigh, she wondered how long nights like this would last. Because in her heart she knew it could all come crashing down. And as she surveyed those patrons already present, the first soldiers of the evening arrived.

She could tell; it was not good.

7. Dark

Today they'd covered a good distance and the trail ahead was clear. Dessa was verra surprised when Uta suddenly said, "We are turning here," as he made a sharp right turn. The annoying mystery though, there was no trail. No path! Or any indication this area was anything other than dense forest.

Dessa pulled up on the reins and sharply asked, "What are you doing?"

Uta was not to be dissuade. Dessa heard through gritted teeth as the big horse did not lose a beat, "Trust me. It's not an option."

Dessa remembered, the last time Uta had taken charge, he'd gone off to find a path to Garwen's kingdom. It had been a true blessing for herself, Torrin and Quillan to know they were on the right path as they were headed out to face the evil tyrant.

So Dessa did the wise thing, she loosened her hold on the reins and let Uta take the lead. Torrin shouted, "What's going on? This is no path."

Dessa twisted in her saddle and shouted back, "It seems Uta has a mission and there is no stopping him."

Dessa heard a responsive 'Ugh' come from Torrin. And, single file, they plodded along.

A few branches reached out to swipe ungraciously across each of them as they made their way through the dense foliage. Hills rose up creating thick shadows in areas, since the sun was making its afternoon journey towards the west.

And then Uta stopped.

Torrin pulled up alongside Dessa, Calandra in tow and asked, "What ye see? It's all looking pretty dark and I'm wondering what this horse is trying to get us into? Or has he lost is everlovin mind?"

Uta snorted and Dessa heard, "Straight ahead, we are spending the night."

Dessa squinted, and through the gathering shadows, she saw nothing but more darkness. And then, as her eyes adjusted to the gloom, she saw it. A bit of darker black. A hole in the darkness?

Spurring Uta forward, they came upon the entrance to a cave. The opening was taller than Uta and just wide enough for a person, or a horse to enter. Dessa dismounted, and said to Uta, "Are you sure?"

Uta just stood and stared at the dark opening. She heard a quiet, "Yes."

"Sometimes you drive me a bit crazy you big horse," said Dessa. She entered the cave as Torrin and Calandra caught up from behind. He thought to himself, 'Hope she don't disrupt a sleeping mathan (bear) setting in for hibernation. Well, better her than me going into such a dark place. I don like them enclosed places, not at all!'

Torrin heard her call out, "Take care of the horses, maybe we can stay in here tonight." He thought to himself, 'I hope not!'

* * *

As Dessa entered the cave, the light dwindled to nothing after just a few steps since it was late afternoon and there was little light to enter. And, the walls were pitch black, there was nothing to reflect what little light came from the modest opening.

She put her hands out to feel along the cold damp surface of the wall. The stone felt like the rough surface of a cat's tongue. Slowly she slid her feet forward, expecting any sort of object to be on her path. And then it occurred to her, as she deliberately moved, she could put her foot right into a large gaping hole and disappear into a black void of no return with one wrong step.

She had heard of caves where people went in to explore and never returned. Oh, how she wished for a flame. Any sort of light would help.

Slowly, after the treacherous idea of falling into black pit had subsided, she got down on all fours and continued forward. The floor of the cave was covered in sand. Fine dry sand, like a beach on a warm day. She mused caves were such interesting oddities. Here in a deep forest, with a beach inside? The world was strange place, for sure.

She had no idea how far she had come, until she looked back. The entrance was behind a good way, and there was little to no light left at that large hole. No one was visible, and she figured, rightly so, Torrin had gathered the horses to find a place to graze.

She slowly crept forward in what was now a cold dark, inky blackness. She put her hand in front of her face and could see nothing. Moving on, she bumped her head on what seemed to be a wall. Reaching right, just wall. Reaching left, empty space.

And then, something else.

* * *

There, in a bit of distance, she saw dense white fog, slowly and silently roiling in the air. And it was somehow, illuminated. Was it far away or close? Hard to tell in the vast emptiness of everything surrounding her.

She held her breath. She held her breath so that no sound other than the sounds of the cave would enter her ears. She listened for voices, for sounds of others. Maybe animals, creatures, bats or anything living in this dark, damp and mysterious accommodation. She listened for clues.

The only sounds that came to her ears were sporadic drips of water falling invisibly through the darkness. As she let her breath out, the sound was loud in her head, almost invasive.

Only the silence of the dark space and the cryptic white fog were there to give her any context to this strange situation. It was not so much as terrifying, it was just totally foreign. Try as she might, she could not make sense of it.

However, Dessa being Dessa, did not shy away. She crept forward through the darkness on hands and knees towards the white fog.

It did not take long to almost enter what seemed to be a thick, white cloud. Darkness loomed just in front of her eyes, but in the air, the white cloud swirled slowly, almost beckoning her forward.

"Chac!" she muttered as her head smacked into a hard rock. The darkness in front of her eyes was stone. She had been focusing on the fog and not paying attention with her hands. Rubbing her face, she stood up and could feel the wall of rock in front of her.

As she made her way around the stone that had impacted her head, she was almost so amused and startled that she laughed out loud.

A small candle with a flame was set in the sand next to the boulder (she could see now, the boulder was quite large), and the light of the candle shown into the deeper part of the cave. As she looked up at the fog, it dissipated into the dark depths beyond her sight.

Now with light, she looked around, curious to see, to understand, to know. The dark walls of the cave sucked in the tiny light, leaving no reflections for the eye to discern most anything. But then she saw odd bits of white.

She was gaining perspective and as she moved towards the bits of white, she discovered that the bits were part of a verra large quantity of cut, split, dried and stacked firewood.

Taking a small piece of wood from the stack, she lit the end on fire from the tiny candle. The flame flickered into an orange illumination and gave her more perspective about her surroundings.

Dessa was in a room. A good-sized room with a soft sandy floor. The area was protected from cold air coming from the front by the boulder that was causing a small knob to grow on her head.

Suddenly she decided to make the most of what had presented itself. Finding the wall across from the woodpile, she leaned her burning stick against the wall. She grabbed a handful of sticks from atop the pile, she proceeded to build a fire. The wood was very dry and caught quickly. Soon, she had a good fire going, and now she could see the whole room in this cave.

Seeing was one thing, beginning to ask the bigger question was the other.

Suddenly, a wave of questions came over her. What was all this about? First the lightheaded feeling along the trail and now this? Oh yes, being able to talk to the horses?

All at once, she began to understand, something verra much bigger than herself was in charge of this journey south to Kalmar. She just hoped, whomever they were, they were friendly.

As our two heroes were to understand from tonight's small detour and adventure along the trail, you must always be prepared to learn. You never know what answers might come forth.

More importantly, you might learn new questions.

8. Kitchen

After seeing the soldiers enter Eskil with what seemed like a verra large chip on their shoulders, Chrisholm went into the kitchen for a moment to gather her thoughts. The huge stove that generally gave her comfort from its constant warmth and cooking just seemed to annoy her.

The stove just sat there, cooking away at the fare for the evening. Bubbling and hissing were the only sounds. She found no comfort in its presence.

She went to the back door that faced the alley. It was not yet fully dark, and she wondered if the dogs had started to line up for the night. Their need in the evening, their need for substance was comforting to her. They were always gracious, yet they were not verra companionable. Most often, they came around, took some food, and went on their way.

Chrisholm mused, 'Why do I do this? Why do I feed them? What song in my heart compels me to be so gracious to creatures who pay me so little mind?'

She was startled by the sound of metal clanging to the floor of the kitchen. The cover to a pot had lifted up and literally flown through the air and landed on the floor. She retrieved the cover and upon investigation found that a potato in the pot had exploded and sent the cover flying.

And then she felt it. Between her shoulders at first, and then the feeling crept up the back of her head and stopped. Turning around, the sad dark brown eyes met hers. Ears drooping, a sallow colored tongue lolling down from one side of a small mouth that was sad and dry.

The little dog was of no particular breed. It was evident though, he was thirsty and starving. She scooped up a handful of scraps she kept for the mutts and proceeded to the door. On her way, she grabbed the bowl of water she put out at night.

Setting the food and water down in front of the little guy, she stroked ears that were too thin and fur that seemed too fine and lacked substance. She expected a quick drink, then a grab for the food and a fast exit.

At first, she was not disappointed. The sickly-looking tongue slowly lapped at the water. The little guy stopped, swallowed and then took a long deep breath.

It was a breath of joy. A breath of thankfulness. He sniffed the food and then did the strangest thing. Slowly putting one paw upon Chrisholm's knee, he faced his muzzle towards her face. He cocked his head and looked at her.

Chrisholm too, cocked her head. Wondering. And then she brought her cheek down to his little face. He gently rubbed his face across her cheek. Took another deep breath and then backed up just a bit. Settling down on his haunches, he proceeded to eat. He did not gulp the food as most dogs do, especially when hungry. He just ate, seeming to enjoy the delight in the gift.

Standing up, Chrisholm watched with interest. The dog licked the bowl clean, took another drink of the water and then in a most gracious way, burped.

She giggled.

He looked at her, and she could have sworn, he winked.

Without fanfare or distraction, the little guy sauntered off down the alley.

She decided it was time to face the soldiers and whatever woes they were carrying into the tavern this evening. But now, she was facing them with a bit of smile on her heart.

She walked out to Eskil's dining room.

9. Light

With the fire burning bright, Dessa was much more comfortable since the cold black darkness gone. Now, she could get her bearings and understand the surroundings of this huge place.

Just as she began to relax, she heard the voice. And then she laughed. The sound of her laughter surprised her after all the dark silence she had endured.

The voice was Torrin, worriedly calling for her. She quickly added more wood to the fire and then proceeded towards the turn where she had so unceremoniously bumped her head. Calling out, she said, "I'm here, its ok. Come on back." After she had called out, it was apparent he could not hear her, because he kept calling.

She had only taken a few steps back towards the entrance when her mistake was obvious. Beyond the big boulder, she was again in the pitch-black darkness of the cave. Turning back, she went to take the tiny candle for a light. But it was firmly attached to the floor of the cave. She grabbed a long stick from the pile of wood, lit it, and used its little fire for light.

As she rounded the corner of the cave, she heard, "Egad, you are OK! I ad visions of returning to Journey and aving to explain to our world how I ad lost ye in a cold dark, unforgiving place."

Torrin stood slowly and made his way to the light. As he kissed her, she could see the worry on his face.

"Sorry, I'll tell you later, follow me." She led him around the corner and he was greeted by the warm glow of an ample fire reflecting off the walls and ceiling of hard rock. She heard him utter something that sounded positive. She did not know what he really said, but it did not matter right now.

As they rounded the boulder, he said, "I am befuddled as te how ye managed all this in such a short while?"

"I did not. It was here. The wee candle was burning, and the wood was stacked. I lit a fire so I could see and then heard ye callin. And here we are."

"It's good for ta night I suppose," said Torrin, a bit wistfully. He was still not fully comfortable with a cave but was willing to make a go for a night. "Let's get our belongings. The horses are good with some grass we found. I've stacked our things by the entrance."

"Wait," said Dessa. "We should build a small fire at the curve of the cave so we can see to get back here."

Together they started a guiding fire at the bend of the cave, and in the better light, as they worked, they marveled at the accommodation. The cave was big, but not so immense that the ceiling and walls seemed to disappear into the air. The sandy floor made for easy travel vs. other caves where walking is a feat of endurance and skill because of the sharp rocks that want to twist off an ankle or knee.

After just two trips back and forth, they had set up a nice camp. The wood was dry and verra hard. The fire it made burned brightly, with warmth and the wood did not burn too fast.

It did not take long to cook a light dinner, and they nestled together in bedrolls out of the wind. The fire had taken the chill out of the rock for now and other than the soft crackle of the fire, the total quiet that enveloped them was almost deafening.

Torrin whispered, "The lack of sound almost hurts me ears. I am glad yer not alone to endure it."

Dessa smiled and whispered back, "I would like to call ye out on bein afraid, but I have to agree with you."

They lay quietly, letting the day's travels end for them. Before drifting off to a comfortable sleep Dessa wondered to herself, 'This be no coincidence. This place? This cave? This candle? Does it mean something? Am I missing something?'

Sleep advanced upon her tired body and mind and she joined Torrin in slumber.

The wee candle, burned on.

10. Question

*Winding back time to a few months earlier
at a place you have not been to…*

Yet…

"Well?" asked the blond lady, pointedly. She was wearing her preferred sparkling blue gown while she slouched comfortably low in her favorite large, overstuffed chair. Her chair was next to his own favorite chair in the smoking room. They were close to a fire in the small hearth that was trying to overcome the chill that had rolled in during this early fall evening.

The huge building was empty except for a few horses in the grand stables and the two of them in this room. Being so large a place, it was always a bit eerie when it was empty. Neither paid any mind to the surrounding quiet of the hallways and rooms.

With no demands on the two of them at this moment, other than the discussion at hand, they were able to move through this conversation slowly. And more importantly, thoughtfully.

Her golden blond hair was a bit askew. She had not tended to her looks since arriving at this most secret, and sacred dwelling, hidden in the dark forest, earlier in the day. And, since it was just the two of them for now, her looks did not matter.

Finally, the question had been voiced out loud. The question of only one word, and it was significant. Since she had voiced it, the door was open to discuss the most important topic that had faced them since the invention of the wheel. And that had been a long time ago.

The question, along with its gravity, lingered in the air. The question hungered for an answer. An answer with dire consequences.

The silence hung between them like wet dew-covered cobwebs in a dark hallway. The usually warm flickering flames from the fire in the room's tidy fireplace felt oddly useless trying to warm the room where the future path of all things was, or was not, to be put into motion to move forward.

He pondered his answer. He did not relish one of the two tasks set before him. For one task, the idea was new, and entirely frightening. A challenge where failure could cost so much. The idea of it gave him pause. The second task was easy, just simple hard work. He relished that kind of work.

She met his pause with a question. A question with an empathetic undertone. More empathy than usual from her. She was caught in a difficult situation and needed him to move forward with genuine purpose and resolve. Most of all, she needed him to move forward and not be worried about the outcome. Usually, she was verra direct and to the point. This time she gently said, "It's not like you to hesitate. Are you unsure, scared, or have questions? I'm here for you."

"None of those," he answered slowly. "It's never been part of me to match wits with someone. Especially someone of this caliber and when so much is at stake. It's not like a long night of Hnefatafl (board game of battling armies) or a nice friendly fight with a broadsword."

He heaved a long sigh and took a long swallow of his drink.

"Don't so fash yourself," she replied. "It wasn't until your very wise deirfiúr (sister) made us verra aware the variables may have changed. We all agreed that we needed to create options."

"Never before have you asked me to perform such a monumental task in so little time. These things usually take a verra long time."

"Yes, I know. But our situation is what it is, and we are presented in a fortnight, the opportunity to begin developing our option with little risk. We will take that opportunity. And I know you will be as successful as you can be. Human nature is fickle you know. Sometimes they rise up to the moment, sometimes they don't even see the moment or the option. The are blind to the possibilities laid before them. I am sure of this one, and I am sure of you."

He sighed and said, "May I ask ye the question that is upon me mind?"

"Of course. There is no pretext here and my intent is you go forth ready to transform him as he needs to be transformed."

"I appreciate you being open here," he said. "So why don't you take on this task yerself. Ye can be anything you need to be, at any time, you really don't need me to take on this man. You could do it."

She took a long sip from her favorite mug and smiled as the amber liquid spread its soulful intensity through her. The bold complexity and intermingled layers of variables in the tastes somewhat matched the bold complexity and haunting variables of their plan.

After a sigh of contentment, she spoke, "I have the others to contend with, which is no issue, as you know. So, yes, I could do it. However, the task you have at hand holds a magic moment I cannot create. Only you can create."

Thoughtful, he tried to understand where that moment might happen, and he came up empty, "This magic moment is no coming to my mind."

She smiled and calmly said, "When they all arrive here. And you walk out to greet them and bring them into this place, the moment will appear. It will appear in many forms for them."

"Go on," he said, now verra interested.

"Your man will know he has come back to where the transformation took hold of his soul and changed him. The girl will realize this is the place of her dreams, visions and yearnings. Our chosen couple will see this as another stopping point along the journey they have travelled. The others," she sighed, "are unknown and not dangerous. They are followers and will go along with the events as they unfold."

"I'm seen' it a bit but not fully," he said. "Sorry for me thick head."

"Ha," she laughed a bit, "Don't fash yerself, its complicated. See, you and yer deirfiúr become human points of light and contact for a few of them. Human points of reference they do and will hold dear. This very place here, is a door to one of their souls. So with this beautiful location, and you and your deirfiúr, they will all find a bit of normalcy, calmness and acceptance. That is important, because when I tell them what is going on, they will be able to understand since they will be in a calm and comfortable, contained by a non-threatening environment. And more importantly, be able to stand up and embrace their roles for the future."

"OK, this makes sense, a bit," he answered. "Which one is gonna do which task?"

She put her mug down on the small ornate table next to the chair. Gently she brought her fingers together and her face darkened. With her eyes closed, she quietly said, "That depend on what happens for the rest of this fall, as all the parts and the people come together. I don't know yet who will carry forth with the various obligations."

"It seems to be a bit of hardship for you, bein the head spryte and all the weight of the future put on yer shoulders," he said in a quiet statement.

She looked at him and smiled, "I get used to it, but I'm getting better at not doing it all alone. I need good help if we are to pull this off. It's too important."

"Do you think the weather will be helpful this time?" he asked, looking intently at her face for any sign of discomfort in the question.

"I have been assured the weather will give you ample cover to succeed. The heavy rains may even provide opportunity since travel will be difficult and the trails verra slippery for regular folks."

"Good. Usually, the weather is a barrier when we have an important project," he lamented.

"I am as surprised as you, but maybe all parties impacted understand the importance of this endeavor."

He stood up and stretched.

She also stood and looked directly at his stomach. Even though she was standing to her usual full human height. She always felt small in his presence, no matter what size she presented herself.

She said, "I must tell you how much I appreciate your willingness to move forward and create this option for us."

He replied, "Thank you," took a deep breath and continued to pop the massive connections of his bones as he enjoyed his stretch. "Now, if you will excuse me, I have just three days to prepare. I will do my best. But I don't know if I can create the same buy-in you built in over two winters of work."

As she dissolved from his sight in the darkness of the night he heard her say, "I have every confidence in you."

He went to sharpen his axe. He had a large amount of firewood to prepare and stack in the cave. The work would help him think about how to drive success at the other task. A task he did not relish. He was still unsure how to take a man who's very being was power and control and turn him into the man that might. NO! He changed the word 'might' in his mind to 'will.' Change the man who will change forever the future of the human race.

He certainly preferred his usual blacksmith and carpentry work.

11. A Surprise

Dessa and Torrin both understood that while travelling on the trail, the bright inviting warmth of a campfire in the blackness of night collects even the most diverse of travelers. Attracting folks, not as a team, maybe more as a loose knit gaggle, or an unorganized club. A team is focused on the team's victory. The members of a club are focused mostly on their own victory (they compete). But at the same time, the club members need the club. They need the larger group's resources, more than just themselves, to enjoy victory. Along this well-worn path, is victory for a night just a victory, or is it more? Maybe here, victory is simply survival and maybe survival against disparaging odds? The trail can be a tough life.

On this mostly cloudy evening, at an unnamed spot along the trail to and from Kalmar, a diverse group of weary travelers gathered at a good fire. Each night, in the dark forest, thick with tall trees, victory comes in many forms, some trivial, some significant. Simply having a warm place to share with others, like yourself, traveling the trail, is a joyful first victory for the evening. And finding a group of travelers for the evening is so much better than spending the evening alone.

Not being alone generally offers the likelihood of sharing food, cooking utensils and the fire. Sharing food is by no means minor. One traveler might carry a large portion of meat in their wagon, and they yearn for vegetables after only a few days. Others are natural cooks and always enjoy trying and sharing new spices. And some weary folks gathering here are simply in need of space in a pan for cooking their meal. And the food they cook, of course they offer to share.

If there is anything to share.

Generally, when travelling folks gather, no one goes hungry or cold. When gathered around the fire, besides sharing of food and warmth, there is the constant chatter of stories, news, and jokes. The evening itself is always warming, because everyone contributes.

It's called the community of the trail.

And so tonight, this dark and moonless night, where a strong chill settles among the branches and ground, the travelers form into a temporary club. They formed under an ancient oak tree. The oak itself seems to stretch as tall and wide as the stars when no clouds obscure the view. The spread of long strong branches provides a canopy of protection overhead from the encroaching cold and thick cold morning dew. Broken bits of its body provide fuel for the fire. An armful of old leaves gives a bit of soft bedding upon hard ground.

Maybe the most important thing the old oak offers is a place to gather. A place to rest, be safe, share food and enjoy an evening that is far from lonely. More than not lonely along the demanding work of the trail, a place to collect among people like yourself.

Of course, sometimes someone shows up who makes the evening much more interesting.

* * *

As Torrin, Dessa and their three steeds arrived to join the forming evening group, the gloom of dusk was gathering. The sun was sharing its final warmth of the day with the long shadows of the forest's tall inhabitants stretching long. When those trees cast long shadows, the time to end the day's journey draws nigh.

A nearby bubbling stream offered clear water for both humans and horse. And where there is water, there is tall soft grass. Uta and Samoot were soon relieved of their saddles and packs. A bit later Calandra was liberated from her large pack and the three wandered off in search of a leisurely evening feed.

A bright fire in the center of the informal circle of people helped to replace the waning warmth of the fall day. Torrin took leave to gather wood for the fire as Dessa pulled together the meager rations they had remaining in their packs.

She turned to the group while holding her large heavy cast iron pan. She knew people would see this pan as a way to cook up a great meal. She loved to share it for cooking and spoke well of Bartoly, Rebecca and of course baby McGowan, as the type of people these folks heading northbound would encounter. Most people did not own such a hefty, well-built pan and Dessa was forever, and every day thankful that Bartoly had fashioned them this large sturdy utensil!

However, as Dessa stood there, holding the pan, as if on cue, the conversation of the group ceased to a strained silence.

Dessa instantly sensed something was wrong. Without showing any tension, or as well as she could, she knelt down next to the fire with her meager supply of food and the pan and then introduced herself.

"My name is Dessa. Torrin and I are travelling to Kalmar and then beyond." She was silent as she unrolled a well-used oil cloth and laid out their small meal on the cloth. This kept the dirt and bugs from getting to the soon to be cooked food.

The uncomfortable silence that had started did not stop. Whatever was amiss seemed to be terribly amiss. Now, Dessa was on her guard. Against her thigh lay the cool blade she carried. Inside her sleeve was the long dagger which had dispatched Hapathius to his eternal rest in hell. She was not worried about defending herself. What worried her was this weird and uncomfortable stillness emanating from this group of people gathered around a fire. Generally there was a great amount of lively talk and fun.

As Dessa cautiously looked up, a large man, slowly stood. He was much larger than Torrin. He had the strong chiseled lines of hard work that leaves a face tough and wise. He simply cleared his throat. His face softened as he looked at the small crowd and then began to slowly speak.

"Good evening," his voice was tight, the way a person sounds when they are nervous. "We would have loved to welcome you to this fire; however, we have an issue that makes us, err, shall we say, not verra inviting."

Dessa looked at the faces of the assemblage gathered around. She had not noticed the sad feelings enveloping every one of them until now. Something was awry.

Verra awry. He seemed genuine, but did not introduce himself?

She stood, made a small curtsy and said to the big man, "Good evening."

He continued, "It seems we all purchased our food for the journey north from the same establishment. After a few days, we have all been subject to the same concern." The big man pointed to a pile sitting at the edge of the woods, far away from the fire. "We seemed to have been swindled into purchasing inedible food stuffs."

Dessa walked over towards the pile and she heard someone say, "I would not get too close to that damnú mess."

Dessa stopped a few feet short of the pile. It was a heap of what should have been food. Instead, it was a slimy mess filled with worms, maggots and bugs. All these creatures were happily feasting on the pile. The pile looked almost as if it were breathing.

She had seen bugs on food before. It was a constant problem; she simply picked them off and moved on. It was a way of life. However, this was just gross. The pile seemed alive. The smell was wretched and within what should have been many days of meals for the travelers at the fire, there was nothing even remotely edible.

"Oh my," she exclaimed as she walked backward, away from the moving slime and stench. She looked at the big man, still standing by the fire.

"We have nothing to share and have had nothing to eat for this many days," and he held up two fingers. "I am sorry, and we are not sure what to do. We can turn around and head back to Kalmar, or we can go forward." He looked again at the sad faces around the fire. "We don't know if there are any stores to be had up north, or how far they are from here. Although we hear the people are fair and friendly, we don't know what to do. Please, you and your companion, please share our fire and fix your supper." His head and shoulders slumped, as if he was a man beaten by the circumstances, and he was completely out of options.

During this lull in the conversation, Torrin arrived with a large armful of wood for the fire. Smiling at everyone, he dumped his load and said in a cheerful voice, "Evening fellow travelers, I see you have met Dessa."

He felt the stares of the group upon him. He felt the sadness of every soul. He looked at Dessa and she suddenly looked alarmed. And then, together, all at once, the entire group looked alarmed.

As one, they hitched back a bit from Torrin, digging their heels into the dusty ground to move back.

As one, they seemed to gasp, and Torrin wondered if his breeches were down around his legs. He had faced death before. He had faced the tyranny of Garwen, and his survival instincts always told him what to do. However, with this assemblage of normal, unarmed kauppasaksa, he knew there was no fight to be had, and nothing in his brain could form a reaction that worked.

He looked at Dessa, wide-eyed and questioned, "What?"

She looked at her wondering lover, or so he thought, and she said, in a quiet voice that meant nothing was right, "Oh my! Why can't we just ever travel like normal people?" And she walked directly toward him.

Or, again, so he thought.

She glided right past him, so close he could feel the heat of her body. As she did, he saw her check to make sure she had both knives secure and available.

Torrin quickly took stock of the group of travelers, now dug in with heels around the fire. Not one was moving, not a one was blinking. They just gazed with large, anxious eyes. No sound or chatter coming from the group.

After Dessa passed him Torrin slowly turned around and watched her walk away from him. Her back was ramrod straight and she moved with authority.

And then he looked over her shoulder. His eyes too widened in anxious curiosity as he took a step back and scrutinized, as she fearlessly made her way towards the edge of the clearing.

12. Foreshadow

Soldiers arriving at Eskil always altered the mood of most everyone in the room. These men (always, only men) were continuously big. And to be seen as a big man in a town full of sturdy sailors means, these men were damnú big.

Of course, they had the audacity to be loud, obnoxious, rude and insolent at the same time. Big was just a start, loud followed. Fortunately, big can be tamed. Chrisholom was good at taming.

Tonight was the standard squad at a table, full of loud men. Casually dressed, they carried short swords in light scabbards. Typical evening group, no uniform, no other arms about. The lunch crowd of soldiers that appeared earlier every day showed up in full uniform brandishing long-swords, morningstars on long poles and war axes for close-in fighting. The lunch soldiers were always on duty, ready at a moment's notice. In the evening, these men were free unless summoned to the fort by the ringing of the alarm.

Soldiers around Kalmar were always at the ready, unless the drink was flowing just a bit too much and they had to stand down. This kind of issue did not occur often, but it did happen time and again, especially if they were celebrating some victory.

As Chrisholom watched the soldiers of tonight land in the tavern they acted as their usual obnoxious, self-centered selves. They immediately took the table they wanted and ungraciously removed anyone sitting there, either with a few words, a glare, or by force. They were always keen on a table away from the door in a corner and with ample legroom.

Ancropolis had explained to Chrisholm the soldiers liked to be able to see the whole room, see the doors and windows and never have their rear exposed to a surprise. And of course, stretch out, relax and make sure everyone in the room knows they are in charge.

Wait? There were usually ten. Tonight, just nine. These men lived by their habits. There were always ten.

Something was obviously up? Their Captain was missing! And their mood was not sour, but was certainly not celebratory, by any stretch.

Chrisholm decided to investigate. Looking across the bar to Ancropolis she indicated she would take care of this group. He cast her a doubtful glance and she just smiled in a way that told him she wanted to investigate what was going on with the town's garrison. He nodded reluctantly and turned back to pumping ale from the cool cellar for other customers.

Chrisholom loosened the tie around her neck just a bit, so her dress moved down and her bosom was a bit more revealing. When it came to chatting these men up, and gathering news from the fort, a lady could easily gain the upper hand. Especially a tall blond with piercing green eyes and the ability to coax the barkeep into samples of free uisgebeatha (whiskey).

Carrying her tray to the bar she gathered ten cups and asked Ancropolis for a flask of cheap uisgebeatha. He glared at her, knowing no coins or payment would be forthcoming for this flask from these soldiers. They generally paid for what they ordered, but when a welcome bit of uisgebeatha arrived at the table unannounced, it was not to be considered part of the evening's fare for which they compensated.

Slowly swinging her hips and making sure she had a wanton smile upon her face, Chrisholom approached the soldiers. She noticed they were taunting a younger man in the group. Something about needing more time than it should have taken to subdue a thief or some poor soul in the town these men had decided to harangue.

"Fesker mah (good evening)," she said slowly to the assemblage at the table as she set the cups from the bar firmly in front of each man. And of course, as she laid the cups, she brushed against each of the brutes. Flirting with a look is one thing, touching someone in a sultry way takes flirting to a new level that always works well with these tough men, and gets them to put down their guard.

The table went verra quiet and seemed to relax a bit. Chrisholm had that effect on people.

As she set down the ninth cup, she reached for the tenth and then looked, puzzled. She looked around, seemed to count, then shrugged her shoulders and put the cup with a theatrical flair back upon her tray. She took a deep breath and began to pour.

One by one she poured a healthy dram of uisgebeatha into each earthen cup. Again, slowly she invaded the personal space of each man in the group. For one, leaning into him and rubbing herself on an arm. For another, putting her arm around his shoulder as a lover might. She physically flirted with each man until she came to the last one. The younger one, the others had been taunting.

Licking her lips to make them shine she said to him so the brutes around him could hear, "My sweet, cute bràmair (boyfriend)," she ran her hands through his long red hair and seductively ran a finger down his cheek. "Ye look like ye need some tender care and a bit of lovin. We need to bring a smile to those verra kissable lips that ye are keepn' scarce from the indelicate ladies of this fair town."

The soldiers roared with laughter.

The younger one blushed a bright red. And smiled.

With that, she put the tenth cup on the table. Taking some time and with some theatrics, she poured the young man a healthy dram in the cup she had set before him at his place. Then she added a splash into the tenth cup. Putting her tray and the flask aside she raised the tenth cup and said to the table, "Slàinte Mhath (cheers)."

As is their duty, they responded with the same and drained their cups. All smiling and happy to start their supper with a lovely lady and a free healthy dram. Even if it was cheap uisgebeatha that burned going down.

"Dinner will be out soon," she told the group. And then, she asked in a seductive voice, "Curious, where is your Captain this fine evening?"

They all looked at each other and one said in a low, grumpy voice, "Trouble at the fort."

13. Never Before

As she neared the edge of the clearing, Dessa bit her lip. She was a bit unsure. To be honest, completely unsure. This was new to her. Never before had she encountered, or communicated with such an animal. But something told Dessa, it was her to meet this beast, for some reason. Certainly a reason that right now was completely mysterious.

Just inside the edge of the clearing, the firelight reflected misty yellow, upon large sad and tired brown eyes. The huge mass of thick brown fur became almost invisible in the waning light. And there stood the largest, and surely the most imperial Math-ghamhainn (European northern brown bear, referred to as a 'mathan') Dessa had ever laid eyes upon. No trophy mount in the big hall of Tarmon's castle compared to the size and profound dignity of the animal that stood before her.

However, as Dessa moved cautiously closer, her view of this huge brown mathan changed. Instead of truly majestic, this once great and beautiful mathan sow exuded sadness. Sadness mixed with forlorn frailty, an overwhelming sense of stress, and utter total exhaustion.

Dessa, guessing some infirmity, approached without caution and came to the head of this massive beast. And her instincts said this seemed to be an exceedingly kind animal. She reached out and ran her hand over the creature's head, feeling the clefts in the skull. The softness of the thick fur was as downy as cattail fluff. In a few moments, Dessa could sense long slow shallow breaths, laboring harshly through the huge body.

The big mathan slowly closed sad brown eyes and seemed to come to a relaxing rest. The overwhelming stress that just moments ago had owned this beauty now slowly fell away. Dessa stood there, moving her hand with caring strokes across an immense amount of brown fur, just quietly being in the moment.

The timeless patter of their heartbeats passed between them. Dessa noticed no sound but the crackling of the fire coming from behind where she had left the fire. Not a human was speaking, she could feel them staring. The mathan's haunches slumped low as a relaxed tiredness took over. A relaxed tiredness that exudes from any living creature who has finally found a destination on a long and arduous journey.

And then in her head, Dessa heard the soft breathy words of a gentle question, and in the frailty of the voice, Dessa heard hope, "You are Dessa?"

Dessa answered back, "Yes, I come from the north with Torrin. What can I do for you? What can we do for you?"

The mathan calmed even more, Dessa thought that if an animal could cry, she would see tears. However, the mathan half-closed its big eyes and motioned with a huge head to the rear right leg.

Dessa walked over and looked. She suddenly understood the reason for the sadness, stress and sense of frailty. The leg was obviously broken below the knee. The end of the leg was dragging, limp on the gound. Useless, and dangerously cumbersome. Hard clumps of dried blood and mud hung from the long thick fur.

Dessa immediately grasped the range of issues. As the mathan walked, the broken leg would drag or catch on anything above the ground. Rocks, roots, logs, branches, all awkward obstacles. Sources of pain for this injury.

Quietly Dessa said, "I am so sorry."

The mathan answered softly, "Thank you, a large boulder flying wild caught me this spring, just after my cub and I emerged from hibernation. I have suffered with this since then. Now she's old enough to fend for herself." The mathan stopped, drew in a large breath and continued, "I am here, to be with you, and your friends." Her big head slowly turned to indicate the silent group around the fire circle.

"Be with us?" asked Dessa, a bit puzzled as she came around to the big brown head. In her mind Dessa thought that this massive animal was at least five times the size of Torrin. One big paw would have filled Dessa's chest.

The mathan opened her eyes. She stared straight at Dessa, and firmly stated. "I wish you to take me. Use me as sustenance for your group. End my misery, and end their hunger."

Dessa's eyes closed, her head spinning. She certainly had hunted her share of big game over the years. However, nothing, nothing remotely like this had ever presented itself. Nothing even close. Not in size or circumstance.

Dessa's hand reached out and she lay her palm upon the mathan's head. The finer fur, just a bit lighter than the rest of the fur around the mathan's ears was so soft, it was almost not there. Dessa almost cried at the tenderness surrounding this huge animal. She could feel warmth flowing off the brown tufted ears. The mighty thump of a strong heart coursed throughout this enormous beast. The heart of a loving mother.

A then a tear did course down Dessa's cheek, and she could not, for the life of her, speak a word.

* * *

In the clearing, all the folks had been sitting silently, most with mouths agape and all of them full of wonder. Maybe full of fear? The from across the fire someone said quietly to Torrin, "What the deamhan is going on over there?"

Torrin brought his gaze back to the group and looked at the array of wide-eyed faces. Quietly clearing his throat, he softly said to everyone, "With Dessa and when she is with nature, it could be anything. With most any day, I am never quite sure until things move forward. However, I can guarantee you, it is important, and you will not want to trifle with the goings-on. But ye should no worry, if there be trouble, I would ave sensed it by now."

Torrin had noticed he felt no trouble brewing. The hair on his neck was relaxed, and the relaxed posture of Dessa next to the huge mathan was normal. Whatever was going on, it was not of a worry.

He hoped!

The tone in his voice and the odd meeting at the edge of the clearing had the effect of keeping everyone in their place for just now. And of course, northern brown mathans are generally gentle and well-known vegetarians, unless they are very hungry. Or cornered. Or angry. It is a widely known fact, a mathan will eat anything if need be. And being eaten was the least of anyone's worries. One swipe of just one of those huge paws would send even the toughest of them to eternity.

As Torrin and the rest of the group looked back to the edge of the clearing, Dessa and the largest mathan they had ever seen, ever heard of, or even mentioned in expanded tall tales around the fire ambled slowly away, together, into the forest. One thing they all noticed was the floppy limp in the mathan's gait.

Torrin could hear from a few mouths, 'ò dhiol' (oh my goodness) muttered under controlled breath as everyone's heartrate started to come back to normal.

Torrin began to rise, he had decided to follow Dessa.

And then he sat down.

It was a wise move.

14. Brewing

"Do ye feel like taking a nice plate to yer dear Captain tonight?" asked Chrisholom to the assembled soldiers at the table.

The group had all been eating for a while now. And for a group of mostly big, seasoned soldiers, they were unusually quiet, somewhat subdued, not like the regular rowdy evening bunch of combatants gracing Eskil's dining room. She noticed they'd been talking in serious tones the whole time. Voices just quiet enough, so as not to share their stories with other tables.

One of the older and larger soldiers of the group answered her question, "That might cheer the commander's morbid mood. He's had his clach (balls) in a knot for the last few days. Bring it here ye lovely wench, add it to our bill."

Everything else at the tavern this evening had been normal. The big pot of stew was getting to the bottom and had been sold for a good number of coins. Ancropolis only had to put a couple of drunken sailors out the door, and they'd really been no trouble to speak of, or ruin of the evening.

Sailors coming off the big three-masted schooners were regulars. The locals loved their stories of lands from far away. These sailors spoke of giant green mountains on exotic islands. Great cities of stone and marble where something called wine or port could be enjoyed. Drinks verra different than the distilled grogs and thick ales common in the north.

The grogs of the north came mostly boiled from foods that had been too long in the root cellar. The leann (beer) or commonly called beòir was brewed in Eskil's cool cellar or brought in by ship from a wide variety of locations. The sweeter treacle drinks or strong dregs were not so common or abundant in this part of the world. Drink here was strong and pungent.

Many times, a few jugs or a cask of these strange and often fruity drinks would arrive at the tavern in exchange for lunch or supper. Usually, the bearer of these interesting beverages would be a first mate or a captain from one of the larger three-masters tied up at the docks. These sailors may have been short of money, but not a spare small cask. And that cask would be to pay for a meal for a rowdy companion the sailor might be pursuing for the evening. Chrisholom had tried sampling these on occasion. She found them interesting, but mostly boring. She preferred to imbibe the strong beòir or uisge beatha (whiskey) of the land. Ancropolis always sampled each and every cask that arrived. He enjoyed hearing of its origins and background. Chrisholm could tell he liked the sport of tasting not only foods from around the world, but beverages and spices.

Ancropolis was a curious man, and that man, was a gentleman. When trying a new drink offered up by a stranger, sometimes he would smile, others, sort of shake his head and mummer a gentle thank you if he was not liking the drink. And she noticed when he went back to the kitchen after a taste, he often grasped his big tankard and swallowed down a hearty share of his favorite beòir. Some of the beverages shared by travelers were, well, just awful.

However, some items were fun, full of taste, color and presented for a lively, or at least interesting detour from their normal fare.

Tonight, Chrisholom decided to use some of the latest import of the aforementioned Port to entice the soldiers into further conversation. Neither she nor Ancropolis were verra fond of the stuff, and they had a half a cask, left by a drunk captain who had taken a shine to her. He had been led away by one of the regular ladies who was sure to lighten his sporran by evening's end.

Unbeknownst to the soldiers and the rest of the tavern, Chrisholom had been experimenting with herbs, honey and all sorts of additives to embellish various drinks. She was close to some amazingly tasty options for their customers. And she had been working to create a hearty drink, one that would please the northern palate. She had been experimenting with a port cask.

Over the last two winters Kalmar had become busier. More people. More ships. More trade. She knew that soon new taverns would emerge. People would have many more choices on where to enjoy their evenings. Chrisholm was smart enough to know Eskil needed to be more than a name. She and Ancropolis needed to have special options for folks. Options that were impressive, fun and not available anywhere else.

So, she experimented, looking to create a buidheach (Drambuie like drink).

She was not ready to share broadly.

Almost ready.

Maybe tonight could be a test?

A mischievous smile was set upon her lips.

15. Caretaker

The mathan led Dessa just a wee bit deeper into the twilight lit forest on a path Dessa could barely see. Dessa noticed the route was easy, no boulders to step over, no logs or branches catching an injured leg.

Dessa quietly commented, "You have taken this path before. I can barely see where we are going."

The mathan replied, "Yes, since the injury, I've had to travel only on easy terrain. I've created or found many trails like this one. The other animals have been incredibly supportive, both of myself and my cub. The wolves decided my cub was off limits. I guess they thought I was suffering enough."

Dessa was again amazed. The animals of the forest decided? The wolves decided? Nature was stronger, more powerful, more intertwined and organized than she could ever have imagined.

Now, it occurred to her, those interesting conversations and experiences among the animals were more than just coincidence. Experiences, that she had not pondered enough. She remembered the big panther, Ailis the Fergal taking Zoltha, Chadus' horse to Garwen's castle. The two must have gotten along. Which is unusual, since panthers are wont to feast on horses. And then there was the conversation with Praritor and Ailis at the Journey Inn, just before the gift of talking to the animals seemed to evaporate into thin air. It had been a close and intimate conversation when they bid her a sad farewell. A lump formed in her throat as she recalled the memory.

When they bid her goodbye, they knew their discussions with Dessa were over. But, how would they know? Was something bigger in nature calling the shots? Was something, or someone in charge? Dessa shook her head as the immensity of it all began to sink in. They knew this odd gift would go away. She was the one surprised. Oh sure, the all-powerful humans? Maybe not so powerful?

But this special gift of conversations with the animals had returned? Had it been returned, or been given back to her for some yet unknown reason?

And now, this injured mathan knew Dessa and Torrin were about in this dark, thick, immense forest. She had known how and where to find them. She knew these people around the fire were starving!

She knew?

All of a sudden Dessa came to the realization that nature is choosing the path. Nature is in control. A thought occurred to her, she could not put it to words or yet understand. But something was coming together, and she shivered, because suddenly, she felt verra small and frail.

And it appeared to her that for a person who knows they can live forever to feel frail, it means something is up. Something bigger than, well, than she knew.

The mathan soon stopped in a place of green soft grass, tall and inviting. She lay down and let out a heavy sigh. "Here is good."

The mathan gazed up at Dessa with large brown eyes, soft at the edges full of need and overwhelming weariness. She looked at the tall redheaded human whom she was asking to end her suffering. And with it, end the hunger of the group around the fire.

Dessa looked back along the short trail they had taken. She could almost see the fire. Almost hear the chatter of the people there at the stone fire ring. The deep darkness of the evening was settling in, and the trees of the forest began to meld into the dark shapes of the night. Leaves flittered to hide and expose stars. Rocks became dark clumps, their characteristics gone until the light of tomorrow's day. And the excited scurrying sounds of the forest's nocturnal animals emerged.

Dessa knelt beside this huge mathan. Her hand found the well-worn hilt of the long sharp blade in her boot.

The mathan closed her eyes and Dessa could feel the stress of hard living, pain and suffering escape from her being. Through the thick fur Dessa's hand found the warm artery in her neck.

Dessa could feel the soft pulsing of blood through the artery, and as she closed her eyes, her tears fell upon her outstretched arm.

16. In For A Penny

At Eskil, Chrisholom prepared an almost too large pitcher of her latest herb and port mixture, her curiosity and a bit of fear burned in her heart. If things were not right at the fort and the garrison commander was in a tiff of some sort, things could go badly in the village.

It had happened before. With the garrison in turmoil, disaster for the residents happened without warning. Any form of normal life was impossible for every person living in Kalmar. If they had even an evening's notice for the citizens, things could turn out much better. Just having a night to prepare, a bit of space to hide important items reduced the stress that abounded when the garrison was in turmoil. Having a day to make yourself ready for irritated soldiers would make the difference between agony and just a little distress.

Two springs before, a report had come to the attention of the garrison that wild Norsemen were raiding the western coast and threatening Falkenberg. By the next day, soldiers had descended from the fort into the town of Kalmar taking whatever supplies they deemed necessary for a three-day march west to Falkenberg. It was nothing short of looting as the citizens stood by helpless, watching horses, goats, cows, sheep and pigs being herded away by armed militia. Any interference resulted in a severe beating or even the burning of the owner's barn. One young man violently died trying to save his favorite horse. None of it was good.

The long and the short was, Kalmar was left verra barren. The soldiers, in their unplanned haste, had taken most of the food. Starvation loomed like a dark and ominous storm, showing upon the face of every being in town.

All summer, it was a mad rush in Kalmar to procure animals, breed them and grow as much food as possible to survive the long, cold brutal winter. Fortunately, no one starved, because the citizens, led by the smart and insightful Borgmästare (mayor) of the town, allowed him to quickly put hard and fast rules in place.

The day after the garrison left, the Borgmästare, Raket0st, called a meeting at Eskil. Ancropolis and Chrisholom were only allowed to serve water. Even if people wanted to order food, it was not allowed. Raket0st needed everyone's complete attention.

Raket0st helped everyone understand the only solution to surviving the winter was to work together. Not a bit, but all the time, share everything, waste nothing and live as one. Breathe as one, closer than neighbors, closer than family. He steadily built purpose into every soul of the town. They knew they all needed each other in their hearts. Raket0st turned that knowledge into desire and then into a fire to survive together and beat the odds.

It was a simple plan and one everyone could easily participate in and understand. All meals would be cooked and served at Eskil. Everyone would contribute what they could. Chrisholom was in charge of the kitchen. Every villager would take turns helping out. Men, women, boys, girls. No one was exempt, even Galgore the disabled sailor was employed to assist.

Galgore sported only one arm. His other had been torn off from a snapped rigging on his ship during a storm. With his good arm, Galgore kept the fire just right in the big stove in Eskil's well-built kitchen. And of course, Chrisholom discreetly gave him a few extra swigs of spirits upon occasion, for she could almost feel the pain he suffered from his injuries.

The plan for the town's survival not only worked out, but it also built a stronger community. Everyone in the area was proud of the fact they would not only survive, but they would also thrive, given a horrible situation.

They would thrive, despite the wretched garrison of troops that bedeviled their lives from time to time.

After a week or so, the garrison returned. Although victorious against the invaders, a third of their troops had been killed in battle. And, as bad news for the town, none of the livestock they had so hastily commandeered returned with the soldiers. The mood of the survivors was not good. The mood of the town was not good, and slowly worsened. Worsened when the soldiers and their leaders realized, a bit too late, that their hasty taking of so much food from Kalmar may have been a mistake.

Only after one day for the garrison to settle back in, Raket0st decided to meet with commander Gustav. Raket0st boldly walked up the rough stone paved avenue along the moss-covered walls of the fort. Although he was alone for this meeting, he knew the towns people supported him, without question. A large crowd of the citizenry stood by the gate, quietly hoping discussions went well.

Raket0st laid out the options to commander Gustav. Join the town in survival, replace what they had taken or they all die of starvation during the approaching winter. And the forecast was clearly for a harsh winter; the summer had been long and hot. Every long hot summer foretold of a long, snowy, harsh winter season.

The matter was not one of power and control. It was simply of living or dying. All of them would live, or die, together. The king would not send supplies, it was too late in the season.

Gustav took a day to consider his options. He knew he could not replace the items; they had all been used or squandered by the soldiers. He also knew, he that if he fed only the garrison, and the townspeople passed on, he was doomed. As much as he looked down on these little peasants, he understood he needed them for labor, supplies, taxes and support. Gustav agreed to participate. And even though he did not like being backed into a corner, he was a man of his word and held fast to his agreement.

After a few days the hard feeling with the soldiers dissipated, well mostly. For some people it took a bit more time. After some bitter arguments, everyone came to their senses, especially as the cold began to creep in towards the longer dark evenings. It worked out because everyone in the town and the garrison had a common purpose - survive the winter. And more importantly, survive the winter together.

Was all this foolishness to start again? Chrisholm was concerned that if something was amiss at the fort, the soldiers might make the same mistake again. This time with dire consequences, because it was already late fall.

Chrisholom resoundly placed the heavy pitcher upon her serving tray, she straightened her shoulders, put on a cheery smile. She was all-in to determine what was going on within those moss-covered walls of the fort.

As she walked past Ancropolis she whispered her plan quickly in his ear. He nodded, set his face stern and then fetched a bottle of fresh clear liquor, just distilled from a batch of almost rotten potatoes.

Many years in the future this liquor would come to be known as 100 proof vodka. Tonight, it was lubrication in addition to the experimental well-seasoned port on Chrisholm's tray.

Chrisholom walked toward the table of soldiers. Her smile bright as she loosened the tie at the top of her dress a bit more and added a seductive gait to her walk, which made her long blond hair swish to and fro across her back.

17. The Right Thing

Their soft shallow breathing had synchronized. Lungs slowly inflating and deflating together, as one. A calm passed between them. A mutual calm, so foreign to the circumstances at hand, settled really as a solace of understanding. This form of kinship, a mutual embrace of souls needing each other in such important ways, verra few ever know.

Dessa knelt in the long grass beside the huge brown form of the mathan. The enormous beast had slowly eased herself to a comfortable position, laying on her side. The broken, mangled leg was positioned prone on the ground, useless and shattered, and out of the way. Dessa's hand grasped firmly the hilt of her knife. She took a deep breath and simply said with conviction, "No."

The mathan sighed. She inhaled a long pondering breath into lungs she had not expected to use much longer. And then, as she slowly released that air, said, "But…?"

Dessa interrupted, "I mean, not yet." Her other hand was buried deep in the soft fur. She could feel the warmth of thick hide under the fur and the down like softness of the inner layers. "Soon, I will carry out your wishes. But right now, where be your cub this evening?"

The mathan flared her nostrils and forcibly cleared her nose, almost a soft bark. It was not loud; it was a sound Dessa had never heard before.

After just a few of these breaths, a young cub appeared in the fading light. The cub stood back cautiously, eyeing the scene in front of her. Not knowing what to do. It had been a summer full of not knowing what to do. Dessa could see trouble on the young face. She could sense worry and tenseness that any young thing should not have to endure.

Dessa motioned the cub to join them and said, "Please lie down with us for the night. One last night. One last time. You deserve one last night."

The injured mathan made some grumbling sounds and the cub took tentative steps forward, "She does not have the ability to communicate with you yet. Please promise me, you will end this with the sunrise?"

Dessa responded, amid tears flowing over her red checks, "I promise."

The cub ambled forward, still a bit tentative and then became curious. She came close to Dessa and sniffed at this creature, who had to be incredibly peculiar. Dessa slowly rubbed her head and felt the cub's warm ears.

After a few moments of getting to know, and maybe trust each other, the cub came to the mother's head. The mathan beast closed her eyes as the cub ran her muzzle across her mother's face.

After just a bit of time, and it seemed too short, the cub lay down with her mháthair (mother) and this strange human. Dessa marveled at their connection. She was sad for what had happened and what must transpire. She knew she needed to do her duty; her greater duty was to bring kindness. She could not make it right; but she could make the situation better, for the long term.

As all three lay together, collectively warm and with a harmony that was hard to describe, they shared deep sleep, as well as a deep peace.

Nature let them rest under a gentle moon, amid the tender rustle of dry autumn leaves in a tender wind.

That is, nature let them rest until Marjie the spryte appeared during the blackest portion of the night. And all of a sudden, things got complicated.

18. Beyond Knowing

"Gentlemen," Chrisholom exclaimed brightly to the assembled soldiers, "Would ye fair sturdy brutes feel strong enough to be part of my grand experiment?" She scanned the inquisitive faces assembled as she placed the heavy pitcher down in the center of their table.

"What you got 'ere, you mischievous young gnèitheach (sexy lady)?" said the obvious leader of the group. His eyes scanned the big table full of men with a bit of a sneer and a leering smile. Everyone else laughed the nervous kind of laugh when your boss makes a joke and you are supposed to laugh, even though it's not funny.

Chrisholom was caught just a bit off guard, she expected pushback at her obvious ploy to befriend these men. But maybe they had been stressing about the garrison? Had they been imbibing just enough to be off-guard? Really, it did not matter. But, seeing how easy it was to break into the group, put her on guard. In the end, her trust in these soldiers was one of simply trusting they were out to get all they could for themselves. Nothing more.

She smiled seductively at the men and replied, "I have been carefully testing ingredients to make new libations for my favorite customers. That be the likes of you!" As she said this, she set the bottle of vodka near her elbow and sat comfortably on an old soldier's lap. Of course, his arm encircled her waist, and a smile appeared behind his long ragged beard.

"Ye are an alchemist of fun ye fair haired troublemaker?" remarked the leader as his hand snaked under her dress and explored her long leg.

"Yes, I do love trying new things," she said lustily. "I'm always up for something a bit different you know (the table snickered at the obvious undercurrent of her statement). The city is growing though, and there will soon be other taverns," she said with a sigh. "We need to keep things interesting at Eskil. I do love ye with me whole heart and I don't want you handsome strong fellows to wander away!"

She did not remove his hand from under her dress, she only stopped his wandering fingers from moving further along by encircling his wrist with her own long strong fingers.

She then moved her lips to his ear and whispered, "I don't mind ye feeling me leg ye big brute, but my husband will spear you through the throat if he sees yer hand in places only his fingers and tender lips belong."

Now, there are some things in life that are just true. The old soldier slowly turned his eyes toward the bar area and looked inquisitively at Ancropolis. The big man behind the bar was not looking at the group, nor at the table. But instinct told the soldier, Ancropolis had already sensed the trespassing upon his lady. The bar owner's shoulders gave it away, a tenseness. An almost frozen sense of stress. The old soldier could see that Ancropolis was not even breathing. Ancropolis was waiting a few heartbeats for things to become right.

The soldier knew, consequences be dammed, Ancropolis would make things right. Right for himself and his lady.

The soldier was not an old soldier because he was stupid or careless. He was old because he paid attention to the things that mattered. Right now, he had a sense that changing his behavior was something that would matter and continue to let the soldier continue to breathe. Because right now, the larger and longer consequences would not matter. Ancropolis was going to protect what he considered his. And this lady was part of what he considered his!

Folklore is a powerful narrator when it comes to understanding a story. Folklore defines how people see, perceive and understand another person. Ancropolis was surrounded by a verra heavy narration of local lore.

You see, not long ago, Chrisholom had imbibed just a bit too much with the evening's crowd of revelers at Eskil.

Everything was really all in good fun. Winter cold was harsh, snow was piling up along the external walls and no man nor beast wanted to be outside. The fire at Eskil was warm, all the bellies were full, and drink was flowing as generously as laughter was shared among the tavern's guests.

Maybe too generously. A young man, a verra robust young man had gotten a bit frisky with Chrisholom. She was, as you might imagine, doing nothing to deter this tall, good-looking, curly-haired redhead to stop his flirtatious behavior.

That was, until she saw the severe and not so much angry, as infuriated look on the strong face of Ancropolis.

Adrenaline had poured into her liquor-soaked blood and sobered her up in just a few heartbeats. She glanced at her redheaded flirting suitor, back to Ancropolis and she then decided to save the flirt's life.

"Ye frivolous sexy man, ye want to hear a story?" she whispered seductively into his young ear (really more boy than man, but at this point, it would not matter). If she did nothing, he would never grow a real beard.

"Certainly, you luscious wench, regal me with your words." He smiled and kissed her hand.

Chrisholom motioned her head toward Ancropolis and said, "Last time another man had his hand up my dress, my dear lover there, tossed a spear through the horny infiltrator's throat. Oh, it did make a mess and I had a tuilli (bastard) of a time cleaning the blood from my dress. But ye know, that beastly man of me own, he just pulled that spear from the man's windpipe, wiped it clean on the still warm deceased's shirt and put it back behind the bar."

The story about Ancropolis stuck and became the folklore surrounding him everywhere he went. The kind of story that generally got told after some juicy unearned gossip about Chrisholm emerged. She might be a flirt, but it never really went any further, she saved her desires for Ancropolis.

So maybe that folklore saved a man, or a few, or kept Chrisholm out of trouble. But right now, a few winters later, this evening, the old soldier slowly removed his hand from Chrisholom's leg. He was wise enough to put both hands on the table, easily seen.

Ancropolis smiled and his shoulders relaxed.

Chrisholom returned her attention back to the table and said, with a heart melting smile, "I want yer honest and most sincere reactions about this batch of brew I've conjured up. It's meant to warm yer soul on a cold damp night, bring a smile to your face and peace to yer evening."

She looked around at the soldiers and she knew they were interested but had never been part of something like this. Usually, they were not allowed to speak their minds. Just follow orders.

By the time the pitcher of doctored port was empty, the vodka was also gone, and the soldiers had staggered out, Chrisholom had all the information she needed. And, they had also liked the drink she'd conjured up. For this, she was overjoyed. The other, not so much. She was not really sure why.

And that's what bothered her.

19. Command

It was impossibly dark. And then it wasn't dark. Dessa awoke with a start from her comfortable position, snuggled warmly with the mathan. She was confused by the light dark issue, and suddenly, without warning sneezed.

"Bless you," said a tiny voice emanating from the blackness of the night.

And then it was abruptly not a black darkness, as fiery pixie dust swirled around the ground with some sort of small person pirouetting in the center of this odd twinkling circle of strange fire that seemed to hover just above the ground before slowly flittering down onto the grass.

Dessa, not really sensing danger, was instantly more curious than startled. What now? Her mind asked as she crept towards wakefulness. A wakefulness climbing from an exhausted sleep that had been warm and deep as she had lay in undisturbed slumber against the warm body of the injured mathan.

A chipper voice, full of laughter emerged from the center of this twinkling circle and now Dessa could see it was a small, blonde woman. A woman of completely indistinct age. She was tiny, she would not even have reached Dessa's knee, had Dessa been standing. The tiny lady's hair was blond, clean, combed and perfect, like that of a princess.

This tiny person (if she was a person?) wore a shiny blue dress, and was moving, dancing and having a good time. All this as the fiery sparks continued to consume the darkness around her.

Dessa cocked her head, watching, getting used to the light and wondered again, what now?

The tiny person in the dress excitedly asked Dessa, "Surprised?"

"What do you mean, surprised?" asked Dessa furrowing her

eyebrows. She was still trying to grasp what was going on here in the opaque blackness of this strange night. An opaque blackness now interrupted by swirling clouds of fiery dust and a small person with a voice like an excited cheerleader giving it all she could at a tied championship game.

It answered, "Did you think we were done with ye?"

"Done with me? What do you mean done with me? And who is we? And as a matter of fact, who mac an donais (damn) are you, or as a matter of fact, what are you?" replied Dessa, more strongly than she might have, had she not been awakened from a warm slumber, after a hard day of travel, ending with a life and death situation from which there was no retreat.

The cheerful voice replied with a laugh, twirled bright pixie dust from her dress and bounced up to Dessa's knee in one graceful leap. Dessa noted this thing was as light as a dried fall leaf, almost not there. The tiny sprinkles of light from the fiery dust settled on Dessa's britches and flickered out. More floated to the ground and slowly disappeared with tiny hisses as it met the dew in the grass.

"My, my, now aren't we the grump!" exclaimed the voice, her tiny hands planted firmly on her hips. Then she sighed heavily, rolling her eyes, "Ok, I prefer to be addressed as Marjie. I am a spryte. You should call me Marjie." A mischievous smile and more twinkling fiery pixie dust was tossed about. "Or maybe, Clamfoot?"

The spryte then threw both of her tiny hands into the air, fairy dust tossed into the sky sending a rainbow of sparks about and then she giggled like a happy child. After a moment, sitting down on Dessa's knee with a smile and a flourish she said, "No, let's go with Marjie! I daresay, I do prefer it."

And with that, Marjie pirouetted into the air spreading a rush of fiery sparks about. Then, with practiced grace she landed on two tiny bare feet, settling upright on the tip of a blade of grass next to Dessa.

A spryte? Whatever is that, really? Dessa mused as she noted such a small creature was packed with more energy than seemed possible. "Aren't you really a fairy?" asked Dessa of this small creature. At the same time Dessa thought she might be dreaming.

Marjie's face instantly took on a solid green color. The color of mold on top of a pond when the sun hits it on a humid summer day. Green, fresh and nasty. Dessa could see and sense the tenseness of clenched jaws. Marjie's hands were tight against her petite waist and her fingers were white from pressing so hard.

After a few breaths, maybe practiced or coached, Dessa could see the stress leave the little spryte and Marjie relaxed. And then in calm voice, one that was obviously calm on purpose, Marjie said, "Fairies are mischievous little deamhans. They make magic and prank the world, just for the fun of it. In my opinion, humble as it may be, they are useless little beings. But we must deal with them, just as we must deal with you human beings. We have not a choice, nor a say in the matter, it's just the way it is. We sprytes are charged with looking after what should be the natural course of the world. Fairies, they just play."

Marjie looked keenly at Dessa, and it seemed to occur to Marjie that Dessa really had no inkling of sprytes. She did not know the difference between a fairy, a spryte, a pixie, a nixie or a stump. Dessa was not toying with her, she was really just curious and not too intimidated to inquire.

Marjie seemed to relax a bit more and the putrid green swamp color drained away from her face and she went from pond scum green to a natural skin, a bit shiny, but less intense. It was a bit unnerving to see it all happen. But Dessa mused, I guess the world is full of surprises!

Marjie fluffed her frilly blue dress, which brought forth a puff of sparks. She flexed her pointy little toes and then sat down in the damp grass with a theatrical flourish and whoosh of sparks. After a bit of a sigh, she slowly moved her face and looked up at the still inquisitive Dessa.

This time there was no smile. There was a fierceness in her eyes that belied joviality. And Marjie said, in a sincere voice, a voice with purpose that held none of the previous kitschy humor of her introduction, "You canna give up."

Dessa sighed as she ingested this directive from this curly haired, fire dusted nothing more than a whisper of a being who had interrupted her warm deep sleep. She mused to herself that all of a sudden, things change, and it's always a shock. A quick flashback of memories flew through her head; she had talked to a wolf and commanded a herd of spiders to attack a man. She had fought evil in all ways possible, had enjoyed passion in the water, upon the sand and in all sorts of places. She had dispatched a rapist who lay upon her chest, learned to fight to the death as a young and lost single girl on the trail. And so much more that was just beyond her memory for right this moment.

What? And now this?

Dessa figured she had seen and experienced just about all the surprises and odd experiences anyone could stand. And she was ready for a normal day. Not like today had been, for sure.

"What?" Dessa said a bit sternly, "Not give up what?"

The spryte slowly folded her tiny glimmering hands upon the bowl her soft blue dress formed between her knees. Sparks shimmered in the blackness of the night, bouncing in small flittering's from her luminescent outfit. The fiery dust almost pooled where her hands lay, clenched together.

Marjie looked up at Dessa with an even fiercer face and said in slow measured words, "My dear, you and boyfriend there carry the message to save humanity from thousands of years of torment and evil. The idea of free will. Living by choice. Freedom of expression, work, purpose. The verra core of the soul. The verra core of life."

Dessa nodded, "Yes, we know. You did sum it up better than we ever have, thank you. But why are you talking to me about giving up?"

Marjie suddenly shot into the air, twirled and showered bright fiery pixie dust over the whole area. The dust became more intense, the sparks bigger, and Dessa could now feel heat.

Finally, after a few more overly theatrical spins Marjie landed again on the tip of a blade of grass. Grass damp with evening dew. The blade did not bend, Dessa was a bit amazed. Marjie stood erect, and proclaimed to Dessa, "I have seen the future, and I know. I know what it looks like if you fail."

Dessa began to speak, and Marjie tossed fiery dust towards Dessa to shush her and then said, "Trust me. Do not fail. It's not you humans we only worry about. It is us. Nature. Every bird, every living creature is counting on you. Even those loathsome fairies."

Dessa opened her mouth to speak, and then it all rushed in. A million things all at once collided in her brain! How the horses helped when she needed them. Praritor the great wolf, at her beck and call. Ailis the Fergal, the monstrously strong panther, always to her defense.

Even the spiders had banded together to support her in her time of need. Nature was there for her. Time and again. Always there.

Dessa took a deep breath and said, "We have no intention of failing at our quest," as calmly as she could muster.

"Well now, pretty words from the pretty girl. So sweet," sneered Marjie. "Do your duty tonight with the mathan. Consider it a gift from all of us, especially her." Marjie elevated up to about head height and said, "Call on us anytime. Oh, and take care of yourself." Marjie gave Dessa a knowing wink, twirled up into the trees with a bright flash of pixie fire, and was gone.

Before Dessa drifted back to a powerful sleep that would not let her stay awake, Dessa turned over a word in her mind that she could not let go, 'Us?"

When Dessa awoke with the sun, she swallowed hard and harkened to herself that she had encountered the strangest dream. Until she looked down and noticed the burned grass and a few holes in her britches from sparks. In her hand was the hilt of her knife, cold with the morning dew. She looked at the mathan, and suddenly knew nature had again come to her aid.

Even more than she understood.

She looked around slowly, the cub was nowhere to be found.

20. Consequence

"Was it fun ye beastly Gnèitheach diabhail (sexy devil)?" inquired a not so humored Ancropolis after the evening's crowd had dispersed.

Chrisholom looked at her lover and said in an even voice, "No it was not fun, at any level, and I need a bath. It was however," and she cast him a knowing glance, "verra much worth it."

Ancropolis raised an eyebrow and went to the great hearth next to the iron stove where the food served at Eskil was prepared. He picked up a large bucket of hot water. "Come, I'll wash ye while you tell me the news ye gathered on your flirting foray. And explain to me why I should let you flirt with that trash. And, why? I might add, should I not practice my spear throwing." He finished the sentence with a bit of a smirk. It was a smoky smirk, and she knew he was half kidding.

She just did not know which half was kidding. Just in case it was not the good half, she picked up a bottle of distilled herbal seasoned vodka and decided not to take any cups (*herbal vodka would come to be known as gin many winters later*).

Entering their room, she closed the door with her foot and moved the brightly painted stone used to keep the door closed to the door's bottom. Making sure it was tight, she dropped her dress to the floor. Ancropolis grinned adding wood to the stove that kept the room warm.

The scrape of the stone was loud in a room where the only other sound was the almost indiscernible hiss of a few candles.

As Ancropolis poured hot water into the tub, he noticed the steam rising amid the bubbles. As he added thin leaves of the lavender soap she enjoyed to the hot water, he smiled. He had felt his own steam rising this evening as she flirted with the soldiers. Now his steam was rising again, for a different reason. He wanted answers, and he wanted her.

21. Deed

At any other time, the invasive drop of cold morning dew trespassing across her cheek would have startled her. She walked slowly back toward the fire ring from last night, along the short path the mathan had taken in the gathering gloom of last evening.

Today, the cold dew did not startle her. As Dessa wiped the cold annoying drop away, a red slash followed her finger in a long sad arc across her face. She could feel the red drip run down her cheek and by this point, did not care. It was just another bit of annoyance in what she was sure to be possibly the worst day of her life.

Her breathing was deep. Even. Heavy. She heard the noisy whoosh of her own breath through cold nostrils and noticed, with annoyance, the heavy fog her breath made in the icy morning air. Oddly, even her nostrils annoyed her, of all days they were clear and overly sensitive. She could not shake the ominous metallic smell of blood permeating her nose, her mind, her verra being.

She needed.

She needed him now.

She needed him to hold her. Help her know their path was right. Know that what she had just done was OK. She knew it was right. It was for a greater cause. It was unavoidable. What she had done had been clearly requested. But it all flattened her heart. She felt like she was spinning out of control.

The mathan.

The cub.

The spryte.

The wretched business of the morning.

The totality of the message mixed with such an act.

Killing had always been part of something else. Something bigger. Killing was always fast, unemotional, tense and dangerous. Maybe for defense, for food or as part of the message delivered to evil. She had never ever been in a position where she had to do anything like she had this morning. What infuriated her most was she had no one to blame but herself for her situation. She had made the decision, and now she had to deal with the consequences.

She felt like an unwilling assassin.

The act had been harsh, and then it had gotten worse.

As Dessa turned the corner from the deep woods and spied the fire ring, she could see, small tendrils of warm smoke whispering into the morning air. The smoke was swept away almost at once by a breeze that seemed to wake with the cool morning. The sleeping travelers bodies lay around the ring, like large logs tossed carelessly, waiting to be transformed into firewood for a cold winter. For a fleeting moment, Dessa had a frightening thought they were all dead.

Until Torrin sat upright as if he'd been hit by a bolt of lightning. He flung his blanket aside and began to run to her.

As he came close, she put out an arm to slow him. He could tell by the look on her face. He had seen the look before, her normally bright blue green eyes blazed striking turquoise. It was the same look she had cast when she needed him to kiss her, and end Garwen.

It was a look that said, pay attention. Something is going on. Something you are going to need to listen to and understand.

He slowed down.

Gently, he encircled her shoulders in a large warm hug and gathered her up. She smelled of earth and leaves mixed with the unmistakable sense of stress. And as he held her, she began to sob.

Torrin stood there, holding her close and let her sob away the anxiety. She felt a bit cold and seemed to be shivering. He could not tell if she was really cold, or it was something else. One part of him wanted to know everything that had transpired. The other part of him was afraid to even begin to know.

He would have to wait until later.

22. Fishing

"It's bad, and maybe it's worse than we know. And the problem is, we don't know, and that is the bigger problem," said Chrisholom. She sat in the tub, as Ancropolis soaped her long blond hair. He needed to touch her, to be near her and reconnect. He knew he would be next in the water, but tonight she was first, she needed the heat. He could tell.

He wanted her to talk. He knew, she needed to talk.

But this? What?

Ancropolis softly whispered into his lover's ear, "Would ye say that again? Maybe say it a bit slower, or mix up da words a bit? Because I 'ave no idea what ye meant and I think it's important."

She turned her head to look at him and gave him a stare that suggested he had turned into a rag doll, or maybe a dumb log. She sighed, turned back as she sat in the warm water and said a bit tersely, "I meant exactly what I said."

"Jus giv me another chance," he answered, being patient. Although at this point, he really wanted to understand so he could do something. Not just wait and wonder. Waiting and wondering was the way of the fool, he was a man of action. In his mind, doing something always brought one closer to a resolution, or at least enough change to get things fixed, or closer to fixed.

Of course, he had no idea what action he was going to be asked to take, and he surely was going to be surprised.

"OK." Chrisholom squared her shoulders, sighed a bit as Ancropolis moved his hands over her soapy skin. She paused and then started again, "Our friend Gustav…"

He murmured, "He may be the garrison commander, but he be no friend of mine."

"Just listen, you big lout," she shook her head before taking one hand that was massaging her upper arm kissing a soapy knuckle. She continued, "The soldiers said Gustav is beside himself with worry. He has found a Völva (seeress, mystic), who has foretold of an eruption of nature."

Ancropolis murmured, "Hmmm? Is our tough leader in the garrison afraid of something in nature? This sort of news does not make a lot of sense to me. I don' think the man is afraid of anythin', let alone some mutterings coming from a crazy lady, ifn she be that, about strange things happening in the forest? From what I ave always heard, a Völva, ifn she be of any value would be pretty much just one step into the natural world of the crazy."

Chrisholom sighed and Ancropolis could feel her pondering, as the water and soap glistened upon her soft alabaster colored skin. She was thinking, debating for a few moments and then she softly muttered, "Oh!"

"Oh?" replied Ancropolis. He was curious and knew better than to push his enquiry too fast. History had taught him to let her muddle in her thoughts and memories if he wanted the whole story to emerge in a coherent fashion. So, he patiently soaped, lathered, rinsed and attended to her, especially her soft parts, while she pondered.

"No," she said, then followed with a "Yes!"

"Hmmm?"

"He has the same problem we have," and she smiled. At least he thought she smiled, because she sat up straight in the water and he could feel her relax too. It was a bit strange, and he was hoping for some clarity.

"He has?" he replied, and then added, "Is this good?"

"Yes!" And she turned suddenly, splashing warm water and soap over her partially clad lover. "Actually wonderful! We must attract the Völva to Eskil! We can ply her with drink and find out what is going on. We can offer to help and then from that we will know what is up."

"Do ya thin' a Völva will be willin to spill her guts to us plain townsfolk? Why this must be a powerful one to set Gustav on his heels, an she mus also be a smart one, if he is a lissn' to her."

Chrisholom smiled as she stood in the tub, her naked form wet and glistening in the lamplight. She undid the knot on the rope around his waist and dropped his trousers to the floor. With a bit of a wonton smile she took a firm grip of his crann. He groaned as she looked him in the eyes and said, "You have a beastly way about you. I know no woman can resist yer charms when ye get in yer head a wanting for her. You will be my bait. I will hook the fish."

She stepped from the tub and led his naked form into the water. She was done talking.

So was he.

They would sleep, but not for a while. She was wanton with lust, and he needed to remind her why he was better than spearing a man through the throat.

As the fire died, the room did not grow cold. And as she slept, her plans formed, reformed and grew in her head. She woke excited to get started.

Chrisholm had no idea, other plans were already in motion.

23. Work

As they stood, his arms wrapped around a slightly shivering redhead, Torrin murmured into Dessa's warm flushed ear, "What 'appened out there? I 'ave be worried sick of you."

It occurred to her, other than her exit to the woods with a huge mathan, he knew nothing. She backed up an arm's length. With her tired face, looked him in the eye, "I'm not sure you'll believe me. But thanks for no disturbing us."

He tilted his head, gave a small comforting smile and said, "You are the dearest part of me life. Surprises is a bit of mystery that just seems to follow you around. Trust me, I'll believe you. It jus takes me some time to fully understand."

Dessa grinned a tired grin and bit her lip. Her shoulders slumped and she said, "You are a kind man. But before I tell you about last night, and there is much to tell. You and this group have a bit of work to accomplish, and it has to start verra soon, actually, it need to start right now!"

"Work?" asked the now confused young man.

"Yes, work," Dessa took a breath and went on, "Seems nature is aiding us more than we know. And we need to take advantage of the opportunity now, or this gift will be lost and that would make today even worse!"

"Now ye is not makn' any more sense than a slug on a beer mug," began Torrin. He stopped as her eyes flashed bright turquoise.

She glared at him and said in an almost savage, yet whimpering tone, "There is a massive mathan just inside the woods," her hand motioned back from where she had emerged. "That mathan just sacrificed herself so that you, and I, and all of these people might eat and carry on!" She was almost yelling.

"What? I?" mumbled a beseeched and confused Torrin.

"Just take care of her. She is everyone's path north, our path south. It was her dying wish she feed us with the verra meat on her bones." As Dessa finished talking, she noticed the others from around the fire stirring. As they began to rise, she shouted at Torrin, her nerves finally giving out, "Just take care of her. Now!"

Torrin looked at the group of hungry travelers stirring from their sleep. He recalled understanding how hungry they were. He knew how frustrated and angry they were that not only was their food gone, but their dreams of heading north were dashed and broken.

No one, not even the hardiest of souls, could make this trip on an empty stomach. He wondered for an instant; Was the most exhausting part of this the hunger, or facing the end of a dream? A dream of a better life?

Torrin looked back towards the woods, and his mind was filled with gratitude. Just beyond this clearing was a gift. Not only of ending dangerous hunger, but a chance to carry on. To carry on a quest.

24. Plan

Chrisholom pulled the blanket over her shoulder and reveled at the warmth of their bed in contrast to the iciness of the room. It was a chilly fall morning, and he had not started the fire yet. In fact, he was still sound asleep with a bit of an angelic calm showing on his face.

She smiled seductively, having been verra satisfied last night, and she knew there was no angel underneath that calm. She sighed and rolled toward him, capturing his warmth and memoires of last night. After their mutual bath, and after the talking was through, they had shared much. Memories of his hands, his lips and his slow, attentive caring still seared through her with a hot smile.

The matted sheepskin still lay on the floor in front of the fireplace. The soft wool had tickled her face as she had taken him. Last night was unhurried, wonderful and special. Neither had wanted their lovemaking to end, she wanted him so badly. She wanted all of him, and he had filled her. She not only had him, she had all of him! His hands, his heart, his words and his parts.

Chrisholom cupped his wilted manhood and whispered in his ear, "All the fires in this room except mine, are out right now and it is verra cold in here."

Ancropolis groaned in reply and then said, "I was hoping you'd put the fire on for us. Ye wicked lass, ye drained me of every ounce of everything I had las night, and I could sleep for days. And your hand is a bit cold!"

"No," she replied, pinching his nipple, which resulted in a whimper. "You get the fire going and we need breakfast." She then added, "Now!"

"What is so the hurry?" he asked through eyes now half open.

"I have a plan and need yer help to think it through."

With that she flung the blankets away and leapt to the cold floor. With a groan he rolled out of bed and made his way to the pile of kindling for starting the fire. It did not take long to light the rich sapwood and spread warm flames.

"So, what is this plan ye have?" asked Ancropolis, still coming awake.

Chrisholm chuckled a bit and said, "I'm not so sure of the details, but ye 'ave ta seduce the Völva."

Ancropolis stood up straight, thought for a moment and said aloud, with his own smile, "I wonder what me mháthair would think of that idea, comin' from yer curious mind?"

25. Team

"You killed that huge math-ghamhainn?" asked Torrin, surprised and a bit shaken. "Are ye daft? It was big as…"

She did not let him finish, she simply stated in a tired tone, "She was hurt. Mortally injured, and living was not in her future. She came to me, actually came to all of us," Dessa hands indicated the now moving small gathering of people. "To save us, give us edible food. A lot of meat with life-saving fat." Dessa motioned to the rotting pile just off the fire circle and said, "To replace that pile of rotten food."

"She knew about these folks near to starvn'?" asked Torrin, still trying to grasp what was going on. The mere fact that this mathan knew about hungry humans in the forest un-nerved him. He looked around, somehow, he felt like he was being watched. Watched from all directions; it was unsettling.

The woods just stood there, looming, large and most of all, powerful! The powerful part Torrin knew, he just did not know how powerful all this dark vastness around him could be when it decided to step up and change the world.

"But how?" his dark hair shook from side to side as he tried to comprehend.

Dessa softened just a bit and sighed. She again realized she'd had a whole night to comprehend the depth of what was going on, and he had just gotten all of it pushed onto his shoulders, after stressing all night. "Please," she pleaded. "Take these good people and field dress that mathan. They need to smoke the meat, render the fat, it will take all day, maybe more. I will tell you all about it later." She began talking faster, "There was much to the mathan's story, and then so much more. My mind almost does not believe it all anyway. I need to settle down. I need to think a bit. I need to get cleaned up!"

She just stood there, trying to give him a moment to reply.

Torrin came to her, cupped his hands around her flushed face, wiped off the still moist blood. He brushed away all the foreign dubisaries (odd foreign material) and gently said, "Ok, I understand, there is much more for ye to speak about? An when ye is ready, I am all ears."

"Aye, there is," breathed Dessa. "Yes, there is so much more to say, but also more for me to figure out. And I need you to figure it out with me. Is jus that…" and the lovely redhead he cherished unexpectedly sat down on the ground and cried.

Torrin knew it was time for action, and to let her be, for now. He wandered over to the group and in just a few heartbeats the team was headed into the forest, tools in hand. Dessa heard all sorts of exclamations when they found the mathan.

As Torrin approached the scene, being the last one in the group he stopped and just looked. What met his eyes was mostly going to be a story that was not so much unbelievable, and it was going to be verra deep.

Dark spots where fire had scorched the long grasses were abundant. He could see the outline of Dessa's form in the dew-covered grass next to the huge mathan. It was all verra confusing.

But the fact of the matter was, there was a lot of joy to be had for these hard-working folks. They were verra hungry.

It was time for action.

26. Invitation

This night, Eskil was near to full. The crowd was excitedly hushed and chatted in muted tones all evening. Of course, the story of Gustav utilizing a Völva to figure out what was vexing him was both amusing, and worriedly mysterious; all at the same time. Many drams of harsh uisge were ordered up from Ancropolis at the bar. He kept up with the demand and was smiling happily at the number of coins coming across to him.

The citizens who serviced the fort had started talking of the odd happenings within the huge stone edifice. It was reported that the main kitchen had been closed and was off limits for a whole day. This while some wild woman conjured up all sorts of deamhan worthy concoctions on the huge stove.

Massive amounts of firewood had been ordered and delivered to the kitchen to boil many pots. Gigantic quantities of steam exited the vents of the kitchen into the town and the smell was just awful. Only Gustav and the Völva were allowed into the main room of the kitchen, used to cook most of the meals for the garrison. No hot or prepared food was available for the soldiers that day, and much laughter was enjoyed at the soldiers plight for 'missing a meal.' The townsfolks took great satisfaction in learning the soldiers may have suffered such misery. Oh dear!

As was told, over and over (and as the night wore on, the story became embellished), at mid-morning Gustav exited the kitchen with nothing on but his pants. His coat, sword, boots and epaulets (that he always wore at the fort) were left behind in the kitchen. The story's mystery escalated when it was said he was dripping wet with sweat. Tears ran down his face and he was muttering something that sounded like 'Never, never, never!'

Everywhere else in Kalmar, for the people, their world was much the same way today, as it was yesterday. The bigger question starting to emerge was one that caused a bit of discomfort, 'What did Gustav know that no-one else knew?'

As the dark of the later evening descended upon Eskil, Chrisholom was careful to make sure the corner table where the soldiers ate was available. No one waiting to eat complained. They knew full well, if soldiers arrived, they would take their seats. Empty or occupied, it did not matter. They took what they wanted.

There was almost an expectation among the citizens that members of the garrison would arrive for their evening supper. If they did not, then the normal routine of the fort was changing, and when their routine changed, something was terribly amiss.

Eventually the big door swung open with a bang and soldiers piled in, single file as they always did for their evening fare and revelry. What made tonight different from the last few evenings was that Gustav had rejoined his team. He boldly led his men toward their usual table. His swagger was his usual self-important swagger. But everyone present could not be fooled, something was different.

He was not really himself.

The tavern was instantly very quiet. And as uncomfortable as it might have been, everyone just stared openly at Gustav.

He stopped next to his usual chair and surveyed the room. Of course, his underlings who accompanied him stood next to their usual spots. As was the traditional custom, no one sat down, until Gustav sat down.

The typically dark beady eyes that gave Gustav his terrible ability to intimidate anyone in his company were bright tonight. Almost joyful. He motioned for his men to sit. And of course they did, without a word.

Gustav stood erect and then said loudly, overly formal, with a hint of sarcasm, "Well now, it seems that we have interrupted your evening's conversation. My sincere apologies! It is imperative for me you enjoy your evening's supper. My men and I appreciate you letting us also enjoy a fine evening supper, at our favorite respite location. Please carry on." He then gave a wave of his hand, removed his hat and sat down. He grinned a bit of a sneering smirk as his gaze surveyed his men.

Ancropolis looked at Chrisholom and pursed his lips. She looked back at him, shrugged her shoulders and began loading mugs onto a tray.

Most of the room turned their attention back to each other and the loud conversations from before that had filled the room, now became a low murmur. Chrisholom noticed that not a person had moved from their chair, or indeed had sat up straight since the soldiers walked in. Everyone was pretty well hunched over to either talk in low tones or hope they were invisible to the large men carrying swords and knives at the corner table.

As she made her way to the corner, tray perched upon shoulder, Chrisholom noticed she did not gain any smiles or nods from the townsfolk gathered about. Even Anton, usually happy and smiling with his friends, was hunched over in quiet conversation. She sighed a bit too heavily, put on a fake, toothy smile and got to the table, making a sincere attempt to look happy. She knew it was mostly in vain. She was worried about what she did not know.

"Gustav," she said as she placed a hand on his shoulder, trying to steady herself and her nerves. "I see you have come back, and we're so glad you're here. We've missed you over the past few days." She uttered a welcoming note to all the men gathered about while keeping her focus on the commander.

After setting a mug in front of each soldier, she again placed a hand on Gustav's shoulder and said in a voice that was supposed to sound welcoming and warm (but she knew it was mostly a frivolous gesture), "We understand there is much going on at the fort, so Ancropolis and I would like to buy you the first round. We have a new uisge just off a ship from somewhere off a coast of some far away place, and goodness knows, it is something that will wipe your cares away quickly."

Before anyone could say anything, Chrisholm walked away. As was customary, giving these brutes a hearty dram was something that calmed them and helped everyone at Eskil experience a more joyful evening.

Arriving back to the table with a full carafe, she poured a heavy dram for each of the soldiers. Finally arriving at Gustav's seat, she planned to give him the remains of her carafe. This was her normal procedure, fill up the commander's mug at the end so he knew he received most of the offering.

Just as Chrisholm was about to pour, Gustav turned his mug upside down, smiled at each of his soldiers and said loud enough for all to hear, "Young lady, I dare say, you lie verra poorly. I know you, and I know your boy style friend behind the bar. You two have been pumping me men as to me whereabouts and demeanor and what news has been happening up the hill. But now I am here, and you both will accompany myself and my men to the fort after we have eaten our fill. Tonight, you will be my honored guests withing the walls of my fort." He emphasized 'my fort' just to make it clear, who was in charge.

He looked up at her, smiled with a sly toothy smile, and then almost as a public display of control, slowly ran his hand up the back of her thigh.

27. Never Alone

Field dressing a mathan is one thing. Field dressing a mathan this size, unexpectedly and without planning or truly having been prepared with all the proper tools on hand, is another. But! Making the most of this gift, as presented and being so very hungry and out of options, made for a very determined and inspired group of people to get to work. Even if they were not entirely sure how to proceed.

Away from the group, and thankfully alone, Dessa made her way to the clear water of the small winding creek. Her only goal was to get herself clean. She was repulsed by the stickiness across her hands. Her knife was grossly gooey with red, and her face spattered in ways she knew was just nasty. As the now almost black redness washed off her knife and hands, her tears mingled with the slow-moving creek. After a moment she washed her face with the flowing water and then she promptly threw up in the grass.

Returning to the stream, she rinsed her mouth clean. Mottled morning sunlight was streaming through the forest by now. The sun was rising, and a bit warm. This also added to her desperation to get the beautiful mathan taken care of so the gentle giant's purpose would remain intact, be fulfilled and not go to a terrible waste.

As she knelt over the slowly moving clear water, her face came into focus amongst the gentle ripples. The memory of the secret people under the water returned. She smiled as she remembered the magic of these people when she was but a wee little girl. And the words of her father, reassuringly strong that the magic would return when we grow older and its more powerful than ever.

The water flowed by and she wondered if the magic was still here, or if it was gone, or would it ever come back? Today was confusing. Yesterday life was an adventure to be relished and enjoyed. Now with the mathan, and Marjie and the command to succeed! She felt a heavy weight on her shoulders.

Dessa wandered further away from the group, found Uta and the two lay down in long grass. Dessa needed the big steed to keep her warm while she forced herself to relax and attempt to take a much needed nap.

As they lay down, Uta murmured, 'Thank you. There are times when I am glad to be a horse. Now relax, you had a hard time last night."

As Dessa eased into a rest. As she let her tired body unwind, she marveled that somehow, are they are all connected? Maybe, we are all connected?

* * *

Just inside the tree line, the weary and hungry group of travelers gathered around the mathan. A full range of questions were racing through each of their minds, and no one spoke. That is until Clare' decided to take charge of the situation and get things moving.

Clare' proclaimed to the group, "Well, we 'ave a gift of not only food presented to us, we 'ave fat and warm pelt for the comin' cold weather. Thank goodness it is a chill morn or this would be goin' bad a'ready." She looked up and then proclaimed, "But the sun is a comin up, we need to get ta work."

Faces turned to her, no one really ready to take charge, or knowing what to do first. Clare' continued, "Who ere has ever cleaned a beast of the forest before? Does nought have a be a mathan, but at least a forest beast. They may a bit different than da animals of da farm."

She looked around at the crowd, no one spoke or raised a hand. They seemed to be in a stupor. Clare' sighed, looked at the big man who had spoken to Dessa at the fire the night before and said, "Buachaill, your family are herdsman. I've seen you dress a goat in less time than it takes to boil water. Why are you standing there like your mháthair is pinching yer tongue?"

The big man looked at Clare', looked at the mathan and back to her.

Shrugging his shoulders said, "Never 'ad anything this big afore, but I'll give it a go. Clare', go run the kitchen, I just ave to get me tools." He pointed to four strong boys and said, "Get yer gloves and things to carry cuttings. Borrow what you need, we'll wash it later, it's gonna be greasy. Verra greasy. The rest of you help my chéile (wife), and we are gonna need a lot of wood for a big, all day cooking fire."

Everyone moved off toward the circle where they'd spent the night. As if by magic, tools and utensils appeared. Axes, saws, knives, baskets, large oilskins and pails. A group headed out to the forest to gather wood. One lady started getting the fire up. Two tall men fashioned a tripod and hanging chain over the coals for smoking and cooking the massive amount of meat.

Buachaill returned to the mathan with the couriers he had chosen. They stretched the mathan onto her back and went to work. As Buachaill worked along he mused this was similar to other butchering tasks he had accomplished in his long life. He had been tending to meat since a young lad, actually since he could walk and hold a sharp knife. This task though, was just so much larger!

Stopping for a moment, Buachaill knelt next to the large brown head. He felt the soft fur around the pointed ears. He stroked the mathan's head from forehead to the end of her long nose. He marveled at how the fur gave way to the solid surface of her nose. And for a moment, he felt sad in her passing. He felt sad for the loss of such a great animal. He always had a moment with anything he butchered. In his heart, he felt he should always be grateful for the soul of the animals that gave nourishment to himself and his family.

Having had his moment, Buachaill went back to work.

As the work progressed, meat went to be smoked. Great slabs of fat were sent to be rendered. Individual parts were taken to a wagon to be turned into sausage and grilled post haste before it spoiled.

The toil, sweat and labor of this team saw the rest of the morning sun's increase and take all the chill from the air. The sun then rose to high noon before it began it's slow descent to the hills toward the west.

A short break was taken at noontime, when the sun was directly overhead, to eat and rest for a bit. After two days of no food, nothing tasted so good. As were the wishes of this gentle brown mathan, there was plenty for all.

Torrin worked alongside the group. The work was not well known to him, and he appreciated his learnings as they made use of every part of the great beast. Dessa eventually woke from her well-earned rest and made herself busy washing things as needed. She could not bring herself to help directly with the work. For her lunch, she ate from their own stores. Vegetables.

When all was complete except for the pelt, Buachaill came to the fire for warmth and a rest. As he sat warming by the fire, drinking a hot tea, Dessa noticed in the darkness a twinkle of lights at the quiet head of the mathan.

For just an instant.

28. Inside

Chrisholm was almost surprised they were not in irons or chains. Of course, there were no options. As odd as this evening was becoming, it was a bit like a pleasant twilight's stroll through the town of Kalmar.

Candles flickered in windows of homes, smoke from cook fires wafted into the night sky, carrying the innumerable smells of supper. Chrisholm noticed sometimes the smell was of strong meat, sometimes heavy spices or a lingering scent of onions. Or, no smells, just a bit of smoke from a fire, calm for the evening.

As they walked toward the fort, she let her mind wander. She pondered the meaning of this somewhat friendly hostage situation. She tried to conjure up what Gustav would need of them? Then she wondered if she and Ancropolis should stop at houses and ask people what they ate? She giggled; that might be fun! It would give them ideas for the food choices at Eskil.

She did not notice what Ancropolis noticed. And in noticing it, he became a bit less nervous, as well as a bit less worried. He occasionally turned his head, watching to make sure it continued, and it did. He smiled and wondered. Really?

* * *

Back at Eskil, Anton had stepped up, with the help of his long-time acquaintances, to clean up and close for the evening. He had wished Ancropolis and Chrisholm 'go n-éirí leat' (good luck) for whatever was in store, and silently wondered, behind his kind grey eyes, if they would ever return.

Quietly, he hoped he would not have to start over again.

29. Unplanned

Buachaill stood stiffly in the gathering light of the morning after the arduous work of butchering the mathan. This morning was cold as many fall mornings in the forest present themselves. The fire had burned very low through the night and all that was left was a pile of warm ashes, waiting for new fuel.

The entire group had worked as a well-coordinated team in a sweaty frenzy until darkness ended their labors. Dark work with sharp tools is never a good idea. However, they enjoyed a well-deserved happy sleep. Bellies full for the first time in days. The starvation threat had passed, and the evening had brought further enjoyment, totally unplanned.

Other kauppasaksa had arrived toward the end of the long day. And as is common on a trail of hardworking people, new visitors usually bring joy. Tonight was no exception.

Joy had arrived in various forms. There was the joy of vegetables to accompany the gift of the meat. The joy of new voices. The joy of news, stories from near and far. And even a few energetic children. Maybe the children brought the most joy. The certainly contributed a lot of energy.

Children do not often travel the trails with their parents. Traveling the dark woods is considered dangerous on many levels. The threat of a wagon accident was always present, as well as attacks from hungry wild animals. Not to mention robbers and miscreants who found children as a source of gold, when sold into slavery.

But these children were close with their parents and pitched right in to help and be part of a day's workday. They seemed to be tame. To a point. That point came about after the meal was finished, the work completed. Then the children changed the energy of the whole group. Almost as a pre-ordained moment.

What brought a change to the whole feeling of the fire circle were the playful exploits that ensued after the work and supper was completed.

Suddenly, without warning, a fast game of tag arose. The younger kauppasaksa attempted to keep up with the antics and speed of the younger children, but they were no match for these well-practiced kids.

Around the camp they sped, kicking up dust in the process. They ventured through the creek with a loud chorus of laughter. The horses attending to the long grass just eyed them and oddly seemed amused by the ruckus.

And for some reason, the children knew to stay away from the site of the mathan. They never ventured close.

Maybe children do understand.

30. Room

How did they get so many verra massive stones atop each other, in such fine form? Where might stones so large come from, so long ago? How the deamhan did they move 'em? These thoughts entered Ancropolis' mind as the old fort came into view in the gentle illumination of the evening. As he walked along, his mouth was agape, a bit like a first-time tourist in a big city.

The soldiers around him said nothing. They just smiled and shook their heads. The looks and puzzled expressions from Ancropolis were

typical of people not familiar with the massive place. The layers of huge stones, high windows and immensity of the old fort was beyond comprehension for most anyone.

The narrow road to the fort was steep and not at all smooth. Jagged points of rock stuck up sharply in countless places where the stones on the old road had vibrated up around loose dirt. Or, where an angular stone had been pushed up by evil frost heaves of the wickedly cold winters. Tracks from wagon wheels over many seasons rutted the pathway up its dark middle. Piles of horse chac often made passage on foot almost intolerable as the sticky, slimy muck adhered to boots in the most disgusting fashion.

And when there was rain, the steep road was almost a chac slide. Not fun, not at all like a good snow slide. The soldiers guarding the parapets often had a good laugh watching folks sliding on their arses down the road in the rain.

Gustav being the man he was, had ordered the road cleared for the day since he was venturing out for his supper. He had no desire to deal with the chac issue, nor the hordes of flies feasting hungrily on the piles day and night. Had he not made such a decree, the amount of horse chac would have been troublesome for his group of soldiers and curious 'guests' approaching the main doors.

Upon the walls of the fort, black moss enveloped much of the rough-hewn stone. Almost as if nature had added its own age-old graffiti. White rivulets of crystalline bleached calcium wound their way beside the endless puzzle patterns of seams snaking in a dizzying array along the vast outer wall. Water had leached nutrients from stone over a millennium of rain, snow and nature's fury. The calcium's powder white added a touch of art to this complex laced pattern streaming down the sides of the giant edifice.

No one alive directly remembered the construction of the fort. So, the stories of its origin were now fables of legends and wonder among the townspeople. Fable and lore told especially well when visiting sailors and explorers inquired about the fort's history.

The construction stories had become theatrically embellished tales of huge men, clad only in sheepskin loincloths. These giant stoneworkers are the favorite characters when fabling is strong in the tavern or around the supper table. In tales of strength, the characters just grow. And at Kalmar, the stoneworkers became bigger, stronger and more powerful. These stories added to the mystique of the fort itself and provided a bit of noble status to the soldiers residing therein.

Other than the steepness and ruggedness of the path to the main gate, this walk did not seem dangerous or scary. Ancropolis mused he had never been treated with such regard by a capturing party. There were no chains or shackles. No leg irons or uniformed soldiers threatening himself or Chrisholom.

As much as it seemed strange, it seemed to be ordinary. Which was a bit troubling all at once. As they trod along, he looked for warning signs, and he found none. In fact, the only sign so far troubling him was not really trouble, it was mostly just a curiosity that had him wondering. That curiosity he figured, would be explored later with his lady, and now was not the time.

More than he knew.

Gustav had not given Ancropolis or Chrisholom a choice about accompanying him and his brood of soldiers back to the fort this evening. That was clear. However, it was not a threatening order, as so many of these orders came to be with the townsfolk. It had seemed more like a cautious invitation.

Often, the soldiers (or as the townspeople referred to them as Gustav's henchmen), would arrive at a farm, or home, and unceremoniously drag off a citizen for some crime committed against the garrison. It could be something such as shorting the fort's kitchen a bit of meat, or a wheel of cheese. It could be taxes not paid. Whatever the crime, the poor citizen was taken to the dungeons, locked up and left in chains to rot until their terrified family could coerce some sort of resolution from Gustav.

The dungeon was no place to be, for any human; be they a typical citizen or some nasty wretch. And the dungeon was a completely disagreeable place to be for any length of time.

Ancropolis had visited a friend locked in there once. His friend had been incarcerated for yelling at Gustav after the soldier's horses had broken his only wagon into useless pieces as they raced through the town.

Fortunately, Ancropolis had packed a quantity of bread, cheese and water in his bag to share. His poor friend was in difficult shape when Ancropolis arrived. The henchmen who had dragged him to the dungeon had been very nasty. Bruises were all upon his face and arms. Cold, wet and disgusting were words Ancropolis had used to describe conditions inside, as well as the physical and mental mood of his friend.

Ancropolis shivered at the thought of being taken to these black, cold, forever impossibly damp stone rooms. Yet he also knew, at this point, fighting to be free from Gustav's invitation this evening was a fool's endeavor. If he went after the disgusting buggers, the best he and Chrisholm could hope for, would be to be injured. And they would be injured by men who really did not care a wit about them or their wellbeing. These would in short, be terrible injuries.

Trodding along, just putting one foot in front of the other and beginning to relax, Ancropolis noticed an outcropping along one massive wall of the fort. In that outcropping was a room or an apartment, or so he surmised. In the center of this apartment was a small window. From that window, light and shadows emerged in a frenzied dance of energy along with shouting and screaming as if a cat had been immersed in cold swamp water. It was almost like watching a thunderstorm on a hot summer afternoon with sound effects telling of nature's fury. And there were periodic loud thumps emanating from the window. These sounded like rocks being tossed together.

"Gustav," proclaimed a somewhat bemused Ancropolis, pointing up at the fort. "What mischief goes on in that far above room? It looks like the deamhan he-self is throwing a party for the wicked fairies of the forest."

Gustav slowly raised his eyes to the room hanging off the side of the fort with its prominent window. He cocked his head and smiled a wayward smile. The smile of someone who knew answers to questions not yet asked. He took a deep breath and sighed as the air left his lungs.

Gustav spoke, "Ah me sweet tábhairne (bartender), ye is witnessing a door that has opened to the stars, the moons and whoever seems to be running the heavens of our future." Gustav looked hard at Ancropolis and proclaimed in a solid voice, "Don't let it trouble ye any. That is where ye are spending the night. Right there with yer conniving galla (bitch). Ye need to make some sense of the gruvelling messages I'm a hearn' from the Völva." He shot the other man a glance and stated, "Don' worry if ye can't, cause ifn ya don't, ye won't have to take care of Eskil, you bein' in the dungeon and all." He snorted and spat a wad of yellow flehm onto the steep road.

Ancropolis looked over to his lover. Chrisholom was walking with a couple of soldiers, chatting as if they were strolling to the market. She did not seem worried or in distress at all. In fact, she smiled as she talked.

As they walked, he turned around, looked again, and thought, this is becoming more than curious?

31. Cleansing

The next morning, Dessa and Torrin had carefully packed all their gear and belongings after sharing a light breakfast. The three horses had happily consumed their fill of soft long grass along the quiet creek. Along with that, they and had enjoyed a restful couple of days. Finally, their packs were full and strapped tight. Saddles cinched, and all was ready for them to continue their journey to Kalmar. Tas they had discussed, they hoped to arrive in the port city after one more night in the forest along the trail.

Both Dessa and Torrin checked to make sure nothing had been left behind. They knew too well, that with all the commotion and work of processing the mathan, the other folks arriving and the general chaos that had ensued, it was east to misplace or forget something that might be very much needed later on in the trip (like a hatchet!). Being satisfied all was in good order, Torrin made his way to Samoot.

Just before he was to climb up, Dessa lay a hand on his shoulder and quietly said, "We must clean up, and I need you to be with me."

Torrin looked puzzled at the redhaired lass and replied, "I thought we jus did?" His arm swung around to include the camp's area.

Dessa's eyes were sad when she said, "We need to clean up that bit of the forest and put things back to their natural order. I dunno why, but the nature of the forest is calling me, and I need to do this. I canna do it alone." She grabbed his hand and led him toward the space where the mathan had her final rest. She heard Uta say, 'Thank you.'

They passed the trees blocking the scene from view. Soon they stood in the depression of tall grass where the mathan and Dessa had shared their fateful night just a short time ago.

Dessa grabbed Torrin's other hand, and she lay down on the grass, pulling him firmly atop with a clear purpose. There was no option in her motions. Her arms wrapped around his back, and she pulled his face to hers. As lips touched, their passion mounted, and the blue sparks, of a time from oh-so-long-ago returned.

The grass that had been bent low from the sacrifice burned instantly. The blue hot heat did not allow for any smoke. The grasses and the ground dried instantly as the fire scoured the area of its past misery.

After only a few heartbeats, it was over. The area was cleansed by an intensity hot as lightning, with no understood source. And since it was morning, the dew on the grasses beyond the fiery heat the two of them had generated, quenched the fire.

Dessa reached her lips to his ear, her teeth teased him before she breathlessly whispered "Tonight, we stay alone, deep in the wood. Tonight, I want you all to myself, and I need all of you!"

32. Door

After the long slow hike up the hill alongside the stone walls, the party of soldiers and their special "guests" arrived at the big, intricately carved, thick wooden doors of the fort. Again, a carefully crafted entrance. The entryway was tall enough for a fully uniformed rider on a horse to enter without bending over. This access to the fort though was designed narrow enough as to not let two horses, or two fighting combatants enter together.

One massive door swung open, and the party entered single file, led

by Gustav. Burly, uniformed guards stood on either side of the doorway under the tall flickering yellow light of triple layered torches ensuring no strangers attempted an intrusion.

Looking straight up, high within the parapet was a wide machicolation (floor opening) on each side of the entry. Ancropolis had noticed exterior machicolations as well. Firelight flickered on the walls surrounding the big holes and Ancropolis figured hot stones, burning embers, flaming arrows and who knows what else would damage an unwanted intruder.

Once inside, both Chrisholm and Ancropolis were carefully searched. Their knives were confiscated with a promise of later return. Chrisholm smiled as the guards seemed a bit embarrassed as they carefully searched her for contraband from head to toe. Ancropolis was not amused.

Gustav and one of his minions beckoned the two innkeepers to follow them to the right upon the pathway that led along the inside of the thick exterior wall. Ancropolis noticed, as they walked, the small courtyard was neat and tidy. A few goats were penned up along one side. Horses tied and ready for an immediate departure should the need arise.

The whole place was quiet, but it was an unnerving quiet. It was as if music and laughter had died here. Although neat and orderly, hardly a trace of any joyful human nature to be seen or heard in any part of the fort. It was a queer feeling he could not put into words.

A steep, narrow stairway threaded its way up the inside wall of the fort toward the room Ancropolis had spied moments ago from the outside. The centers of the narrow stone steps were worn into a shallow valley from ages of boot traffic. Ancropolis mused the narrow steps would be easy to defend against anyone trying to fight upward toward this mysterious room (which actually now appeared to be a small apartment) with a window.

There was no banister. No handrail. No handhold of any sort.

Everything here at this monstrous stronghold of a fort was about defense against outside evils and maintaining control.

Everything!

Or so the inhabitants thought.

33. Tonight

Dessa and Torrin traveled south for one more day. They travelled toward places where so many more folks lived than they ever could have imagined or even known about. As they would soon discover, they found more folks with a wider variety of beliefs and customs than they knew existed.

With dusk gathering and the shadows growing long, they and the horses hunted out, and found a cozy private place to camp under a wide tall pine, a bit off the trail. Wood for a fire was plentiful a little deeper into the forest. Lush end of summer grasses for Uta, Samoot and Calandra were thick and tender. After building a nice cooking fire, a light supper was easily prepared and eaten while they recounted their day on the trail. This included smiles over the folks they had met, and other interesting tidbits of the day.

As the sun set with its vast crimson rays touching the edges of thin clouds on the horizon Dessa said to Torrin, "Listen."

She gently touched her fingers to her lips with a soft smile and had said 'listen' not in a way to indicate danger, but in a way to indicate something interesting. Her eyes were almost a hint of blue green, and full of joy.

Torrin was quietly full of happiness, and he relaxed seeing her eyes were so far from turquoise. She was in a happy state, long past the stresses of the past days. It felt good to be back to normal with her. Normal with just themselves.

Together they had been lounging side by side with their backs resting against a large log from a downed tree. Sharing a blanket, their shoulders were almost touching. They sat so close they could sense the peace of each other, feel the warmth not only of each other's body; the warmth of each other's soul.

This was the repose of lovers who not only enjoyed their mutual close company but reveled in its intimacy. This shared moment was comfortable, and a time for stress and hard times to diminish into the gathering night. Time for the stress to evaporate from both their body's and mind's together. It was time to let the travels of the day and the anxiety of worry be lost to the forest.

Since she had told him to 'listen,' Torrin cocked his head, looked at her with a mildly quizzical face, slowly closed his eyes and did as she beckoned. He heard nothing but the intermittent sharp and soft snapplings of their fire (a fire not crackling too loudly). The campfire also gave off the mild hissing of water and sap boiled from the ends of logs, not yet quite dry. The only noise from the trees was the sound of a few newly dried leaves as they murmured a light soft swish among the branches, soon to fall to the ground and return to the earth that created them for the warm and sunny summer days. Other than those few soothing sounds he heard nothing of consequence.

It was so quiet; he thought he could hear the almost soundless breathing of the horses nearby. That was not what he was hearing. Really, what Torrin heard were the sounds of nature's gift of the void. After a few moments he could feel the quiet restful joy of tranquility. Close, but not quite the tranquility Dessa had roused him from along the trail just days ago. However, that desired and longed for feeling seemed to be within his grasp.

As hunters will tell you, sitting quietly with nature, becoming one with the heartbeat of the forest is sometimes the most calming feeling ever experienced. Nature's gift of the void; the void of sound calms the soul and slows the heart to a gentle steady pace.

Torrin smiled and said at just above a delicate whisper to the happy red-haired lass beside him, "Ah don' hear but nothin' but nature's void." He did not want to break the spell of the larger-than-life peacefulness that seemed to surround them.

Dessa's quiet, slow and delicate reply to him was, "That's what I mean. Listen to the quiet. It's the void of sound that lets the too much noise in our heads escape. We ave been surrounded by friends and noise and oh so much activity for what seems forever. And I ave missed these times of almost deafening quiet." She paused and then added, "An I ave missed sharing it with you. Us!"

As they let the noise and stresses of the past diminish into the evening air, she moved closer to him. The wee space between them was now gone, and she laid her head upon his shoulder. He reached out and took one of her hands into his.

Very slowly he traced a line from her fingertip to her wrist, feeling and experiencing the softness of her being. He marveled at the lines of veins that crossed her hand and the texture of the few soft blond hairs decorating her China like skin. He let himself enjoy the curiosity of the wonder of it all and let his mind wander to the amazement of all those hands could do. All those hands would do.

Together, they lay down, pulled the blankets over them, barely kissed and let the shared immediate warmth mingle until the chill of the night was gone from them both. They were careful not to create sparks and too much heat and start a fire. They both knew from experience that an untamed fire could truly take the romance out of a moment such as this one they were sharing.

As Torrin stroked Dessa's soft curls, she stretched her hand lower and explored. With her ear upon his chest, she could feel and hear his long sigh as she explored. It was almost like the purring of a large cat, and she smiled. Before long, she began to toy with the reaction she had expected.

A reaction she wanted and needed tonight. Rolling over together, she lay under him. His one arm wrapped gracefully under her shoulders and his other arm was free to let his hand continue to toy with her hair.

As they made love, he watched her face and marveled at her smiles, reactions and the soft humming sounds she made. Just as he had marveled at the magic of her hand. And it occurred to him he was verra blessed.

After a fashion and enjoying the aftermath of each other, they let all their selves relax, for the first time in what seemed like many nights.

It would be a bit before they would again enjoy this level of peace, solitude and intimacy.

Their campfire burned low, and the breath of the forest sighed to a gentle pause as nature and our lovers succumbed to their much-needed break.

Dessa brought her lips to Torrin's ear and whispered, "I love ye, and tomorrow, our world will change."

34. Völva

A well dressed, serious-looking guard stood at the bottom of the stairway leading to the small apartment. Gustav dismissed the other soldiers who had made the trek up the hill and introduced Chrisholm and Ancropolis to the guard. "This brave and wonderful man is my second in command. He is the Captain of the guard here at the fort. His name is Bourdicca and he has been working with the Völva, attending to her needs since she arrived. He will take us up the stairs and into her chamber. Mind you, this is a chamber of much mystery. I daresay, it will be like nothing you have ever experienced before."

Ancropolis and Chrisholm greeted Bourdicca. He seemed every part the professional soldier and efficient leader of troops. A tall man, well groomed, resplendent in a clean uniform and he produced a sharp salute when introduced. Ancropolis thought to himself that this man had found the perfect role for himself, a soldier. Sharp as a good knife, yet a bit humorless.

Bourdicca took the lead with Gustav trailing closely behind. Climbing up, Chrisholm held as best as she could to the rough rock along her right side since there was no handrail. She felt as though she was scaling the wall with nothing to hold onto except sold stone with her fingernails. Her fears soared and she imagined she could be blown off these thin steps by not so much as a stiff breeze. As the whole party climbed higher and higher she began to shiver and held her breath.

Ancropolis sensed her terror and quietly said, "Me bràmair, don't be worrying, you will be fine, I will not let ye fall. Just a few more steps, now breathe and trust me."

An interesting defense strategy mused Ancropolis. Climbing these stairs with the wall to your right meant your only free hand would be your left hand. Most people are right-handed and having only your left free puts an attacker at a great disadvantage. The people designing this stone stronghold put a lot of thought into every aspect of defense.

Bourdicca climbed the stairs with no issue or hesitation. He reached a point near the top of the long stairway and stopped at a narrow door. Ancropolis mused this door most likely led to the room they had spotted from the outside. The wood appeared to be thick and strong. Steel straps and rivets ran across the heavy planks in five places. The door looked impenetrable.

The long and narrow stairway continued past the door, along the wall up to the very top of the fort. The walkway at the top held battlements sporting defensive blocking merlons with a wide crenels every few feet. The door where Gustav and Bourdicca had stopped, however, was in itself a curiosity. Not a handle or hinge was to be found. Whoever was inside was completely in control of who might enter since the door swung into the room. Forcing your way in was not a practical option. There was no room for leverage, no handle for pulling and no hinges to break off for entry.

Above the door was a small rectangular hole that looked like it was part of the room. This hole was large enough to drop defensive objects on an attacking opponent. Rocks, hot oil, balls of flaming sticks, iron spheres, ash for blinding, or any other device suitable for defense of the room could be used to keep the occupants safe and defend themselves.

Bourdicca, standing at attention, rapped gently on the door and said quietly, "Madam, we have brought you the people you requested. Please open the door so we may enter and deliver them to you forthwith."

Instantly, insanely loud screeching emerged from inside the room along with yelling gibberish that seemed to have no words but was filled with intense emotion. Something was thrown through that small window over the door. Whatever it was, it sailed through the air and landed in a wet splat on the hard packed dirt of the courtyard. Both Gustav and Bourdicca took a step backward down the stairway and waited.

More screeching ensued and then after a few moments, the door swung open to the inside. No one was there in the doorway; it was simply an empty space. Steam, smoke and putrid smells emerged from the opening. Gustav and Bourdicca disappeared one by one, up the final steps and into the room.

Still standing on the steps, trying not of tumble to the hard ground below, Chrisholm said to Ancropolis in a shaky voice, "Do you think we should go in?"

Ancropolis answered, trying to sound unshaken, "Aye, we ave not but a choice. If we back down these terrible stairs, we're just going to ave to climb them again. You heard the man, she asked for us for some strange reason. Go on sweet lady!"

Chrisholm did not move and so gave her a wee push from the back and said, "Go ahead, you know it will be all right, an I'm tight here behind ye."

She entered the room with him close behind, she could feel his breath on her neck. It felt good to be off the steep stairway. When they entered though, what they came upon in this upper apartment took them both by surprise.

One oil lamp burned upon a high ledge lending a dull glow to the entire apartment. The place was nothing, but a single room made from roughhewn stone, just like the rest of the fort. In one corner a small fireplace smoldered, sending smoke into the room and up through a grate in the ceiling. The fire was too low though to produce much heat, and the gray damp smoke just lingered in the room. A huge pile of ashes surrounded the fire, indicating no-one had really tended to this important part of the room in quite a while.

A compact table with four study wooden chairs occupied the center. Upon the table were a variety of different colored glass jars. Each contained dried leaves or other strange oddities that looked to be medicinal. On one corner of the table stood a bucket that looked as though it held steaming water. Stones of various sizes were strewn about the place, all painted in mismatched odd colors. Some of these stones still sported wet paint. To put it mildly, nothing really seemed to make sense.

And near the window she stood. The Völva!

Her back was to the door as well as to her visitors. She stared out the window that led to the street and seemed to be breathing slow and deep, like she was having a hard time controlling herself. With every long exhale, some gurgling from within her small body emerged like the sounds of the dying. This ragged gurgling poured uncomfortably into the ears of all in the room. Then, in a startling fast motion she raised both her arms straight over her head and shrieked a long fearful howl that would have made even the biggest, meanest wolf cringe. All four people in the room jumped at the retched sound and looked at each other with a bit of distress.

The Völva whispered in a hoarse, gravel toting voice that was just loud enough to hear, "You two be gone! Don't return until Ancropolis descends the stairs and requests the roasted gourd."

The Völva turned and looked at the two soldiers. Her long gray hair was matted, knotted and askance in every direction. Green snot ran from her nose and dripped in gross little gobs upon the stone floor. She spat something foul from her mouth and then with a swiftness that belied her apparent age (she looked like she was wretchedly ancient) she plucked the bucket from the table and poured the steaming liquid over her head. Now being drenched from head to toe, she looked at the two soldiers, pointed to the door and screeched, "Now!"

Gustav led the way out in a manner so fast Ancropolis and Chrisholm thought for sure he would overshoot the stairs and simply sail through the air. Bourdicca was just as fast, and they were safely on the ground in just a few heartbeats.

The echo of their footsteps had barely faded when they heard a screech, followed by, "Close the scruvuling damnú door," screamed the Völva. She took a few steps backwards and pushed her back tightly against the wall, just near the window.

Ancropolis walked over to the large wooden door and gently closed it tight. Two sets of thick iron hooks were affixed to the interior of the door. A matching pair were affixed on either side of the door along the wall. Long stout beams leaned against the wall and were used with these hooks to secure the door. Ancropolis looked at the Völva with the question on his face on whether or not to add the beams to the hooks. This would securely lock the three of them in the room.

The Völva slowly nodded yes.

He picked each one up and with some work and twisting slid them both into place. He was amazed at the heaviness of each timber and wondered how this petite woman could manage to lift them. A question he figured that would find its answers in due time.

Ancropolis turned back to the Völva and took stock. She might come up to the top of his stomach, maybe not. She surely could only see a bit out the window, as her eyes barely made it to the top of the sill. Her arms were scrawny as new saplings. Although her eyes were bright, and she seemed maybe to be in good health. The woman was a compact package of mystery, for sure.

The Völva looked at the door, tight and secure. Then she looked at Chrisholm and Ancropolis and seemed to size them up. After this, she tilted her head, as if accepting them and she promptly sat down with a huge sigh on one of the chairs at the table. Putting her head in her arms she emitted a low growl from somewhere in her soaked body. To put it somewhat kindly, she looked like a skinny, gray, old, drenched rat.

Then in a completely different, soft and kindly voice the Völva said, "Will one of you please get me a blanket? I am freezing. That little show with the water might not have been a good idea. And young man, please get the fire going properly. This smoke is killing my sinuses."

Ancropolis looked at Chrisholm, shrugged his shoulders and made his way towards the fire.

35. Yes!

The next morning Dessa emerged from the woods at their little campsite. She had gone off to take care of her morning personal needs and worked to get herself straightened as she walked. She was smiling as she watched Torrin kneeling by the fire, stirring the porridge mixture of oats, berries and nuts in their sturdy pan.

She tended to the horses, packed some things until he called her. Sitting together, against that same log where their tenderness had begun the night before they set the pan on a log between them.

Before picking up their spoons, they softly held hands. They held each other's hand and let a few moments of quiet pass between them. It was a way of gently thanking nature for their food. It was a way for them to stay connected through what might or might not be a long and wonderful day. Or, as they had experienced, a terrible day.

The two of them had formed this habit, pretty much quite by accident. Or maybe by intent. Either way, it did not matter. When Ipi had taught them meditation, the act of becoming centered to quiet their minds, hearts and body, they had started to practice centering together each day.

They started holding hands before meals after the terrible fire at the Journey Inn. When all was in ruin around them, they needed a moment to stop and take stock and let their minds catch up. Both had notioned they had been doing this quiet connecting and centering since after their first kiss, so long ago. When they had entered the stream at Rebecca and Bartoly's cabin, they had pressed their lips together to warm the water and then silently lay blended, enjoying each other's company, compassion and melding of soul.

Of course, that evening had ended in heated passion beyond expectations. Those times were certainly repeated, but never on a busy morning before travel.

So, soon after the Journey fire, one morning, before they began their breakfast, Torrin had taken Dessa's hand in his. She started to ask what was going on, but Torrin just smiled. He put a finger to his lips, slowly closed his eyes and softened his breath. She took the clue and followed.

Since that special morning of finding a new way of being one, being together as they would not ever be with anyone else, they had kept the practice.

Oddly, the timing was always spot on. The quiet between them was wonderful and on some mornings, Torrin could sense the feeling of their moment spread. Even in a room full of people chattering over their breakfast, there seemed to be a pause, as a sense of gentleness permeated the room.

Even now, being outside, Torrin would feel the forest quiet and all around him, a peacefulness seemed to ensue. More than once on a cloudy day, the sun would shine as they finished their moment.

And their moment always ended with a smile.

So, this morning, as they smiled at each other, Torrin began to move his hand to his spoon. The scent of warm porridge had invaded his nostrils and was making his stomach do a bit of a dance in anticipation of the warm meal.

This morning though, Dessa broke the tradition and held fast to his hand. As she brought her eyes up to meet his, he began to panic. Her normally blue orbs now gleamed a bright turquoise. Her beautiful almond shaped eyes only did that when she sensed trouble or danger.

The hair on the back of his neck stood up straight. His head instantly hurt, and he immediately longed for the peaceful moment that had just passed between them both.

"What be the trouble?" he hoarsely whispered.

"Me bràmair, there really is no trouble, other than me finding words for ye right now." Her eyes slowly turned back to their bright blue. She pursed her lips and went on. Since she had started, she now could not stop, and knowledge like this was best not kept secret longer than necessary.

"But your eyes went to the turquoise?" he said. "You only do that when danger lurks, and ye never cry wolf. Ye are havn' me a bit worried just now."

She sighed and let a small smile turn her serious face more pleasant. "I would guess it's not so much a danger, it's just me. I am, a bit scared."

"Oh deamhan," replied Torrin. "Kalmar is just a town with people and you and I together can get through anythin' and ye got nothing to worry about. It's just a bunch of people all gathered about. Kalmar compared to going after Garwen is gonna be…" she pressed a finger upon his lips to quiet him as she gazed with intense eyes at his face. He could feel the heat of her staring upon him, and his stomach flipped a bit, wondering what mischievous on-goings were now coming his way, on what should have been a quiet, perfect morning?

"We," she looked him fast in the eyes with soft tears puddling in her own and softly said, "are going to have a baby."

36. Anomaly

After descending the stairs at the fort, Gustav and Bourdicca stood in the courtyard, both looking up at the little apartment on the side of the fort. Gustav said to Bourdicca, "That woman is a befouling mystery to me and I canna for the life of me figure it, or her, or all, or any of this out. It's beginning to hurt me head."

The soldier standing next to him replied, "Aye, she seems so much a mystery. But how do ye know she is privy or understands to the goings on that ave ye vexed so?"

Gustav sniffed a bit and began, "Last summer, things began to get strange. I could not put my finger on it, still cannot. But it was right around the time those folks to the north ended that bastard Garwen."

All Gustav heard was a questioning, "Yes?"

"One day, on patrol, we were out west, making sure there were no wandering deamhan lurking in the forest. We made camp and it was a warm, crystal starry night. We had been slogging through swamps, and it'd been a hard day. I dunno if I had a dream, or if what I remember was real. But it shook me to the core."

Bourdicca turned to look at Gustav and quietly said, "Ye know, the whole garrison is worried to the deamhan's wrath about what is goin' on with ye. It might be better for all of us if we knew what we were facing and we could be prepared, some. Yer not alone here boss, but we can't do yer bidding if ye is hiding somethin'. Even if it scares ye. And the way ye have been carryin' on, the men are getting worried they may never get home in one piece."

Bourdicca stood stock still. He had never spoken like this to the commander, and was a bit nervous. Even more nervous than that crazy lady up in the apartment could muster in his soul or spine. So, he quietly waited a bit to see what would come. A conversation, or a stiff reprimand?

"I don't want the men to think I've gone crazy or soft or turned on them." replied the commander. And the reply was in a soft tone, one that made the intently listening Bourdicca even more nervous. He had never before felt any bit of compassion from Gustav.

The commander continued, "I think it has to do with strange antics of the animals of the forest. And it made no sense at all. I was told by Raket0st to contact the Völva. He assured me she was in touch with all the natural wonders of the forest and could tell me what was going on. I had no idea she would be so..." He paused for a moment to find words and then went on, "Such an anomaly of everything normal." Gustav shook his head back and forth as if trying to get the vision of what was happening in that upper apartment to go away.

Bourdicca took a long deep breath and said, "How about we go up to yer private room, open that wee cask of yours, share a dram and get this off yer chest. I won't tell a soul, and we might be able to make sense of some of the things that have cast such the vex upon ye. There is a good chance ye will feel better."

Gustav snorted, thought for a moment, looked at Bourdicca and then said in his normally caustic voice, "Fine, but if I hear one word of this from anyone, your head will be on a stake. But to be honest, right now, with what happened to me out there, I am in a befuddle, and don't like it one bit."

37. Together

Dessa smiled as she picked up her spoon and began to eat the cooling porridge. She felt like a weight had been lifted from her shoulders since she had shared her news of the impending baby with Torrin. He just looked at her, mouth agape, eyes wide and with pretty much just a silly look on his face. Dessa said, "Eat before it gets too cold."

Torrin replied, after a bit, "Eat? Eat at a time like this?"

He jumped up knocking the pan of porridge askew, which Dessa barely rescued before the contents became one with the ground.

"How long have ye known?" sputtered Torrin. "Do you feel ok? Why have ye not told me earlier? Who else knows? Oh dòigh nàdair (way of nature, in a positive manner)!" And he fell to his knees in front of her and kissed her deeply.

As to be expected blue electric sparks burst forth from their bodies and began burning the grass and small sticks all about them. Dessa smiled as she pushed him away. He immediately stood up and stomped out the small flames.

"Chac," he muttered. "See, I'm a fool, I've almost gone and jus cooked ye alive." He just stood there, smiling and breathing like he had run a marathon and was unsure what to do next.

She began to giggle like a little girl. "What?" asked a puzzled Torrin.

Dessa could not talk she was giggling so hard. After a few heartbeats she regained composure and with a wide smile said, "Oh you are such a dear sweet man. I 'ave wondered how you would take this news and am so happy you are happy, and my worries were unfounded."

Torrin sat down on the log, picked up his spoon and started to eat. She could tell he was deep in thought, and she began to eat with him. From experience she knew he needed a moment to collect his thoughts.

So, she let the silence happen and waited for him to be ready to chat.

Presently, he asked, "When?"

"When what?" she asked.

"No, let's discuss that later," he continued, changing the course of the conversation, "Why were you worried about telling me, about you carrying a babe, I mean us having a babe?" He was talking faster than his brain to keep up, so he ended with a sigh and said, "Why were you worried?"

Dessa thought for a moment, "Well we don't sit in one place verra long, we are on the trail with adventures, and I was worried you would see a baby as getting in the way of our purpose." Her eyes teared as she described her concern with the purpose they shared.

And then her face turned serious when she remembered she had not yet told Torrin of the visit by Marjie the spryte. She had not yet explained that their purpose was a quest initiated by something so big, it was not understandable. Something so big she had not yet had time to truly consider the implications.

Torrin spoke with quiet affection, "Ye have nothing to worry about. I love ye, we are in this together and we carry on to our purpose, however all this turns out. Together. And that means all of us." He smiled, looked down towards her midsection and then said again, "When? I mean, when did ye know of this wonderful news?"

Dessa stood and said, "Let me show you," as she walked toward Uta.

She returned carrying two small leather bags, both tied at the top with brown sisal. The bags were each just the size of her palm. One was a light tan color; the other was dyed dark red, almost the color of her hair.

She explained, "Ipi showed me how to measure the time between my monthly flows. I'm not consistent with the moon, so we had to measure with these wee stones."

Torrin looked at the bags, scrunched his forehead, looked up and said, "Go on. If Ipi had something to do with this, it's going to be interesting."

"Ipi and I were down at the waterfall one day, cooling off, enjoying a good bath and a nice relaxing soak. Ipi looked at me with a smile and said, 'Lass, ye is ripe to be with child,' I think I sort of blushed and told her we did not know if having a wee one was in our providence. Ipi just guffawed and said, 'If that big brute Valterra could get that sweet lass Kaitlyn with child, you will have no worries. If'n ye want one. But as I see it, the way you two is carryin on, you arc bound to flower from your seed soon.'

Torrin blushed himself a bit and said, "So what did she show you?"

"Well, I asked her, how will I know if my womanly flows have stopped and that a good many days have passed; because the days all run together and I might not notice for a while, and it's a good thing to know. Just because I was a wanting to know." Dessa smiled a bit shyly.

Torrin sat quietly and waited, listening carefully.

Dessa held out the light tan bag. "This is Ipi's counting bag. She put this many wee stones in it." Dessa poured a small pile of stones into the palm of her hand. "The number, she gave it a name, I think she called it twenty-eight. Means not much to me, but she explained it to be the number of days between my monthly flows, give or take a couple. The flows do stop when one is bearing a child."

Torrin rearranged his legs and stayed planted on the log, intent on trying to understand what he knew to be some sort of mathematical system. Math was not something he was good at or knew much about, so he was quiet and curious, except to say, "I guess that makes sense that the flows stop when you are with babe. I never put no mind to such thinking, but please carry on."

Dessa, rolled her eyes just a bit and smiled. She figured men would not think of such things since they were pretty much not involved in the monthly ritual. She returned the small wee stones back into the light tan bag, then continued her explanation, "So this is what Ipi and I named the Dessa bag since it matches my hair." She smiled a bit, tucked a long curl behind an ear and continued, "My instructions were to find a wee pebble every morning and put one in the Dessa bag starting with the first day my flows stopped. And I need to do this every morning until it starts again."

Torrin was beginning to understand some sort of comparison was coming, hoping he didn't have to count numbers; he couldn't do that sort of thing.

Dessa opened the red bag and Torrin noticed it held many more stones than the light tan bag. "I had started this counting before we left for Garwen's castle. Figured I needed to get into the habit if it was going to be accurate. The last time I had me flows was a few days before the fire."

And then continuing to show what was going on, Dessa opened the red bag and poured the contents into her palm. It was a large pile! Many, many more than the number of stones held in the tan bag. Dessa looked up to Torrin and said, "The first stone in this bag went in while we still lived in Kaitlyn and Valterra's magnificent room.

At that moment, both Torrin and Dessa realized that this babe was probably a result of their shared intimacy upstairs at the Journey Inn, just before the fire consumed the magical place. A fitting tribute to a future that would be better for all involved, in so many ways.

Dessa came back over to Torrin, gently took one of his hands into hers. With the other, she poured the tiny pebbles she had collected over the past many days into his palm. They filled his palm, overflowed and spilled to the ground.

They both listened to the gentle tinkling, swishing and tiny thunking sounds the pebbles made flowing over each other and landing on the soft grass. There were obviously many more little stones here than contained in Ipi's tan bag. Yes, there were many, many more!

"Ye asked me when I knew," said Dessa. "I compared the stones while we were on the trail, early that day when Uta began talking to me again and all of nature put me into a bit of a trance."

She sighed and continued, "There were so many stones in my bag, I figured there was no doubt of me being with child, and I was going to tell you around the fire that evening. But then the mathan arrived and our world went to helvete (hell). It has taken me, actually taken us, some time to get back to our verra own story. But we are back, and we are here, and I love you."

Torrin looked up with tears in his eyes. His face was blotchy red, and he moved his lips, or tried to move his lips and could not speak. She could tell he was running a full set of emotions through his brain and body, and she had to let them take their course. As she had done for herself.

Dessa sat quietly, chewing on the porridge. She was ravenously hungry and was not going to miss this meal. Torrin finally cleared his throat and seemed to be ready to talk.

And then he began to talk quickly, and with an overtone of concern in both words and the look on his face, "We should turn around, go back to Journey. Really, go back to Tarmon's castle. At least find Kneafsey the midwife, she will take care of ye. We'll take Kneafsey to Tarmon's and Sanura can watch over ye, care ta your needs. And we need to get word to Accalon and my mháthair that she is going to become a seanmháthair and your athair will be so proud to become a seanathair and it's all so exciting and if it's a boy he is heir to the throne in Tarmon's kingdom and Quillan is going to be an uncle..."

She really was not sure how to stop him from going on, and was a bit concerned he might not hear her anyway if she said anything. Dessa looked around at their camp and thought for a moment. Would this be a good place to spend another night? The morning was getting on and they had already lost a lot of daylight for travel and maybe they needed a rest? Maybe they could use a bit more time together to relax before they entered Kalmar. She had a feeling all would be verra busy at this town, a town that was totally foreign to them both.

Then she mused at how quickly so many thoughts could come to her brain in such a short fashion. She looked up and realized she was the one missing the conversation, not him. Torrin was chattering away, all excited.

Torrin stopped to breathe and Dessa put her fingers on his hand still holding pebbles and quietly said, "So, there is a bit more that has come up. Really just come up. I know ye have said that every day is an adventure when we is together, yet this one is a bit beyond even me."

She paused, collecting her thoughts, "I need ye to meet someone. Well, I think she be someone. Anyway, she is, or seems important. She showed up that horrible night. During the night when I slept next to the mathan, before..."

She had to stop and find words. The pain of the experience still roiling her emotions. She felt tears welling and had to swallow hard.

"So, meeting her, and listening to what she has to say may focus yer thoughts on our decisions. It might affect what we think about our direction of travel and, much more."

Suddenly Torrin was awash in a powerful memory. The memory of Safon, the kind lady who taught the new mothers of Trebor's kingdom how to take care of a new babe. Her final words came to him in a flash and struck him like a bucket of ice water. He could hear her dying message from his parents, her voice, strong and caring:

Go forward to build, not to destroy,

But defend at all costs.

Your mission is to hold true the promise,

Keep it true, protect it, make it the future for all.

Torrin looked at Dessa, his eyes wet with memories mixed with the news of today. And he said, "We be our destiny together."

38. Meeting

Chrisholm calmly held the wet gray head of the Völva against her midsection as the older woman clung tightly to the blanket. She was shivering, trying to warm what seemed to be not just her body, but the dark torment of something bigger that was trapped inside her in this cold, damp smokey room. Nothing but musky odors invaded their breathing.

In the corner, tending to the fire, Ancropolis moved ashes from the fireplace area, added wood and worked to gain a hotter fire so the room could become less like a cold dank root cellar. As sticks caught to the flame, he went to the big door, removed the timbers and opened it. The open door coaxed a draft of fresh air to move through the room. The smoke had been almost blinding, and he was starting to wheeze.

Presently, the smoke cleared, the hotter fire began to move the warmer air up to the open grate at the top of the room and the apartment slowly began to take on a more habitable atmosphere. He added more wood to the flames from the big pile of split logs arranged against the wall. The wood was split into mostly thin long pieces about the length of his thigh and was well dried. It caught easily and burned well. The added heat was verra welcome and the exit of the dampness joyful.

As the smoke cleared, Chrisholm found some drinking mugs. Ancropolis found clear water in a skin. The skin was hanging on the wall, a stout, dark wooden peg holding it up. Ancropolis looked at the peg and marveled that it looked as old as dirt. He felt the wood and was surprised that the touch revealed not a wooden feel at all, but one like rock. The wood that had held items upon this wall for eons had turned to stone.

With the room warming, Ancropolis decided it was time to secure the door. Anyway, the cool breeze had become annoying now that the fire was hot and the room's air was much clearer. He reset the timbers to secure the door.

Chrisholm sat kitty-corner at the table when the small gray-haired lady finally stopped shivering. Mugs of water were now in place for all of them, and Chrisholm took advantage of the moment of calm. She then reached under the blanket that surrounded the old lady and took one thin blue veined hand into hers. She could feel the cold dampness of the woman's skin and waited for a moment before setting forth her inquiry, "I am Chrisholm, this is Ancropolis. Who may I ask are you?"

This tired looking person, not at all as fierce as when they entered the room looked up into the kind eyes of the young woman seated next to her. She took a moment, enjoyed some water from the mug in front of her, smiled gently and said quietly, "My dear, I am the future you have known in your heart for a long time would come." She took a deep breath of the cleaner air, made a pleasant humming sound that sounded like joy and then continued, "And you are the future I knew would arrive."

Chrisholm looked up at Ancropolis with a bit of seriousness on her face, looked back at the old woman, who was now regaining some normal color and said, "I did not think you would arrive here so soon."

Now Ancropolis was looking puzzled.

The old lady gave a heavy sigh, simply said to him, as she pointed to the window facing the outside of the fort, "Young man, would you be so kind as to look out that wretched window and tell me what is going on down below at the street level?"

39. Camp

Torrin's mind went from 'When did you know?' to 'Who am I meeting?' to What is going on?' It was almost too much for him at this moment. He sat down with his head in his hands and thought, 'I'm going to be an athair, now I need to meet someone, or something in the forest, here, a long way from anywhere? Can this become any stranger or more weird?'

Then he looked at Dessa, his face softened, and it occurred to him, 'Yes it can get weirder!' Really! He had escaped from a dragon, almost froze in the winter forest, was rescued by people who ran a lodge no-one knew about in the woods and then fell in love with a redhead who could converse with the animals.

OK, he thought. Bring it on! He stood up, put his arms around the tough young lady he was dedicating his life to and said, "If ever I want some variety in my day, I just turn to you." He kissed her on the forehead to avoid making more fire and said, "Who might ye be making introductions to, this fine morning?"

Dessa hugged back for a good long moment and said, "I dunno how long afore she arrives after I summon her. I will put out a call in a moment. Let's plan to stay here tonight, enjoy some quiet time together before arriving at Kalmar."

"She'?' he asked.

"I believe it is female," answered Dessa. "I'm not sure what we might get, anyway, it's going to be interesting."

Torrin said, "Well, whatever it is, I'm never disappointed in your escapades with nature. In the meantime, I'll gather more wood for a nice fire. Maybe we can find a better spot and pitch the tent, and I'll see if I can root up some vegetables."

She stood tall, kissed his cheek and promptly set out into the forest to summon the spryte. He just watched her go. He thought to himself, 'I'm the luckiest man alive.' And then he made his way toward Calandra to fetch his hatchet from her big pack.

* * *

Dessa strode into the woods. The gentle chipperings & twerpings of numerous small forest critters subsided as she invaded their sanctuary. Moving through the heavy timber was fairly easy, since little undergrowth was to be had in this area. The sun was blocked by the dense canopy generated by the huge trees in this part of the forest. Moving on though, it took just a few moments to spy a brighter area. A brighter area where one of the huge trees had capsized to the ground from some storm or lightning strike and left a hole in the canopy for sunlight to stream in from above.

Around the downed tree bushes and saplings grew because of the sunshine flowing to the ground. She navigated her way through the new undergrowth and stood next to the downed tree. The trunk came up to her chest and the quiet of its massiveness was almost unnerving, considering this tree had been swaying with the breeze for ages.

Dessa climbed up onto the colossal main trunk. The length of the massive log that now lay soundlessly across the ground was a quiet testament to the power that brought this monster to the ground. The long, huge trunk was so wide Dessa could comfortably lay down on the smooth bark and not worry about rolling off.

And she did just that for a while, to enjoy the warmth of the sun, the peace of the forest. As she lay there, eyes closed, the forest yet again began to stir. The chirping of birds returned, the scratching of tiny feet on bark, or the rustling of the dried fall leaves as small creatures darted to and fro in their element. It was the peaceful symphony of the forest.

And of course, with the sun, and the quiet peace, Dessa slept.

Until the monkey sitting on her chest started tickling her.

40. All Is Good

Ancropolis looked out the window of the apartment in the fading light at the road below. Flaming torches on either side of the doors they had used to enter the fort cast flickering shadows that danced eerily on the road. The firelight from the torches also danced in the eyes of the dogs.

He could see a great quantity of dogs. Dogs of all sizes laying along the side of the road. Not a one made any sound and not a person on the street seemed to notice them.

The Völva said, "Are the dogs still there?"

Ancropolis turned from the window, a bit bewildered by what he had seen and said, "Yes, there are a great many of them, up and down the road. What is going on?"

The Völva replied, "Oh, it's simply a sign from nature that Chrisholm is the right one. Tell me, are they calm or carrying on?"

Ancropolis again looked out, "They are all as docile as sleeping puppies and making not a sound."

The Völva slowly stood up, grabbed a small stool and approached the window overlooking the road. Standing tall on the stool she softly said, out the window, "Braw."

Ancropolis peered over her shoulder and noticed all the dogs looked up at the window, as one. Somehow, they knew. After the Völva uttered her 'all is good,' message they all stood up, stretched and went their separate ways. No barking. Not a sound, except a few clicks of nails upon stones of the road.

The Völva stepped off the stool, raised her arms over her head and stretched. The sounds of her joints popping echoed off the walls. She took a deep breath, walked over to the now hot fire and warmed her hands.

Chrisholm said, "It certainly was..." The Völva shushed her with a stern, "Quiet."

"Yes, I know, it was easier to get to me than you thought. Now we have work to do. We must set them up for success, or this all goes to helvete."

"We?" asked Chrisholm and Ancropolis together in unison.

And then after a moment, Chrisholm said, "Set who up for success? And what do you mean?"

The Völva sighed as she turned her back to the warm flames of the fire that was taking the damp chill out of the little room as well as herself and said, "Why our dear captain and his sidekick who just left. They are part of this project, just as you two of you are, and we need them to buy into the plan."

"What plan?" asked an incredulous Ancropolis.

41. Monkey's Business

Dessa's eyes popped open, and her first instinct was to fling this unruly animal off her chest. But the animal was pinning Dessa's arms firmly to her sides. And in an instant, Dessa knew she knew nothing of this furry, brown skinny creature. What damnú was this thing? Since Dessa had never seen, nor ever even heard of a monkey, she had no idea what was sitting on her chest. And tickling her with its long, skinny furry feet?

Suddenly it all came together and between giggles she sputtered, "Ok Marjie, get off of me."

"But how did you know?" said the monkey as it rolled backward in a summersault off Dessa and sprung nimbly to its feet. The creature balanced perfectly on the big log. And then before Dessa could say anything, it did a handstand, holding itself up with one long, brown furry arm.

"I figured anything that doesn't make sense and is a bit crazy, is going to be your doing," replied the redhead, sitting up, crossing her legs at the ankles.

The creature jumped to its feet and said, "My, my, aren't you the smart one," In and instant it dissolved into Marjie's former self, blue dress, perfect hair, clear fresh looking skin and little feet. Except, this time, no sparks.

"No sparks?" asked Dessa.

"It's daylight," replied the spryte. As expected, with a bit of her typical flourish, she sat down on the log, her little legs sticking out in front of her, toes wiggling a bit. "No need to light things up right now. So, what did you need from me?"

"I want you to talk to Torrin and explain the importance of what we are doing and help him understand why we need to go on," said Dessa.

Dessa continued, "And I am a bit curious too. Curious to understand more about all this and why its important and who cares and whatever else I need to know."

"My guess is he wants to head back to mommy now that he knows you are carrying his little wee future inside you." Marjie grinned.

"There is that," said Dessa. "I must confess, I'm feeling a bit of the same."

"That's just buggers my dear," Marjie, said frowning. "There's not a lot of choices here, and you two are dug in verra deep." Marjie groaned and disappeared into nothing.

42. Kitchen

The Völva gently said "Young man, please go down to the courtyard, ask for more drinking water, a jug of wine, candles, a bit of food and bedding for the two of you," said the Völva. "You'll be staying the night here."

Ancropolis moved toward the door and began removing the two beams that secured the door from any outside interference. He again marveled at their weight and wondered, almost aloud, at how this pint-sized, incredibly old lady could move these heavy beams. Before he said anything though, his mind caught up to his wondering and told him that if she was this strong, maybe he should be a bit more careful in his words.

Before he was able to open the door, the Völva said, "Please don't tell them I'm, well, how you might call it. Normal. I have had to keep them on edge, for good reasons, which I'll explain later, unless I get too deep into the wine." She smiled, and continued, as she piled ashes into a bucket, "Also, after you head down the stairs, I'll be throwing ashes out the door and screaming some hysterics for theatrical effect. I don't want you to get the ashes in your eyes. Knock when you return, we'll open the door. Please don't be too surprised by what you see when you come back in."

Ancropolis looked at Chrisholm with a wondering question written all over his face. Chrisholm just smiled and nodded toward the door.

As he opened the big door, he heard a huge intake of breath from the little gray-haired woman and hysterical shrieks were spewed forth. He ran as fast as he could down the narrow staircase. And as promised, he could feel the dry powder of ashes falling on his head as he neared the bottom. Continuing to sprint, he held his breath until he was clear of the dusty storm.

Looking around, he found a guard and asked where he could procure the items the Völva requested. Of course, this being a verra organized operation, he had to ask three different people at different levels for the same thing.

As Ancropolis went from person to person asking questions, he wondered how they got anything done around here.

Finally, he was ushered into the big kitchen of the fort and had discussions with the folks working in the sweaty place. They were happy to oblige and got to work. These people were generous, and kind enough to give him some wine as he waited. He got curious looks. He could tell; they wanted to ask questions. Unlike the big room at Eskil though, these folks in the kitchen kept to themselves and although quiet, they were not unfriendly.

43. Question

Torrin had been busy setting up a nice campsite for the evening. There was now a neatly stacked pile of dry split wood. The horses had been unpacked, and the tent was pitched on a bit of higher ground in case of rain. A nice assortment of beans with various spices were under the cover of the big pan near the fire, soaking in warm water to go with their supper.

Dessa was impressed when she arrived from her excursion in the woods. She felt a bit guilty, having taken a warm nap on the long tree. But then, she'd been frazzled by the experience with the mathan. And then of course with Marjie showing up and making everything a bit more critical.

He looked up and said, "Couldn't find him, or her, or whatever yer supposed to call upon?"

Dessa knelt by the pot, removed the lid and stirred the beans with a clean stick before saying, "My dear, if you think I am alone, or we are ever alone, especially when travelling, you have not been paying attention."

Torrin nodded that he almost understood, but then looked around again. He was expecting to see a wolf or a panther or some other large, imposing 'ruler of the forest animal' entering the campsite to do something magical. Seeing nothing, he walked over, sat next to Dessa, stretched out his legs and said, "Yes, I suppose you're right."

"Yes, she is right," came a gut-wrenchingly loud and almost thunderous voice from the treetops. The earth shook with the power behind the words, and Torrin almost jumped to his feet.

Dessa gently said, "Really? Stop with the drama and just come here. We need to talk. You need to help us, and from what I can understand, you need us to help you."

With that, Marjie appeared, perched, perfectly balanced on the toe of Torrin's boot. She was dressed in her typical blue dress, arms folded in front of her, and she had a stern look on her little face.

His first instinct was to kick the intruding thing off his boot. His instincts had become a bit tame though, and he squelched the thought before he did any harm. And at the same time, he decided he should not trifle with something that could appear out of thin air after proclaiming an announcement with an earth-shattering voice. Even if it appeared to be a tiny lady in a blue dress.

"So here you are, up close," said the spryte. "Not bad, I've seen better." She hopped off his foot, walked over to a nice flat rock, cleaned it with the swipe of her hand and sat down with a bit of a plump.

Torrin thought to himself that she must like her sound effects.

The silence of the little group was interesting. They all looked at each other for a few moments. Dessa decided Marjie was just waiting to see what would be forthcoming from Torrin and herself, so she kicked things off.

"This creature here," Marjie frowned at the word creature, a bit of green seeping into her pretty face. Dessa quickly went on, "is really no creature at all, she is a forest spryte and…"

Marjie cut her off, "Good afternoon Mr. Torrin. I represent nature. I represent everything there is. The mountains, the trees, the creek, the animals, and everything. Well, that is, mostly everything. I have trouble with the weather, it is frisky, temperamental and does not like to cooperate." She sighed a bit, and continued, "I'm even responsible, as much as I can be, for even you!" She pointed a slender finger at Torrin, and some shiny sparks sailed out and landed on his coat. He pushed back at the surprise.

"I thought the wolf and the cougar were the ones watching out for nature," replied Torrin, dusting sparks off his coat. He looked at Dessa, she raised her eyebrows, indicating it was a good question.

Marjie sighed and said, "Interesting thought. We sent those two merely to watch over and protect you from evil. They both did us all a great service. Although not as much of a sacrifice as Sebastian. They did grouse about leaving family for days on end, but at least they did not have to die."

"Sebastian?" queried Dessa.

Torrin somehow instinctively knew the answer. His eyes narrowed a bit became dark. He shuddered.

Marjie answered, "Sebastian was the last dragon. He wanted to go out in a blaze of glory and sacrifice himself for the better of all he knew and loved. He was ready to go, since no mate was left for him and he was tired of living alone. We sent him to gather Mr. Torrin here from the water where he lay and fly him to the creek near Journey."

Torrin and Dessa looked at each other, back to Marjie, and Torrin said, "That dragon, that dragon flew with me in his belly?"

"Oh, my yes young man!" clapped Marjie excitedly. "It was a short flight, over one small mountain, but he loved the challenge, and he knew, if it all worked out, you would put him out of his misery and loneliness. And at the same time serve a verra valuable purpose."

"What? I mean, that whole thing was no accident? Now nothing makes sense!" inquired, or maybe stated, a now incredulous Torrin.

"Oh, we sent Garwen's nasty brood to waylay you and toss you into the creek. Sebastain was waiting nearby and swooped in after those stinking little boys were out of sight. You were still knocked silly, so gulping you down was easy. He made the flight, and you passed the test."

"Passed a test?" asked a now verra curious Dessa.

"We thought he was the one," continued Marjie, "But we had to be sure. If he could escape Sebastain and drag his injured self to Journey, it would prove our suspicions that he had the gumption to succeed. And he did, and the rest is history."

"You really planned all that?" it was not a question, just as before, it was more of a statement from Torrin, and he did not look happy.

"Oh my, yes we did!" said Marjie, using her favorite phrase. "It has all taken more time than we hoped, but all good things do, like growing a big strong tree. Yes, we had a plan, and we had to test things, and you did just fine."

Dessa was quiet for a moment, and then asked, "Was I part of a test? Did you, I mean, was all I went through something that was planned?" She was remembering a jumble of wretched moments. A horrible marriage to Darius. Escaping down the castle walls. Outwitting Tallon and having to defend herself to the death, lying in the damp leaves on her back while Hapathius threatened her with the ultimate violation.

Marjie groaned, "Oh my, yes dear. Not all planned, completely, in every detail. Some of it just happens the way it's going to happen. We can't control every nuance you know. That deal with Hapathius was something we did not foresee. However, you did just fine, rose to the occasion and did a verra fine job." Marjie smiled at the memory.

"But!" interjected a fairly agitated Torrin.

"No buts today," replied Marjie sternly. "Evil exists and we needed to use it to our purposes to test you both, and then we needed the evil to be gone. Garwen was the perfect source of our need for something evil. Both for people and events. Garwen and his despicable brood served us well, and you both took good care to obliterate him, which we appreciate."

Torrin stood up and angrily exclaimed, "You tore me from me home, you had me athair killed, you tormented me mháthair, burned a perfectly good kingdom to the ground, killed good people and you expect me to sit here and just listen to you and be pleased with whoever or whatever this 'we' is you refer to? Don't bet on it little lady, I don' care who you are or what you represent, you are bad, and I am not going to let you torment me, or Dessa any longer!"

Marjie looked at the angry man. Right now, he assumed he was much bigger than her tiny frame, nestled comfortably on her rock. In his mind, he carried two daggers and knew how to use them. In his mind, given this situation, he felt he was a powerful man. Or so he thought.

Marjie simply crossed her arms and said, "Well now, this answers a hard question I have been asking, for a while, and makes things much simpler. Bye."

And with a swoosh of fiery fairy dust, she was gone.

44. Supper With Wine

Ancropolis carried a large flask of dark red wine. He led a small troop of men from the fort's kitchen, all in single file up the stairs to the compact apartment where he assumed the Völva and Chrisholm were still waiting for food to arrive. These kitchen folks were all clad in the formal wear of serving staff. This formal wear consisted of dark short sleeve shirts tied at the neck, a white apron and all varieties of assorted breeches. Ancropolis figured the formal uniform for the kitchen ended at the apron and they could wear what they wanted for breeches. Some wore lighter breeches, and some wore heavy garments. Ancropolis figured the heavy material was for working nearer the hot fires of the kitchen.

Anyway, the men were all very courteous, professional and seemed eager to please. Ancropolis and Chrisholm would find out later in life that kitchen duty was a much sought after position at the fort. Kitchen folks rarely went into battle. Plus, you almost never went hungry, there being food about the place most of the time. So, this group of men never wanted a bad review or mention that could jeopardize their position. Ever.

These culinary professionals put on quite a fancy feast. A heavy tablecloth was unfurled and covered the center table. Four candles adorned the middle with a small arrangement of fresh flowers. Crystal clear water in a carafe, a pitcher of ale, a flask of red wine and a hefty dram of scotches accompanied the meal.

In addition, the food delivered consisted of boiled potatoes, fried greens, and a well-seasoned heavy pork dish. This all filled several serving dishes, jam-packed to almost overflowing. Three large bowls, one each for the apartment's occupants, were set out, accompanied by sturdy wooden spoons, carved from old oak. The spoons were as smooth as a well-polished rock.

Topping off the evening was a baked curiosity sporting a glazed cinnamon topping over fluffy bread rolls filled with a mash of nuts and honey.

Now, mind you! All of this was delivered with utmost grace and panache while the Völva sat like a hunched cat in the window frame. She was perched above the heads of all these culinary gentlemen, screeching unintelligible mutterings and spitting toward the road below at regular intervals.

After the meal had been set out and the kitchen help safely escaped, the Völva jumped down and softly exclaimed, "Isn't this nice!"

45. A Cask

They had made the long trek to Gustav's private office, just off his apartment near the back of the fort. Bourdicca waited until Gustav motioned for him to take a seat on the visitor's side of his desk. Even though the commander seemed to be showing his human side, Bourdicca made the wise choice to determine protocol not be broken.

Gustav extracted two wooden goblets from the cabinet behind his large formal work desk. He then proceeded to move two small bronze statues from a shelf behind his chair. One statue looked like a bear and the other resembled a dragon. Bourdicca had never really noticed these strange works of art before. He had always found himself rigidly upright, at attention when standing in front of the commander, and this huge desk. His job was to either report or listen. Not pay attention to the art adorning this large dark imposing room. He mused that there may be yet more oddities to discover this evening.

He was right.

Gustav removed a plank from the back of the shelf, set it on his desk and then procured a well-crafted, small wooden cask from a dark space behind the shelf that had been so well hidden. The cask was a little bigger than a man's head and polished so well it reflected the flickering yellow fire of the candles doing their best to bring shadowy light to the room. The cask sported bright brass bands, and the polished wooden staves alternated in colors of dark and light wood.

Bourdicca marveled at the well hewn cask. He never knew his boss had a penchant for artistic features. And then it occurred to him, he really did not know his boss, this man, very well. Actually, come to think of it, no one at the fort knew the man well.

Gustav detached a large brown cork from the bung hole on the top. He then proceeded to pour a wee bit of amber liquid into both of the goblets.

Bourdicca was instantly amazed at the variety of aromas emanating from the liquid. He was used to the fare in town and the casks and flasks of the men. But this was heavenly. A fine fragrance of peated malt, sea air and a faint touch of smoky wood fire floated up to his nostrils. He gently breathed in a long deep breath through his nose, and said, "That is the nicest scent I have ever experienced in me short and dutiful life. And if'n I never experience it again, I will be sad. But to have, I am blessed."

Gustav looked at the man on the other side of his desk. The man who made this company of soldiers run as a solid unit. He saw the man who had made Gustav successful for many winters in this cold and foreboding place. And Gustav saw a man who cared not only for the work, but for the people.

Gustav then proceeded to add an additional healthy portion of the amber scotches to both goblets. Setting the cask down on his desk, he replaced the cork in the bung hole. Then, setting the cask aside, he picked up his goblet.

"Slàinte Mhath, Bourdicca," said Gustav. "Yer not only a good soldier and a wonderful commander to the men, ye are a blessing to me, ye bein' here and takin care of business so well. I don' think I have treated ye with the respect and care ye deserve."

Bourdicca said, "Thank you, we must pay attention for each other's safety and success, every day, every project, every endeavor. I sense there is change in the air. We must be vigilant to fend off anything that threatens us."

Gustav said, "I could not agree more." And the two men shared a respectable and hearty mouthful of what they thought to be the best scotches available in the north country.

Since both men were ones to appreciate a fine scotch, they did not just toss back this gift, that was now ready for consumption in their goblets. After the first small mouthful, they both swirled the amber liquid in the goblet and slowly drew in a full breath of the vapors emitting from each of the polished cups. As is customary with fine drink, one must close their eyes and allow the smell, taste, heart and emotion of the creation seep into the soul of the drinker.

This they did. They shared some quiet time between them. They shared that space where people who appreciate the fine art of whiskey let the experience bring them together.

Gustav was impressed. Bourdicca did not gulp this creation, he appreciated it to the fullest. It was a bit of a test by Gustav to see if he could really trust this man with the story he was about to share. Because, if told correctly, it could also change this Bourdicca. Change Bourdicca's view and attitude towards people. The experience had changed him. And what happened continued to morph him as oddities around him churned.

Bourdicca, looked up and said, "This is wonderful, and where do you want to start with what is going on?"

Gustav said quietly, "Well, the best place to start is when I woke up with my face in the mud and then I started to fly."

46. Forward

"I'm thinkin that din-no go so well with the wee creature," said Torrin, adding wood to the fire. "Don't think she admired me thoughts." He was shuffling around, a bit slumped over, Dessa could see he was deep in thought and a bit distressed.

Neither Dessa nor Torrin had really talked much since Marjie had vanished in her usual swish of sparks. Neither knew what to say, or how to start the conversation that was needed to be had between them. Now at least, Torrin had got things rolling.

Dessa thought for a moment and said, "Well, ye could be right, or not. As I'm thinkin here, neither of us knew what we were going through, or why, or by what, and did we even know there was a purpose? We were simply responding to what was happening in our lives. For me, a lot of it was just simply surviving."

"So true," said the dark-haired man, sitting down next to her. "I ave felt like we've been running hard dealing with life and did not know all this fell into a plan of sorts. I. Well, we, just had to do what we thought we had to do." He was talking slowly, trying to get his thoughts in order.

Dessa said, "Yes, and then we thought we had to go spread the purpose, but all this now going on, just has me jumbled up and questioning."

"Hmm," mumbled Torrin. Then he stated, "I ad no idea we were part of someone or something's grand plan! I guess in foresight, we should ave asked more questions and looked around deeper. I mean, when ye came inta the clearing at Journey almost dead up on yer horse, I was not thinkn' this was part of some grand master plan ta get us together and test us and... I guess I'm not sure of what?"

Dessa laughed a bit, "I guess when you dragged your injured leg onto the porch at Journey you were not thinking of meeting the spryte who was in charge of things and being in her service."

"No, not at all," sighed Torrin.

Dessa turned to Torrin and finished by saying, "With where we are, together, and this bit of us growing inside me, I am just not sure what to do. It all seemed so right just a short while ago, now it's, it's, or I'm not so sure. Especially now."

Torrin gave himself a moment to think by adding more wood to the fire and stared at the hot coals under the burning logs. He watched the alternating black and dark red areas dance among the glowing embers. He paid curious attention to the small bits of smoky log that flittered around in the flames, noticing the different colors and was just quiet with a stern face and puzzled expression.

Dessa said, "Maybe we turn around, let Marjie and nature deal with their issues all by themselves. Torrin nodded in agreement.

Quiet once more fell between them as they pondered together their options. The fire burned brightly and they were not really sure of what to do.

That is, until Marjie appeared floating over the fire, seeming to ride the smoke that rose to the trees. Her eyes were ablaze with energy, arms folded across her front. She said sternly, "You two enter Kalmar tomorrow. It's not an option. You will be guided to the destiny that awaits you. Leave here early."

And, with a swoosh of sparks that filled the camp, she was gone.

Torrin said, "I don't know about you, but I'm thinkn', at this point we don wan ta trifle with someone or something that can fly, make fire, change size and get around like she do."

Dessa gave a heavy sigh and said, "You are right, tomorrow, we head to Kalmar and see what happens."

47. New Perspective

At that same moment Marjie delivered her stern message far to the south, back in the fort at Kalmar, Bourdicca ever so slowly set the polished wooden goblet holding his scotches onto Gustav's huge desk. He was not sure what to say. Hearing from Gustav that he was 'face down in the mud and began to fly,' seemed to be verra senseless and not at all like the commander he reported to on a daily basis. Something was going on with the man, something big, maybe transformative and Bourdicca did not want to spoil the moment.

Gustav saved Bourdicca from having to speak and risk losing the feelings of the moment. Gustav began, "We were on our third day of patrol in the woods. It had been raining. Oh, raining so verra hard for that whole damnú gray day. I decided to go on patrol with the men, to get into the field, get my patrol legs back, get a taste for reality again! It was getting dark, and we became separated. To put it bluntly, and it's embarrassing, I was lost."

Bourdicca picked up his goblet, enjoyed a mouthful of the aromatic amber wonder, and placed it back onto the desk before saying, "Yes, I have been in that situation, and it's no fun, whatsoever. Please tell me what happened. You obviously found a way back to camp?"

Gustav laughed, "If I could have made it back to camp, then this story would not be verra interesting. In fact, we would not be sitting here enjoying these magnificent beverages. But, alas, this was not the case, and this is where the story turns into, shall we say, a life changing moment."

Gustav took a deep breath and continued, "I had been getting a little panicked and then I lost my footing on a steep and verra slippery slope of mud and rocks. After a wet slide, I went down, face first into the mud. Not a particularly comfortable way to land. The nasty cold, dark and wet stuff seemed to suck me into the ground, and I was pretty much trapped. When I tried to push myself up, my hands just slipped in the wet goo. For a time, I made an effort to work myself around to try and get up, and then all of a sudden, I felt myself rise from the muck and found myself moving forward along the path. It was as though I was flying through the rain, dripping mud and believe me, I was a bit taken aback, confused and disoriented!

Gustav took a medicinally large swallow from his goblet to calm his nerves ensuring he could go on with this tale.

"I looked to my left and could see that a verra large man; Oh verra large, had me by the scruff of my breeches and was carrying me along the way."

"You don't say?" said a fairly bewildered Bourdicca.

"I do say, my man! I do," responded Gustav.

Bourdicca could see the man across the desk relaxing a bit. It was either the scotches or just finally getting this story off his chest. Maybe both? Anyway, Gustav was going full tilt with his tale and Bourdicca was not going to stop him with any silly questions.

"This man carried me for a time, in the dark, in the rain. He was not even breathing hard with the added burden of my entire body, my wet clothes or my broadsword. He never bumped me into a tree, never lost his step in the slippery mud. He just kept walking and chanting."

"Chanting?" asked Bourdicca. "What the deamhan was he chanting? And I canno imagine his size or strength." Bourdicca was at this point beginning to wonder if this tale was a dream, the result of too much strong drink or a fantasy, somehow created in his commander's mind? He kept his mouth shut though and listened.

Gustav set his goblet gently upon the desk. He looked at Bourdicca and said, "If you laugh at this…" and was then so choked up, he could not speak.

Bourdicca said, "You have no worries."

Gustav cleared his throat, his face a bit pinched, and began to speak, in almost in a manner of a person reciting a poem, yet it was not a poem, it was so much more…

"He kept chanting:

May my deeds be the hammer to shape not only my future,
but that of generations to come.

May the forge of my heart, craft this world into a place
worth living.

May my fire stoke yours.

May my resolve remain stalwart in the face of adversity,
and serve to embolden the weary.

May my hands be stayed in anger,
but never idle toward peace.

May the song of my heart be that which I sing the loudest.

May you find respite, in my presence."

As Gustav finished, Bourdicca, with a quizzical look on his face said, "That is a powerful message, could ye repeat it for me?"

Gustav did, this time with a bit more resolve, his face clear.

Bourdicca then asked, "How did ye come to know the words so well? Was there more, or ave ye added yer own text?"

Gustav's eyes closed gently, and then he completed his story. "This man, he carried me to a place in the woods. A massive log cabin with a stout stone hearth, a fire blazing inside. He set me down on the floor inside and went to a pot at the fire. He just kept repeating the words I jus told ye."

"Did ye ask him where ye were, what this place was?" asked Bourdicca. The second in command was a bit concerned because if there was a place like this, he and his men should know about it. Yet, he had no inkling.

"Oh yes, I was all about questions," answered Gustav. "But the big brute just kept repeating the verses over and over. He gave me a bucket of warm water from near the fire to wash myself. He set food on a plate for me and kept the fire blazing, so we were warm. But then he did the strangest thing, and it took me a moment to understand."

"I canna think of much stranger happenings going on," said Bourdicca.

"Then just listen, because it gets more interesting," said Gustav. "It finally became apparent that the big man was a blacksmith. As I looked around the room, all the tools of a smithy were about. The big man, he picked up a large blacksmith rounding hammer with one hand, and with the other removed a large chunk of bright red metal from the fire, which I now understood to be a forge of large proportions. Setting the hot metal upon an anvil, which must have weighed as much as two large men, he began to pound it with the force of a whole company of soldiers. All the while chanting his words."

"Yes, that be a strange behavior," replied Bourdicca. "I'm wondering how you escaped?"

"I was fascinated," responded Gustav. "I had no thought of walking away. There did not seem any danger, and the big man could have caught me in a fast moment anyway, so why bother?"

"True," agreed Bourdicca.

"This time, when he finished his verse, he looked up at me, pointed the heavy hammer at my chest and said one word, 'Repeat.' I answered to him, 'Your verse?' He simply nodded yes, and I started out as best as I could while he pounded away on his metal. I think I got out just the first phrase and then could go no further since I had not been listening with an intent to repeat."

"What the deamhan did the man expect?" exclaimed Bourdicca.

"Oh, he expected all of it," sighed Gustav. "He bade me to take his hammer and pound the metal as I spoke. This I did, and he spoke the verses with me, over and over and over."

Gustav took a gentle sip of his whiskey and continued, "When I tired of pounding the metal, he relieved my hand of the hammer, and we just kept repeating the verses. We would stop to drink water and eat some, in silence. But then back at it."

"When did it all end?" asked Bourdicca.

"Well, my fair man, it occurred to me that it would not end until I had the verses memorized. So, I put myself into knowing the words. I put myself into shaping the metal. And soon it happened."

"What happened?" asked the now bewildered Bourdicca.

"This," said Gustav. Reaching under his desk he held up a beautiful, bright, shiny, pure silver serving platter. The shiny metal had been pounded into a flawless circle, with perfectly spaced hammer marks around the middle. It was nothing short of an amazing work of art. "This was finished just as I was finished memorizing the verses, and me arm was as about to fall off from pounding this metal. And then it all fell into place in me head."

"What fell into place?" asked Bourdicca.

"I'd been having thoughts of something amiss in the forest, something off with nature. Like I said, these thoughts started after Garwen was culled from the earth. And then it hit me like a trip to the gallows." Gustav looked sternly at Bourdicca, he took a sip of his drink and then said in a low voice, laced with emotion that was undeniable, "The issue was me."

Gustav took a long thoughtful drink from his goblet and Bourdicca did likewise. Both sighed together, enjoying the moment. As is the way with a good scotch, there shall be no rushing or fast paced anything. Savoring the art of the beverage, appreciating the time it took to create, and honoring the labors invested in its creation are a vital part of enjoying the experience. Now a beer or ale may be consumed quickly. However, a good scotch must be appreciated. And a large part of the relationship between two scotch enthusiasts is sharing that time of appreciation concerning what they are enjoying. Doing so calms the mind, softens the heart and brings joy to the soul.

Gustav continued after they had enjoyed their moment, "I have been playing the tough soldier for as many winters as I might remember. But the world I have created does not find respite in my presence. I need to be the verses if I am to understand what nature and the future have in store for me. For all of us." And Gustav swept his hand around, indicating the fort, the village and everything they could imagine.

"You want to be a better version of your best self? asked Bourdicca.

"That my man is a spirited and wonderful way to put it. I like those words. Thank you." Gustav pondered for a moment, and continued, "I want everyone at the fort to be proud of the work we do. Proud to serve our king and proud to protect these people. We have it backwards. We have had it backwards since the first winter ever arrived."

"What is backwards? quired Bourdicca

"We look at the people here as serving the needs of the fort and the king. We need to change that thinking. The king keeps the realm intact. The army, be as it may, is charged with keeping the people safe. We treat these people like they are a disease we must conquer. They are not a disease. They are the people who count on us, and we count on them because only together, can we survive or thrive or whatever."

"Well spoken," said Bourdicca.

"Sure, but I'm not knowing how to make it happen," lamented Gustav, leaning back in his chair, his eyes full of question.

They both would find that in life, when we are open to the question, the answer will appear.

48. Supper

Across the courtyard, up the narrow stairs in the little apartment hanging off the side of the fort from where Bourdicca and Gustav were enjoying a drink, the Völva and Chrisholm sat at the little table, now complete with food and drink. Once more Ancropolis tended to the fire before taking a seat. The room had cleared of the men from the kitchen, and the door secured with timbers.

Besides the candles on the table, the kitchen workers had also delivered four stout candles on lengthy firm posts. These candles were placed along the walls in various locations to add light to the small, usually dark apartment. After the candles had been lit, their flickers danced in a soft golden glow across the table, on their faces and everything contained in the little room. Now with the fire warm, the candles lit and food to consume, the space took on a much more civilized and gentler feel.

Almost.

The window looking over the road proved to be a bit cumbersome though. Since there was no glass, a cold breeze had been harshly blowing across the occupants. Both Chrisholm and the Völva commented on the cold air and how annoying it was to not let the room be comfortable.

Ancropolis found a large leather hide rolled up in a corner and secured it across the window opening. The breeze was now tamed. This brought smiles all about and it was finally time for all to sit down and enjoy a meal.

The Völva poured three goblets of wine and held out her hands for Chrisholm and Ancropolis. They each gently grasped the offered pale slim hand and the Völva stopped and waited. After a few heartbeats, she quietly said, "Please, you both also join your hands."

They did.

The Völva bowed her head and said, "We thank the spirts and all that is good, for this food, this room, and for the community we are so blessed to know. May all of everything be better for our presence." She paused, she let go of their hands and said, "Let's eat, I'm famished, and I have not had anyone to dine with since I climbed those ghastly narrow steps." She looked up and smiled.

Neither Chrisholm nor Ancropolis moved a muscle. Their curiosity was to the boiling point. Finally, Chrisholm blustered the questions she knew they both were thinking, "Who are you? Why are we here? What is going on? You act as if we should know you. But really, we have no clue!"

The Völva said, "Oh dear, you know verra well who I am." She then took a healthy drink from her goblet and looked at both of them with a smile.

49. Back

Bourdicca had consumed all but his last precious swallow of the mystic amber liquid in his goblet. There ensued a silence between the two men, a silence of thought and pondering.

Before long, Bourdicca queried, "I am curious, how did you ever make it safely back to yer camp in the forest with the men?"

Gustav smiled in his reply, "The big man simply walked to the door, motioned for me to pick up this silver tray and follow. He seemed a man of few words. So, I followed. We walked out of the huge blacksmith shop. It was late morning. We had been up all-night hammering and sharing the verses back and forth. The sun was up, the birds were chirping, the forest had that clean smell it gets after rain. A bit earthy, damp, yet washed and crisp. Especially invigorating walking through areas in the sun, bright between the trees and the falling leaves, it was glorious.

"So ye both walked back to the soldiers at the forest camp?"

Gustav continued, "We walked together most of the way. He knew exactly how to go, straight through the woods, not a path in sight. He just walked like a man possessed, and when we topped a ridge, he looked to the next ridge, spied our camp and said, 'See?' I told him yes, and he left me, going back the way we had come at a dead on run. I could not thank him or add inquiry."

Gustav stopped talking, rubbed his chin and then finished, "I had so many questions, I wanted to know if I could return to spend more time with him, find out where he comes from, what drove him to do what he did? Why? Just why? Yet he was gone in a flash, like a dream. And I ave wondered if it was a dream, until I look and feel this solid silver platter. This work of art. I know, something more must be in store. And I know I could never find the shop again."

"It's a bit of a deep mystery to me," said Bourdicca. "We could send out a scouting party to find the building ye speak of. It being large with a fire burning, it canna be that hard to find."

"Yes, I have thought of that move many times," replied Gustav slowly and thoughtfully. "However, the man did no want to be discovered, and I feel he would not be verra glad if a squad of soldiers came a knocking on his door. There be something a bit deeper goin on and I do no need ta rush this. There be no threat to anyone, so we play this out and see what is happening."

Bourdicca thought for a moment and instantly admired the courage and forethought coming from his commander. Bourdicca replied, "I ave ta agree with you. This man, he be a mystery for sure. An ye got no name from him?"

"No, not a name, not a wif of where he be from, no dialect or markings upon him to give me a clue," replied Gustav.

Bourdicca added, "Waiting and watching seem ta be the best path forward."

Gustav finished the conversation with, "Almost, I am looking for answers and talked to Raket0st. When we sat here in my office, sharing a dram, as we are, he told me to find a Völva. And then she appeared at the fortress door. Something strange is happening, and it is happening now." Gustav sighed.

50. Morning

In the early part of the morning, sometimes a traveler can experience a few mysterious and magical moments when deep in the forest. This only happens when the wee light of dawn breaks the darkness into something of an enigmatic fog. And the magic occurs for just a brief few moments. Its moments when darkness no longer prevails, yet the light does not yet rule the day. This mystic phenomenon only lasts a few heartbeats. It is dark, and it's not dark, all at the same time. Shapes are emerging, yet not yet visible. Then suddenly, shadows of the trees appear and finally the light of the sun fills in all the elements and it's daytime. Again, the light rules! Of course, the long shadows of the trees travel through the day from the west to the east, but the morning can be a magical, mysterious period.

Torrin was partly awake for that verra break of dawn upon their camp. A fleeting thought came to his only half-awake brain; he and Dessa had been through the dark, the fog, the shadows and then to the light. But now, did they seem to be returning to the dark? Or was all their trouble the dark, and now they would be entering the light?

This thought diminished as fog will disappear when the sun comes out when he fully awoke. Very gently he laid a hand upon Dessa's cheek. For a few moments he let the warmth of her sleeping breath curl around his wrist. Then he softly stirred her awake.

She gurgled a soft, "Not yet, I'm warm and only halfway through a wonderful and fun dream."

Torrin sighed, laughed a bit and commented, "Aye me sweet bràmair, but I don wanna get off on the wrong foot with yer wee spryte lady again by not making it to Kalmar. We must get a move on and be on our way."

Torrin rose and got to rekindling the fire for some quick cooking. The coals from the night before were still hot below the top covering of white flaky ash. He lifted a small oilcloth and picked up the tiny kindling sticks they had stored the night before so the wood would be dry for the morning fire. Then on his knees, he began to softly blow on the coals. Soon flames rose up. He added larger sticks and bits of wood, and as he had done so many times. As the flames reached up, he warmed his hands over the fresh fire.

Making his way to Dessa, he knelt down and said with a big smile "I could pull yer blanket off, or get to tickling ye to get ye up. What's it to be?"

Dessa opened her eyes and spied the warm flames of the fire. A smile crept to her face, and she said, "Ye do give good care to me, especially on a cool morning. I do love ye." She sat up and kissed him quickly on the mouth, careful to avoid any sparks.

Torrin smiled back and went to get their breakfast from the big pack Calandra carried. As he walked near the horses, he felt a pang of envy that Dessa could talk to them and he heard but nary a sound, other than the occasional neigh or wet whinny. But things are what they are, and he had an idea he was going to experience more of that in a short while.

They cooked a quick meal of porridge and shared some dried beef. They had not taken any of the mathan meat or fat. Dessa could not bring herself to be part of that gift. Torrin had agreed, somewhat grudgingly; anyway, they did not really need the meat. And tomorrow, they were sure they could procure more stores from the town as Dessa still had her gold from Gale.

Although, they were not sure how to use the gold. Coins and metal for trade were not part of the northern valley at Journey. They had grown up mostly with a system of barter or just owing someone something in return.

The early morning sun had chased away all the shadows when they cinched the big pack tight onto the wide sturdy back of Calandra. A few moments later, their own smaller packs were secure on Uta and Samoot. Torrin stirred the fire to make certain it was safe for them to be on their way. Dessa filled and then carefully sealed their canvas water skins, and she checked with all the horses to make sure they had eaten their fill.

As they mounted up, Torrin took one more look around to make sure nothing was left behind. He smiled when he saw the tightly stacked, small pile of wood left against a wide tree. A large armful of leaves covered the top to help keep the wood dry. It was their habit, leaving a campsite better than they had found it. And dry wood for a traveler caught in the rain was a very welcome gift. Torrin and Dessa had come upon stores of wood and other niceties at campsites along the trail, so they were always conscious to return the favor (someone had once left a small glass bottle of a tasty, yet strong drink. They still laughed at that find; it had been fun!).

Dessa, aboard Uta, steered Calandra by a lead as they made their way back to the main trail to Kalmar. The sun was now bright through the trees, and the morning chill of a fall day had succumbed to a warmer, more pleasant temperature. Some leaves fell quietly as they wound their way along the path that had taken them to their restful campsite, away from the main trail.

When they found the trail, Dessa released the lead from Calandra, and they all broke into a slow trot. There was no talking or banter this morning. They were on a mission to reach Kalmar and get to the next stage of whatever mysteries awaited. Both Dessa and Torrin kept glancing at the forest, expecting Marjie to appear at any moment.

But all was quiet.

They passed some kauppasaksa along the way. They briefly exchanged pleasantries and inquiries about how long it would take to reach the city.

Torrin asked Dessa, "When we get to Kalmar, where do we go?"

She replied, "Not sure. Something tells me we'll know what to do or, we will be informed as we need. I'm not worried."

51. And Morning

Chrisholm slowly awoke in the room where she, the Völva and Ancropolis had spent a quiet and peaceful night. She noticed early morning light creeping around the edges of the outer window. The light was bright and crisp against the leather Ancropolis had secured to the window blocking the cold breeze from the previous evening. The room had cooled considerably throughout the night. Just as she had desired the other day, she did not want venture from her warm blankets. She lay there, listening to the quiet breathing of the two others. Her mind wondered what mysteries would arrive or be solved today.

Before long, stirring began next to her and Ancropolis awoke. He kissed her on the cheek and quietly told her he was going down the stairs to the privy. The ladies had a small privy in the corner of the apartment to use, and he wanted to give them a bit of privacy (and of course wanted his own privacy).

While he was gone, Chisholm took care of her morning business, and by now the Völva was moving about and did the same. Chrisholm began tending the fire and the Völva sat quietly on her bed, legs crossed, hands stretched out, and her eyes softly closed. Her face looked serene.

Chrisholm had never experienced anyone meditating before and she was curious about what the Völva was up to, and more importantly, why?

The Völva explained, "My dear, it's called meditation, some call it centering. It doesn't matter what you call it." The Völva smiled a bit and continued, "Anyway, it's my time of the day to connect my soul with the spirit world and nature. I practice meditation every morning. Calms my nerves, gives me insight as to what to say and do on a busy day. And, for what it's worth, I like it."

"Could ye teach me?" said Chrisholm. "And why do ye call it a practice, ye seem to have this worked out pretty well?"

"Well, my dear, it's called a practice because it takes some mental tenacity and many times practicing the process to get your thinking where you desire to get your thinking. Don't worry, you'll see. Now sit up on the bed, in a comfortable position, any position is fine. I just like this one."

Chrisholm smoothed her skirts and sat crossed legged on the bed. Her hands in her lap. She closed her eyes and said, "Now what?"

"Think of nothing," said the Völva.

"What?"

"See, it's an interesting practice!" grinned the Völva, "What I mean is to get into a calm state of mind, you start with removing all the thoughts you have that distract you from being in a peaceful way."

Chrisholm made a quizzical face and said, "OK, sounds easy, let's see how it goes."

The two of them sat quietly with no sounds in the room. A soft and gentle peace settled between them for a few moments.

"Chac," muttered Chrisholm, "All sorts of thoughts are racing around me brain. This is impossible!"

The Völva again softly smiled, never opening her eyes and said, "Now dear, you understand why it's called a practice. Here is a tip for people just starting out. Close your eyes gently, take three deep breaths, verra slowly. Then, imagine a large gray stone in your mind. Nothing else and just hold that thought of the stone for at least three more long, gentle breaths. See if that works for you."

Chrisholm slowly brought in three long deep breaths and let them out. She muttered a low 'hmmm' of satisfaction and then the sounds of her gentle breaths could be heard. She then said again, "Chac! I only got to two and then thoughts came creeping in. This is hard, but I think I'm going to like it."

"Mm, mm," said the Völva, "That's better than most people. Most folks can't even get the gray stone up for a moment. Keep it up, you'll enjoy it."

Just then the big door opened and Ancropolis walked into the room. He carried a steaming pot of aromatic tea and a large loaf of fresh, warm bread. He looked at the two women, perched on the bed and just said,

"Now that is interesting, you two look like ye is sittin for a painting."

The Völva said, maintaining her meditation pose, her eyes still shut, "Your lady here is learning the practice of meditation. You might want to learn too, for its verra relaxing, calms the heart and the soul."

A short laugh emerged as he responded, "I don't see meself learning that trick."

The Völva's eyes popped open, she smiled and said, "Whatever you choose sir. Anyway, I am done for today. I like to meditate, but can't compete with fresh bread and hot tea on a cool morning. Come on let's eat. And after we eat, you, young man need to go see the commander, and request the roasted gourd. We have a journey to take, and we leave towards dusk."

Ancropolis asked, "What be the significance of a roasted gourd?"

As the Völva tore off a large chunk of the fresh bread, she said, "People, such as yourselves use hollowed out gourds with candles inside to ward off spirits during Samhain (Celtic precursor to Halloween)."

Ancropolis nodded that he understood.

The Völva continued, "So, since our friends downstairs link me to the spirit world, I figured that roasting a gourd was a good way for them to keep, yours truly, linked to the spirits. Well, at least in their minds. It also gave them something to do."

Chrisholm sat down at the table and poured tea for herself while she asked, "So are ye really a Völva, or someone who is just clever enough to trick Gustav and company inta thinkn ye is one?"

The Völva finished chewing her bread and spoke quietly, "There be Völvas out there that be real, no doubt. Although I've never met one. Also, there be many who call themselves Völva, and they are a total fabrication of even the idea of connecting with the spirit world, let alone being able to know the future."

Both Ancropolis and Chrisholm were sitting very still, waiting.

The Völva finished by saying, "Maybe it be not so important that a lady can see the spirits and the future. Maybe it be, the company she keeps that be the big difference. You'll see, this evening."

52. Arrival

"I think you needed a good workout," said Dessa to Uta. The big mare was huffing a bit as they headed along the path at a slight downward slope at the Kalmar's entrance. 'I suppose ye are right, as long as there is good grass and a long night's sleep ahead,' replied Uta.

Samoot and Calandra had kept up with the good pace Dessa and Uta had set for the day. Torrin, as was his normal traveling self, admiring the forest and now the array of buildings. There were a lot of buildings! More in one area than either of them had ever experienced. And a great number of people walking along the road.

"I think we have arrived," said Dessa.

"Aye," said Torrin, "But I'm not seein where we should be heading, or stopping or whatever?"

Dessa said to Uta, "Where do we need to go? I'm sure ye received verra clear instructions from Marjie."

Uta was quiet for a few moments and then replied, 'Find Eskil and Anton, it's all I know.' No more instructions were forthcoming.

Dessa looked at Torrin and said with a bit of wonder, "That was somewhat helpful, but really, not so much."

"Did ye get a response from the big beasty?" asked Torrin.

Torrin's question was rewarded with a wet whinny and snort from Uta. Samoot seemed to join in the conversation with another snort. Calandra, being the more staid of the bunch, said nothing.

"Seems she does not like being called a big beasty," commented Dessa. "Anyway, what she said was to find and an Eskil and an Anton." There was nothing more forthcoming from Madam Beasty. But at least it's something."

"Hmmm. Eskil could be a person, but most likely a place, the name generally is associated with cooking. Anton is a favorite name for boys. So, we is probably looking for an Anton in a place called Eskil."

Dessa stopped the big horse and asked a woman passing by where she could find an Eskil and or an Anton. She was still not sure what these were, person or place, so asking seemed to be the answer. Or was it?

The woman just kept walking and did not even look at Dessa. Dessa looked back at Torrin and said, "Not like the good folks of the valley!"

A bit further on, an older man was slowly walking along the road, and Dessa tried asking again.

"Aye, ye is headed that way me little gnèitheach. Jus down the road a bit, on yer right, afore the road turns to stone an rough bricks."

Dessa decided she did not like this place! A woman ignored her, and a perfect muigean (disagreeable person) of a stranger called her a sexy woman at their first meeting. Both were verra inappropriate. She spurred Uta forward, her face tight and her eyes a dark turquoise. She heard Torrin mutter a quick 'Thank you' to the man as he and Samoot passed by at a steady trot.

In just a few moments, a tidy building that looked to be a tavern of sorts appeared on their right side. A small livery was next door, and they headed in to have the horse's needs attended to and boarded for the night.

A young boy appeared and helped Dessa off Uta, then tied Uta to a post. "You don't need to tie her," said Dessa, "She is well mannered and won't give ye any trouble."

The boy looked at Dessa with a bit of a stern expression on his face and said, "This is the rule of the master, if I don't tie up every horse, I'll get beat fer sure. Go into the tavern and find McGill. You pay him, three penningar for the night. Includes feed and water. Ye need to be gone early in the morning or ye pay again, no exceptions. Don't worry, I'll take care of em good, and I does like a nice tip." He moved to tie up Calandra and then on to Samoot.

Dessa asked, "Pay? What is that?"

The boy stopped and looked at Dessa as if she'd gone daft. "Money lady, like this." He dug into a sporran at his side and produced a coin. "Avan't ye ever seen money afore? Where did ye come from, the ever lovn' moon?"

Torrin walked up, looked at the coin and said, "I've heard of this stuff. We were talking about it around the fire. Might ave been a bit around Journey, but I've never needed it afore."

The boy just said, "Well if ye not payn', ye not stayn'."

Just then Dessa remembered the gold coins Gale had given her. She reached into her pack and produced one. It was a verra different color than the one the boy was holding, but she hoped it would work. The small bag that held the gold still smelled of the fire at Journey, and the singes on the bag reminded her of the importance of this quest. "Like this?" she asked.

The boy's eyes went wide, and his mouth opened like he was going to speak, yet all that came out was a gurgle. Finally, he muttered, "Wow, never seen one afor, heard bout 'em, never seen one. Can I hold it? Please?"

Dessa thought, Ah, some manners. Of course, when he wants something. She handed him the coin. He hefted it in his hand, put it in his mouth and bit down. "Its real ahright, wow! McGill will make change, and ther's gonna be a lot of it." he exclaimed and handed the coin back to Dessa.

Change? Thought Dessa, what is that? As they took their leave, she stopped, quickly turned around at the big entrance door and snatched the satchel from her pack where she had stored the coins. She grimly smiled at the stable boy and walked away. She was sure she heard him mutter, 'damnú.'

They walked the few feet to the door of the supposed tavern and stopped. People scurried about along the road. A few horses and some wagons plodded their way along. Some people looked kindly, but most sported a stern face about themselves. A few of doors down, two soldiers walked along, one carrying a nasty looking flail with vicious spikes on the ball, the other carrying a long-spiked pole. They seemed to be on a patrol for some reason. The two looked in windows and opened doors as they passed. There was no request for entry or a simple 'Hello.' They just carried on as they pleased. It seemed odd, it did not seem verra friendly.

Torrin continued along the front to the end of the building to look around. Dessa heard him say, "Come here, you need to see this!"

She joined him after scowling at the guards, and they had scowled back at her. Torrin said, "Look!" and pointed. She first saw water and then her heart stood still for a moment. They were looking at Kalmar harbor. Wooden boats of all sizes bobbed on the gentle surf. These boats ranged from simple rowboats to huge three-masted sailing ships. The masts, ladder shrouds, booms of all sizes and interconnected mass of materials were something they had never, ever even imagined, even though they had heard of them from travelers. They both just stood there, transfixed at the sight.

Torrin said, "Can ye believe it? People ad talked about the big ships, but I ad no clue as to their size. Oh, me glory!"

Dessa said, "Now I understand how all these goods and kauppasaksa are arriving to head to the north. It seems there is a surprise every day for us. Let's go inside, pay the man McGill and maybe we can get something to eat. We need to figure out our next steps."

When they entered Eskil no one paid them any bit of attention. Torrin commented, "Guess they are used to all sorts of folks comin and goin, being a busy port and all."

They walked up to the bar where an old, wizened man was taking care of customers. When he had finished serving a couple of others he smiled and made his way over to Torrin and Dessa.

"I am Anton," he said. "You two need to get a good lunch in you, pay McGill and be off later this afternoon. You have a trip to make towards dusk. It's an easy way for ye. Just stay on the road, go past the big double doors at the fort and wait at the end of the big wall. Make sure you arrive before the shadows of the buildings are across the road from west to east. The fort is easy to find. McGill is the man in the black hat. He will make change for your gold and don't worry, he is honest. I'll be over to your table with food and drink soon."

Dessa and Torrin looked at each other and together said, "Marjie."

53. Exit

Ancropolis finished his tea and asked the two ladies at the table, "You want me to bring the commander? Do you need anyone else to come up here?"

The Völva said, "Yes, have him bring his number two, that man he calls Bourdicca. I'm not sure if he will be of any use this morning, but it will be difficult to go get Bourdicca after we are gone on our way. And Gustav seems to like having his number two around. Also, don't be surprised at how things appear when you come back up. I need to keep up the theatrics. I do have an image to maintain!" She sighed and said, "I think I am getting too old for this. Now go, go on your way!"

Ancropolis opened the door and started down the stairs. When he landed on the ground, smoke was billowed out the hole over the door and the vent in the roof. And then, the smoke turned green. He shook his head in amazement and looked for someone so he could find his way to the commander.

It took a bit of searching and asking. No one seemed glad, happy or eager to be taking a stranger up to Gustav's private environment. Ancropolis kept getting handed off to one person and then another. Finally, he was given to a sturdy man who was different than the others. He was impeccably dressed and told Ancropolis that the others had tiadhans made of mush (translation, soft balls). They were all afraid of the commander, for no real reason.

After walking with this soldier for a bit they arrived at a long circular stairway. There were many windows. Some with glass, others covered loosely with a course burlap, and some open. The mix of coverings created a confusing pattern of light, dark and shadows. They climbed tight irregular steps where the intermixed sunlight and shadows caused Ancropolis to stumble twice. He had to stop and close his eyes

to let his head clear so he could proceed along the confusing stairway. Again, Ancropolis thought, easy to defend.

Eventually they made it to the top. After passing through a large, armored door, they entered a small antechamber. The soldier guiding Ancropolis was careful to shut the armored door tightly. Protocol again, to be followed!

Once more, Ancropolis marveled at the masonry, the sheer amount of hewn stone, the craftwork of the masons and all the details. This place just did not end. The soldier approached a stout wooden door to the left and knocked. A few moments later Bourdicca appeared. The soldier who had been leading Ancropolis saluted, turned on his heals and marched out.

Bourdicca looked around to see if anyone else was present and then said, "Ah, one of our visitors, what can I do for you?"

Ancropolis smiled and said, "I need to see the Commander."

"I will take any messages to Gustav young man. What say you?"

Ancropolis replied, "No, I will see him, the Völva has a request." He was trying to decide if he liked this man or not. Ancropolis was totally unsure.

Bourdicca frowned, he was obviously used to being in charge, unless Gustav was present. He said, "Please wait for a moment while I check with the commander." He turned on his heel, disappeared through the door; it shut tight with a bit of a theatrical slam. Ancropolis found himself alone in the anteroom, with nothing to admire but stone walls and various closed doors.

Footsteps echoed off the stone walls before the stout door opened. Bourdicca appeared with Gustav close behind.

Gustav passed Bourdicca, his eyes bright with question. He asked, "What message is from the Völva?"

Ancropolis grinned, knowing that both men were eager for news to move this all forward. He simply stated to them, "Herself requests the roasted gourd."

He heard sighs of relief and an exclamation of, 'finally!' He was ushered into Gustav's private office while the commander finished a discussion with one of the men from the fort.

54. Lunch

Entering the Eskil Tavern and Inn, Torrin found a table with two chairs by a large window and sat down. It was a relief to be off his feet, out of a saddle and sitting on a comfortable chair. He noted this enormous window was the largest piece of glass he had ever encountered.

Dessa took some time to pay McGill and collect her 'change,' whatever that was. When she came to the table Torrin had procured there was quite a lot of this stuff called 'change.' Her little sack of coins was verra full.

Torrin asked how it went. Dessa replied, "He was quite excited abou the gold coin. Said he had seen a few in his day, but never one that old. He bit it, just as the wee stable boy did and he pronounced it just intact and wonderful. I inquired as to the reason for the biting of the coin. He was verra amused that someone with such coins would not know. He dug in his sporran and produced a coin like our gold. He said the real gold was softer, and ye could feel the difference in a bite. I tried it. He was right. Our real gold is softer and there is not a bit of strange taste. The other coin was hard and had harsh flavors like biting on a horseshoe."

She dropped the sack on the table and went to tell the horses they would be leaving later in the afternoon and to eat their fill now. They would not be enjoying a full night's rest at this little resting place.

As Dessa entered the livery through the large double doors, she saw the stable boy lying on the floor, surrounded by blood. He had a massive cut on his leg and was bleeding. There was no sign of how it happened. But that did not matter, he was close to dead already.

Dessa ran!

Dessa ran to Eskil, burst through the door, looked at Torrin and said, "Come, the stable boy has been injured. Now!"

Torrin rose from his comfortable chair as quickly as he could manage.

Although, he was a bit stiff from all the riding, and it took him a few heartbeats to stand up straight and start moving.

McGill beat him out the door.

As Torrin rounded the corner to the livery, he saw the young boy on the ground, McGill at one side, Dessa kneeling next to him on the other side.

Dessa looked at Torrin and said, "Get out your small knife." She looked at McGill and said, "Please move, we can fix this."

McGill looked up at Dessa and shouted, "Lady, this kid is bleeding to death, there is nothing you or anyone can do for him. Whatever happened tore his leg up like meat through a butcher's grinder." With that McGill moved to the top of the boy's body, picked up his head and moaned, "Oh ye little ponach (young lad), don leave me, yer such a special friend!

Torrin paid no mind to the grieving man. He stepped around him, knelt, and deftly cut the boy's breeches from crotch to ankle. The material opened up and they witnessed up close, a verra bloody mess. His bones were white, against the dark red of his blood. Blood that was running out of him and pooling in his pants leg. Muscles, tendons, and bits of dirt floated in the gore.

Dessa looked up at Torrin and asked, "Do you think it will work? I don't remember anything so bloody and terrible before." Her eyes were a dark turquoise.

Torrin took her hands, looked at McGill and said sternly, "Put his head down and back away. We can't know what's going to happen to ye if yer touching him."

As Torrin finished talking, Anton and a few others turned the corner and entered the livery. He could hear gasps of horror.

Turing his attention back to Dessa, they both raised up tall upon their knees, met in the middle over the boy and they kissed verra gently. Their hands went down to just over the top of the nasty injury and together they moved their clasped hands toward his foot.

Small blue sparks flew around them, heat rose from their hands.

And then!

Nothing happened.

They both looked down at the boy, Dessa had tears in her eyes and

Torrin said, "Again." His voice indicated, there be no option.

This time, their lips met hard, blue sparks lit the interior of the livery. In his mind, Torrin was a bit worried for all the straw and hay about, but figured dealing with all that would come later. He was also aware of the shouts of worry and despair coming from the now assembled crowd. And deeper in his mind, he knew that if his own child ever needed help, he hoped someone would be daring, kind and brave enough to never stop.

The gash responded, bone emerged from end to end and mended. Parts meshed together, skin emerged from his ankle. Like a sock unrolls up a leg. This new skin stitched itself clean to the lower part of the boy's thigh. As they noticed the leg healing, Dessa and Torrin ran their intertwined hands up to the unconscious head of the lad, and then ever so slowly back down to his feet.

Their lips parted, they sat back on their heels, hands still clenched over the you lad's inert body, continuing to move slowly from foot to head. Back and forth. The heat dissipated, and they watched. They hoped and they almost breathlessly, waited.

Finally, the young man took a breath, turned his head and threw up. Dessa smiled and expelled a bit of a laugh through her partially open lips. If a person has the strength to expel their stomach, they have the strength to live. Ipi had taught her that when they had spent many an evening discussing ideas around healing. Throwing up was a good sign.

They looked at each other, Torrin smiled too, and then little by little they unwound their hands. When they released each other they both had to sit back and be still, for they were totally and completely spent. Both panting a bit, sweating and they shared a bit of a grin.

Dessa looking a bit pale lay down on the damp floor. Torrin said, "My bràmair, what is it? Are ye OK? Ye sick?"

Dessa just lay there, breathing softly. After a moment, she said quietly, "Sush, I need a moment."

Torrin felt a bit shaky as he stood. He held himself stable with a hand on the livery wall. He then looked down at McGill and said, "We think he will be fine, but is going to need a few days of rest. He needs to eat, and make sure it's good food. He will gain strength over some time. You need to let his little body catch up and fully heal."

McGill just sat on the dirt floor, his mouth agape. He was shaking his head in utter amazement.

Walking around the foot of the boy, Torrin came to Dessa and knelt next to her. He kissed her on the cheek and could feel her whole being warm from the kiss. She fluttered her eyes open, turned up to look at Torrin and smiled. She whispered, "We did it."

"Yes," he murmured in a low voice. However, I am worrying the people here are going to think of us practicing of witchcraft. Let's get to our lunch and be on our way. Did ye warn the steeds of our early departure?"

She shook her head no, as he helped her up. Together they found the three horses, quietly chewing in a clean stall. Dessa gave them the news. All Torrin could hear was a loud wet whinny. He heard Dessa say to Uta, "Relax, we have not pushed ye on this trip except for today. Or are ye getting old and frail an I need to be rid of ye?" Torrin heard another loud wet snort as Uta blew a lungful of air from his nose.

Dessa said, "We can talk later, just relax and eat."

Dessa and Torrin turned and walked back toward the livery's big entrance door. The boy was sitting on a stool, drinking some water from a goblet. McGill was standing next to him, mussing with his hair. The crowd had dispersed, since there was nothing more to be seen here. McGill seemed to try and speak, yet no words came from his lips.

Torrin knelt next to the boy and said, "Take it easy for a couple of days, let yerself heal right." He then stood up and followed Dessa to Eskil. When they walked in, a soldier was waiting for them, sitting at their table.

55 Dust

Bourdicca followed this time, letting Gustav lead. Gustav was not in a rush, but he certainly was not taking his time, and he waited for nobody. Up the narrow stairway they climbed. Ancropolis was third in line, wondering what it was all about.

Of course, all of them were wondering what this was all about! And maybe more importantly, was all this, whatever it was, coming to an end?

Or maybe, it was coming to a beginning?

Just previously, Ancropolis had been given a bit of the cold shoulder by Bourdicca while in Gustav's office. Obviously, Bourdicca did not like taking orders from a 'visitor,' or his having any of his normal responsibilities of controlling who gets to see Gustav usurped.

Once inside the massive office, Ancropolis was now greeted warmly by Gustav and motioned to a seat. Gustav had offered a beverage, and Ancropolis politely declined, thinking that getting back to the little room quickly was more important. He did not want Chrisholm to sit in green smoke verra long.

Gustav inquired, in verra serious tones about what Ancropolis had learned while staying with the overly dramatic and almost crazy Völva.

It occurred to Ancropolis that knocking down the dramatic persona the Völva had built might not suit them all at this point. He rubbed his chin for a few moments, totally lost in thought before replying.

"To be honest with me self, I don really make much of all the shenanigans. I do know, when I arrived this verra morning with fresh bread and tea from yer verra fine kitchen, she and my love were communing with some spirits. It was all verra strange and mysterious." Ancropolis looked away, took a deep breath and finished, "Ta be honest, its makin me skin crawl and I'm looking forward to movin on with all this."

Gustav was silent for a moment and then said to Bourdicca, "Tell the kitchen to prepare the damnú gourd, let's get this under way."

Wordlessly, Bourdicca left in a hurry.

Gustav turned to Ancropolis and said, "Thank you. Other than my short encounters with this woman, I've had no other information about her. The connecting with spirits is not surprising. Are you surprised your lady was part of this behavior?"

Ancropolis looked hard at Gustav and said with much conviction, "Me sweet Chrisholm has always been in touch with something beyond me comprehension."

* * *

At the top of the steps, Gustav knocked on the door of the apartment and it gracefully swung open from his knock. Fetid smells emerged, along with orange smoke and some chanting. Ancropolis smiled, it was certainly a lesson in theatrics, one he would never forget.

The three men entered the room, Chrisholm sidled up to Ancropolis and held his hand, as though she were frightened. They looked at each other with a grim smile, a smile that foretold dismay, or disaster.

The Völva was dancing on the sturdy table. The table was now in the center of the room and the long candlesticks delivered by the kitchen folk were gathered tightly around the four points of the table. It looked just as though she was trapped in a small cage.

The Völva was chanting nonsense, twirling her skirts as she spun. Each turn missed the candle flames by just a breath.

When Ancropolis closed the door, the Völva stopped dancing. Stopped chanting. Seemed to stop breathing. She looked down at Gustav and Bourdicca. Her wide eyes seemed ablaze with fire or fury. It was not obvious, but it would not matter.

One at a time, the Völva pointed at each person standing before her. She sneered some sort of unintelligible remark. Then clearing her throat, she spat green phlegm out the little window high over the door. Putting both hands on her hips, she let out a loud "Well now," and promptly jumped onto the floor.

Pulling herself up to sit on the table, she sat down with a long sigh. Immediately, she threw both arms straight up and said, "Sit down, right where ye are." And then, one word at a time, with full effect she said, like a tired mother berating a miscreant child, "We. Are. Running. Out. Of. Time!"

The four of them sat on the cool stone floor, like children, sitting eagerly in front of a teacher.

And then the Völva spoke, "Ye called me here. Ye summoned me here," she pointed to Gustav, "Because yer world is in a plux. Somethin is bothern ye, and ye is worried sick to death. Sick to death yer gonna lose control."

The Völva dropped her arms to her side. Sliding her hands forward, she tightly gripped the edges of the table. Her fingers were white, her nails were bright pink. It looked like it hurt, but she paid no attention to the grip of her hands. Her face just stared at the four on the floor in front of her, like she was going to tear the flesh from their faces.

The Völva's voice asked in a guttural tone, "Did ye bring the roasted gourd?"

Gustav unfolded one hand and showed the Völva a small brown, shriveled item. It did not look like a gourd, but maybe it had been?

With a low growl the Völva said, "Give it to the woman."

Gustav handed the brown shriveled item across the group to Chrisholm. And she held it in her hand, palm open, displaying it for all to see.

The Völva instructed, "Place the gourd on the floor, smash it with a log, see if the inside survived the roasting. See if the truth survives the heat of the scorching fire!"

Chrisholm set the brown, well roasted gourd down. Turning to one side, she grabbed a log from the woodpile. Taking in a long breath of air and with a mighty swing, she brought the log down upon the gourd.

It exploded into a million pieces. The gourd basically exploded into dust.

Four faces turned to the Völva, looking for an answer.

"Just as I thought," shrieked the lady, sitting on the table. "The gourd is like your life, and you cannot exist in the world that is coming. You will soon be dust. Saddle this many horses, she held up all her fingers on a thin white hand. We depart near dusk when the bottom of the red sun touches top of the west tower. This evening, we ride with all haste to meet with the vast fortunes of nature and determine yer fate."

56 Thanks

Torrin and Dessa both sat down at the table where they had left their belongings. At a quick glance, nothing had been touched, for which they were happy. Seems they might be needing the gold coins for certain things, and they would be unhappy to be without the gift Gale had left with Dessa.

Now, they found themselves sitting at the table directly across from this newly arrived soldier. The uniformed man did not stand, nor introduce himself. He just stared, blinking occasionally. As if in a stupor, he simply sat, breathing through his mouth, which hung annoyingly open. Torrin was reminded of a dog who might sit and stare, maybe nip at a fly now and then.

A few moments later, Anton arrived holding a large serving tray with two bowls of steaming food and three mugs of ale. He served the soldier first, giving a gentle halo to the fellow. The soldier did not respond, in any way, shape or form. His eyes did not even move.

Next, Anton served Dessa, then Torrin. After he had set down the food, he said to them, "That Jasper is a lucky lad. Ye performed either magic or a miracle in that stable. I don know how ye did it, but it was amazin. I'm sure McGill will show his appreciation when he returns. Enjoy yer lunch."

Torrin took a long drink of the ale in his mug. It was well crafted and cool from the cellar. He thoroughly enjoyed the treat, and he smiled at the gift of a fine refreshment, especially wonderful after days on a dusty long trail that had held many mysteries.

After he set down his mug and wiped the bit of froth off his lips. He then looked at the soldier and said, in a voice that was obviously forced to sound respectful, "I feel as though ye want to say something, but afor ye do, let me introduce us to ye." He glanced to Dessa, smiled and then said, "This is Dessa, daughter of King Tarmon and Queen Gersemi of the north. She is the love of me life, and the wholeness to me soul."

As Torrin was speaking and introducing Dessa, the man across the table looked down, grabbed his goblet and drank half the contents in one seemingly large gulp. He ungraciously set his mug down and stared back at the two across the table. His expression did not change one bit, nor did he acknowledge anything about the information offered.

Torrin continued, he was determined not to be bested or disturbed by this rude and obviously belligerent curmudgeon (disagreeable person). "I am Torrin McKenna, son of King Trebor and Queen Ethelda, also of the great north. How may we be of service to ye?"

The man picked up his mug, drained it, set it down. He simply said, "Humph." With that, he stood up, turned on his heel and left Eskil, grumbling and muttering.

Dessa and Torrin looked at each other, and she said, "Let's eat and get out of here." Torrin nodded in agreement and they both began to eat the still hot, verra meaty stew Anton had served. Torrin was happy to see a nice slice of hot fresh bread atop of the stew, and it melted like fresh churned butter in his mouth. He decided he liked this place verra much and the fare they offered. Even tho some of the people seemed to remain a bit of a mystery.

Dessa asked, "Did that soldier just bother yer verra heart?"

Torrin laughed and said, "No, not at all. I'm thinkin he is afearn' of us more than we might know. Or something? I dunno. But yer eyes stayed blue and the hair on me neck made no fuss. So, I figured there be no danger. If'n ye had looked at me with those beautiful eyes of ye and they ad been turquoise, it might have been a verra different conversation."

Dessa looked down and noticed Torrin still had his seanathair's knife perched on his lap. She grinned to know that at least this time, he might have been more prepared for something bad before she was.

They had almost finished the stew when McGill re-entered Eskil. He was holding his hat and looking anxious. The man rapidly looked around the place, spied Jasper's two benefactors and came quickly to their table.

"I dunno how ye did it, maybe I don wanna know," he was talking verra rapidly. "But I wan te thank ye, so much! I've raised the boy since he were born. His momma died bringing him into the world, an his pa was lost at sea in a huge and awful storm…"

Dessa interrupted, "Please have a seat." McGill sat down, he seemed verra nervous, his hat was still tightly clutched in his hand. She continued, "It was our pleasure, we help where we can."

"How did you learn to do that, that healing?" gasped McGill. "I've never seen anything like it." He smiled, and relaxed a bit.

Dessa answered, "We never really learned it from anyone. Just sort of discovered it by accident one day. Takes us both to do it though, cannot do it alone! Not sure where it comes from, but it is pretty handy on occasion." Dessa finished her ale. "How is the little guy?"

"Amazing! He tol me he wanted to get back to work. Canna believe his tenacity! He loves taking care of the horses so much more than being around any people. But I told him to go home, get something to eat and just rest a wee bit. He looked at me like I'd gone mad, cause I've never said anything like that afore. But he is a good lad, and he went on his way home to rest up."

McGill then leaned in like he was going to share a personal thought and he softly said, "As much as I appreciate what you did, some of the folks who saw you in action are a bit afraid of what they'd seen. There were rumblings about witchcraft and such. I'm not a believer in such things, but people can get on about it, you know."

As McGill finished speaking, a scowling man stared at them through the window and then quickly walked away.

All three looked at each other, Torrin said, "Thank you kind sir, we appreciate the advice."

McGill stood up and said, "I ave ta look after da horses for this afternoon. Don worry about yer bill, it's on me." And then he left.

Finishing up their ale, Dessa said, "So much for having a restful night in an inn. I could have used a bath!"

"You and me both."

With that Anton appeared, started clearing the dishes and remarked, "Seems you two have good timing. The shadows are telling me it's time for you to leave and McGill paid your bill. Anyway, it seems, you have provoked a bit of a wicked fuss in the town here among the more superstitious. We've already had a handful of people inquiring about where you are staying tonight. Something tells me you might want to get up to the fort and see what there is in store for you. I hope it works out, and thanks for what you did for helping young Jasper! He is a bit short with folks, but he be a ard worker, every day."

Dessa and Torrin were surprised when they walked into the stable. Uta, Samoot and Calandra were all facing the door, saddled and ready to go. McGill said, "Anton give me a eads up. I think ye should sgiot (scatter away from here)."

57 Accused

The red sun was beginning to set over the west tower as Gustav mounted his dark muscular steed. The horse had been immaculately brushed clean. All the components of his tack were well oiled and any brass was perfectly shined. He was very well prepared for travel.

Gustav calmly surveyed the courtyard of the fort. All was in good order. When all was in order in his life and all around him, it brought him solace. Bourdicca approached, hand raised, "Commander, a verra menacing report from the village. We must attend to the issue post-haste, and it requires your attention before we depart!"

Gustav growled under his breath. He had grown weary of this constant need for direction, and orders, and his blessing afore anything could happen. It seemed this was required for anything at all! From time to time, even Bourdicca got on his nerves. He glanced at the three riders ahead of him, ready to depart. He looked at the guards, standing by, waiting for his command to release the doors and free them to venture out to some unknown fate or undertaking. Venture out to what he hoped were answers to his vexations. He stared at Bourdicca and said, "What is it? This better be vital."

"Witchcraft sir, witnessed and proven! Dangerous and powerful witchcraft the likes of which we have never seen before. My captain, of the town patrol, reported a large group of townsfolk witnessed closely, firsthand two strangers. They assaulted a young boy to the point where he was bleeding profusely. Then they tried to burn him and yellow sparks flew from their bodies. These sparks almost burned the stable to the ground. The stable next to Eskil. He interviewed the two strangers, and reported they are verra terrifying and obviously filled with evil power."

"Bring your man to me," huffed Gustav.

The soldier whom Dessa and Torrin had encountered in Eskil

marched up and stood at rigid attention. He saluted smartly and simply said, "Sir!"

"Tell me," said Gustav. "And make it brief."

"Sir, I spoke with this many folk all afternoon in town," he raised five fingers. "They all reported this couple from the north assaulted Jasper, the stable boy, pinned him to the ground and produced long yellow sparks, like lightening between their bodies over the prone lad. Almost set the stable ablaze."

"Captain, can these dangerous strangers be apprehended safely by you and your men or do you need my help? I need your word on this!"

"Sir, we can, if we are well prepared and keep them separated. They can only exert their powers when together. I questioned them at length at Eskil. They are verra cagey, menacing, and it was a challenge to get any truth. I was able to pressure them for information. They are from the north. Am quite sure they have escaped from Garwen's kingdom, and were wizards Garwen had used to torture the citizen of that wretched kingdom."

Gustav pondered this information for a bit. He had never encountered this sort of wild excitement before in Kalmar. Especially something so amazing and witnessed firsthand by the townsfolk. Wizards? Really?

He ordered the soldier, "Bring them in for questioning. I will interrogate them, one at a time upon my return. Chain them in separate rooms, in the lower dungeon. That will chill their menacing powers. And keeping them in the dark, separated, keeps the garrison safe. Keeps the town safe as well for the time being. Good work. Now go, do not fail!"

The soldier saluted smartly, turned on his heel and marched off.

Prepared? Thought Gustav. Hmmm? He jumped off his steed and walked away, seemingly full of purpose. The Völva watched him march off. She did not do anything except twirl the mane of her horse.

Gustav emerged from the tower, wearing a knapsack. It looked full. Other than curious, it meant nothing to anyone. He barked an order to open the doors, and the guards promptly put their backs into the job of releasing the heavy doors.

First the Völva, then Chrisholm, followed by Ancropolis, filed through the narrow doorway in a slow and orderly fashion. Bourdicca then headed out and surveyed the road, making sure it was safe for his commander to exit.

It was not entirely uncommon for some disgruntled soul to attack the commander. The attacker's warped thinking? Life would improve in the town if the commander was dead and gone. Seeing the coast clear, Bourdicca motioned for the commander to exit, and then he stood tall in his saddle, guarding, watching carefully.

And off at a fast trot, away from the town, this adventuresome troupe begin their quest. The fort loomed dark and large on their right as they rode up the stone paved street in the waning shadows of the day. Gustav was hopeful the Völva knew her way and this journey would not be too much of a distance to ride. He was concerned, because this little group was wholly unprepared.

They had no tent, no food, and just the minimum of weapons. Gustav thought for a moment, he must be daft to have left the fort without several guards.

The corner of the fort appeared and sat solidly, just as it had, for longer than time itself. As they passed the corner, three horses of magnificent presence came into sight. They were tethered to a tree, and Gustav thought it strange for such stunning steeds to be left alone, totally unattended along this road.

Two people emerged from the woods, looked curiously at the Völva and proclaimed together, "Ipi? What a surprise!"

58 Ride

The Völva looked down at Dessa and Torrin standing along the road and then screamed loudly, "Onward! Let's ride!"

The couple, mysterious to all expect the Völva ran to their great steeds. And in what looked like one fluid motion, easily mounted their horses and took up the rear, following the troupe out of town.

Uta said to Samoot, "Bet you a bag of oats, we're making thunder along this trail tonight."

Samoot responded, "You're on. Last time we did that, we changed the world, for the better. I hope she knows where she is going. I canna see a thing!"

Soon, the Völva reached the edge of Kalmar. The stone road ended and turned into a simple dirt path. This path was a tad narrow, obviously not used a great deal, and never for a wagon, it was much too narrow. However, narrow or not, she let loose into a full gallop.

A strong breeze swept the dust from the pounding hooves across the path and into the trees. Bourdicca was thankful for this cleansing wind. He really hated breathing trail dust. He did note though, he had never ridden this hard on this trail and was a bit nervous about their speed.

In a surprising turn of events, the Völva suddenly took a hard right, to the north and headed at full gallop through the forest. There was no path, no trail. The night was gathering its normal gloom, and trees were looming dark. Bourdicca was now entirely alarmed at their pace. There was no clear route here. This was not possible!

Regardless of the trail, or lack thereof, on they thundered over hills and splashed boldly across streams. Some streams large and flowing with a bubbly white current cascading mightily around boulders the size of a horse. Some, barely a trickle, hardly enough water to create a flow. All these steams graced the foundations of wide valleys carved by glaciers eons before humans made their homes in this part of the world. And by some miracle, or grace of nature, no tree or branch reached out to thwart the progress of any horse or rider. In fact, nothing touched any of them as they raced through the gathering gloom.

The heavy breathing of the horses gradually began to form into a pulse of what seemed to be one single remarkable, rhythmic cadence. Huge heaving breaths, full of hot vapor exploded from their enormously flared nostrils into the chilly evening air as they thundered on. The group did not stop, did not slow down, and pressed on as evening shadows turned to their normal darker black, and night wrapped cool dark hands around the earth.

After what seemed like an eternity, and a distance that would have taken days to cover at a normal pace, the Völva finally slowed. Walking her horse for a bit to let it cool, she rounded a corner at a copse of thick pines. The heavy branches created a dark wall of intimidating forest. A wall that seemed normal, unless you looked behind the towering branches.

A building of immense proportions emerged from the dark, hid behind the tightly knit wall of trees. The Völva nimbly leapt off her horse and skipped through large wooden double doors that seemed to grace the massive front of the place. They could all hear her call, "Zachariah, we have arrived. Where is supper?"

* * *

The rest of the group arrived one by one in a single file. Their horses were still breathing a bit hard, but were cooled adequately from their walk. Murmurs arose from all the riders as they encountered the big building. Well, that is from everyone except Gustav. He knew where he was, he knew it well.

Samoot said to Uta, 'You owe me a bag of oats."

Uta snorted, 'No, you owe me a bag of oats.'

'That was not the bet, replied Samoot, you said…' Dessa pipped up, "You two be quiet, you'll get fed. I wish I knew where we were, and what was going on. And now I'm going to go find out!"

With that she jumped down and walked up to and past the horse the Völva had been riding. Dessa was determined to find some answers and figure things out. She had spent too much time in her life wondering what was going to happen, and wondering where she really was. All this wondering was bothersome for her.

Little did she know she needed to understand the questions first.

Dessa strode purposefully through the large front doors of the building; she was confident Torrin would attend to the steeds in good fashion.

Torrin watched her purposefully enter the massive structure and understood he was in charge of the horses, and again, wished he could talk with them. He was not sure what to do, so he brought some water to each one from a bucket he found on the ground. The horses were thankful, and he could have sworn they smiled.

* * *

When Dessa stepped through the big open doors, she stopped in amazement and gasped. Never had she witnessed a building of such magnitude. Not in her father's kingdom, not in the forest, or anywhere. Even Journey paled in comparison to this monster!

A few doors and windows were scattered about, leading to who knew where? The floor was like solid rock! Large flat stones of granite had been formed to fit together with a small gap in between each stone. Just the floor itself was an amazing feat of engineering.

At one end of the room a fireplace burned brightly, taking the chill from the room and adding yellow dancing lights throughout. The large mantle log over the firebox was held up by timbers as big around as Dessa. The mantle had been carved into a forest scene of animals, plants and trees. The moon looked down upon the scene from the left corner and the sun shone from the right. The details were amazing. It was spectacular work of artistry, engineering, patience and size.

Walls rose up to the height of five tall people. Thick timbers were meshed together to create heavy walls. She noticed, with a bit of pride, the walls had two layers. Just as her people had designed the hunting cabin where she stayed when this adventure had begun, after her escape from the castle. The cabin where she had narrowly escaped a run-in with Sgail, the evil cougar. Dessa even now had a distinct memory of her hat stuck to his long-curved fang. The thought of it still gave her the shivers.

Here the two layers of walls were each built from thick logs. All the bark had been removed, and the bright white of the wood was strong and mighty. Smooth tan colored chinking (mortar-like substance to fill the cracks between logs of a wall), was thick, inserted as a weather-proof link between the logs and looked as old as the dirt on the trail. Between the walls, dirt was packed solid as insulation. The distance between the interior and exterior walls was about equal to a large boot. She mused, this seemed to be the favorite building plan of the north. The design would ward off the fierce cold of winter and the heat of summer.

Long rafters, each the thickness of an adult and longer than the walls were tall, long and straight. These stretched from the walls' edge to the overhead beam, supporting the immensely wide roof. These rafters were evenly spaced, and not too far apart so they could carry the colossal snow loads of the fierce and unrelenting winters.

And then, there was the main beam! This beam ran from one side of the building, all across the top to the other side. One long, continuous log. More than long. More than big. It only could be called colossal! Even the stumps along the lengthy trunk, where branches had been removed, were large.

As Dessa was pondering how any people might have raised such a colossal log so high above the ground, she felt a large hand grip her shoulder. The grip was not tender, nor was it hard or harsh. It was similar to a grip she would get from Gale in the stables as she grew up. Firm, without question, yet considerate and resolute.

Turning her head, she looked directly into the chest of what must be a verra sizable man. She looked down at his large black boots, buckled smartly around verra large feet. Bending her neck back as far as it would travel, she looked up into the expansive dark eyes of the biggest man she had ever laid eyes upon.

Dessa exclaimed quietly, "Oh my!"

The huge man calmly looked down at the redheaded lady with kindly dark eyes, smiled just a bit and said, "Hello Dessa, my name is Zachariah. Please call me Zach. How may I be of service to one who has done so much?"

59 An Answer

Chrisholm just sat there in her saddle. Her mouth open, tears streaming down her cheeks. She held onto the reins as though a strong wind was going to blow her out of her saddle, and she needed to hang on for dear life.

As Ancropolis approached Chrisholm, he noticed he could see his breath in the dark chill air. A slight breeze whispered the vapors away, and he thought, it won't be long afore winter lays its icy hand upon our lives again.

Looking up at Chrisholm, he saw her distress and said, "Me bràmair, what is it?" He lay a comforting hand upon her leg and then turned to look at the immense structure looming ahead of them. He then looked back at Chrisholm, and he could see she was staring at the building, tears coursing down her cheeks. She was unable to speak or utter any sort of intelligible sound. Her face was showing blotchy red patches, and she was swallowing hard.

He simply asked, "It's here, be it not, this place? Is this the building of yer visions? This is the place that keeps a creepn into yer dreams at night and makin ye ask so many questions?"

All she could do was nod a yes as she stared at the building.

Suddenly he felt a bit weak himself. He felt unsteady knowing they were now going to face something that had been festering in her brain for a long, long time. And he was confident of one thing for certain, he was not sure he was ready to do so. But, he considered, there is never a good time for the hard things in life, so why not now?

He now knew. The dogs following them up to the fort and seeming to stand guard until they were told all was well with both himself and Chrisholm? Or maybe all was well with just Chrisholm? He did not know. Then the curious event of commander Gustav sent to fetch them, courtesy of the Völva. The Völva treating them like they had been acquainted all their lives. He understood with a shake of his head that it was time for what she foretold to move forward. Yes, it was time, he could not avoid it.

The memory of all those mornings, when she would wake with a jolt as if hit by a rock came rushing back to him. Ancropolis was usually awake, just resting there with her warm softness sleeping next to his long frame. She would awaken and let forth a small whimper.

Over and over again again he would ask, "Where ye there?"

She just lay there, letting her breathing come back from the jolt of awakening from the strong dream, and eventually murmur something. She would say things akin to, "It's jus so big." or, "I canno find my way into a door."

Her dreams took her to a place, and now they had arrived. Arrived at this place.

Ancropolis glanced again at the huge building and then grasped the reins from Chrisholm's softly gloved hands and lay them over the horses neck. Then, he stood tall, wrapped an arm around her waist and lowered Chrisholm to the ground. She stood on shaky legs. Her body leaned against him, and he could feel the heat seeping from her body as she assimilated their surroundings.

Chrisholm turned to him. She wiped the tears from her cheeks and said, "No matter what happens, and I don't know what's in store, please know I love ye, with me whole heart." And she kissed him, holding his face with both hands.

She then squared her shoulders and walked toward the large open doors, finally walking inside.

She did not look back.

60 Worry

The very same evening, far to the north, Rebecca found Bartoly sitting on one of the stools inside the big hearth that was the glorious center point of their beautiful kitchen. A goblet of wine in one hand and he was mindlessly poking at the small fire with his other. The look on his face was one of deep thought. One she had seen when he was conjuring up a thought for a new device or invention to help the people of the valley.

However, something told her this was different. She set little MacGowan down and he scampered away to play. She took the stool next to his, put her head on his muscled shoulder and quietly said, "Me sweet Bartoly, are ye gonna share ye thoughts or do I ave to get ye beyond thinking drunk to talk to me?"

He sighed and put his goblet down. This freed up his arm, which then encircled her shoulder. They sat there for a few moments, letting the warmth of each other and the surrounding huge hearth melt into them before he spoke.

"Rebecca, ye know I don keep anything from ye." He sighed and continued, "Sometimes I jus don know the right words ta express me thoughts, when the thoughts get deep, or they is running at me like a charging buck." He paused, his shoulders slumped and he finished his thought with, "Like right now."

"Oh, ye big lug," she said playfully. "Are ye cooking up another idea for the next big invention to help people live a better life, or improve der farm?" Rebecca was smiling, "Out with it."

"Aye, if it be that simple, I'd be in the barn, the forge hot and there would be hot metal flyn' about. No, this one is one I have been expecting, and did not realize it would be comn' so soon. It just makes me a pine a bit for our friends, cause I misses them so."

"Oh, do ya have a feelin they is with Zachariah at his big place there in that dark forest?"

"Yes," he sighed, "and I hope it goes well. For all of them. For all of us. We all have a stake in this, and ifn it don go well, I canno imagine the future."

Rebecca spoke in a comforting tone to Bartoly while running her fingers through his dark curls, "Relax. We both know Zach has a way with words and people and situations. And I have no doubt Dessa and Torrin will do the right thing. Plus there be a bit of involvement from nature to make things go right. I remember when my not so sweet and innocent deirfiúr, Gwendolyn, had made advances te Torrin, it did not go well for her."

Bartoly shuddered at the thought. He remembered the story. A story told time and again in the valley about the beautiful fair-haired lass Gwendolyn having her life end with a large log impaled through her chest just as she and Torrin were to couple as one in the forest.

He said to Rebecca, "Ye don think that bit with yer deirfiúr was just a terrible accident?"

She shook her head as she muttered, "My dear, there be no doubt in me mind, not for an instant that the natural world was to have no-one but Torrin and Dessa for each other. And nothing, no one and no situation was going to get in the way of that matchmaking."

Bartoly replied with a simple, "Oh My."

Rebecca concluded with, "And I bet you a back rub after MacGowan goes to bed, our friend Zacharia has a wee bit of help to make everything go as well as it needs to go. Whatever that is."

This brought a smile to his face, and she kissed him on the lips.

As she turned to attend to MacGowan who was now playing with his blocks on the floor, she thought to herself, 'I certainly hope it goes well, for all our sakes, and especially his.' She picked MacGowan up and gave him a warm motherly hug.

MacGown said, "Ma-ma blabba."

That made Rebecca smile.

61 Welcome

Stepping sideways from the big man, Dessa delivered a formal curtsy and said, "It is my pleasure sir." She glanced about and swept her hand around the big room while saying, "This structure is truly, just truly, completely magnificent! I am almost at a loss for words at its immensity."

"Thank you, you are verra kind," replied the big man, "It has taken a long time to get it in shape. We've had a lot of help over the winters, and we are verra proud of the place."

"We?" inquired Dessa. "Who else, if I may ask, shares these beautiful and overly impressive accommodations with ye?"

"Oh, it's mostly just meself and my sweet deirfiúr here. Well, most of the time. We seldom receive guests, such as yourselves. Usually, our visitors be a bit wilder and more diverse. But we are honored te have ye, you bein so important."

Dessa wondered about all that. He had given her a lot of information. Wild visitors? Diverse? We? Being important? And who are these others? Dessa took a deep breath to calm her racing mind. Which helped a bit until Ipi showed up.

The Völva walked up next to Zach and exclaimed, "There you are little deartháir (brother)! I've been looking all over for you." She was carrying a goblet, made of clear glass with a red beverage in it. "I see you've met Dessa. Good. We'll have to get everyone settled and have a nice supper. I see you have prepared quite the spread for us in the refectory. I am famished after eating at the fort all week. And I must say, those fires you built to chase the chill away are delightful!"

Turning to Dessa, the Völva said, "It is so good to reconnect. It's been a while dear, give us a hug."

Dessa and the Völva shared a brief embrace and then Dessa said, somewhat excitedly, "Ipi, what the deamhan is going on here?"

Ipi replied, "Oh in due time, we are in no hurry and there is so much to discuss and review and decide. Oh my!. Let's get your wonderful steeds put to rest in the stables and then get everyone gathered up and make our way to the big room. We can all talk at supper. And, as I said, it's a magnificent supper! I'm thinking you will never forget this meal. We'll show you to your rooms later."

With that, Ipi, also known as the Völva, turned on her heel and walked briskly toward the back of the huge room. She disappeared through one of the tall doors.

Dessa stared a bit and said to Zach, "There is more to this building?"

Zach replied, "Oh this is just the entry, I'll get ya a tour by-an-by. But first, I must attend to the steeds out front. I'm figuring yer men out there are wondering what to do and havin' a man be hungry and a bit lost is not a kindly thing to have around when ye are the host of an event as important as this one bein."

'Event?' wondered Dessa.

62 Again

Bourdicca held the reins of Gustav's horse as the commander deftly dismounted. And just as everyone else had, Gustav stretched and took a few steps to get his balance. It had been a hard ride, through a dark wood on little to no trail. To say the least, it was stressful.

"Well, my man," said Gustav. "This is where the giant took me. He carried me through those big doors and eventually into his immense blacksmith shop. Something told me we would arrive here. And goodness knows, we have! I want to meet this man again!" And with that, Gustav followed in Chrisholm's footsteps through the tall front doors.

Bourdicca looked at the building, then looked at Torrin and said, "De ye have any idea of what's goin' on ere?"

Torrin, remembering his upbringing, did not answer. Instead, he said, "Good day sir, my name is Torrin McKenna, from the north, Queen Ethelda and King Trebor are me parents. May I please enjoy the pleasure of knowing whom it is I am addressing?"

Bourdicca was a bit impressed that this man, whom he had taken for a common horseman had such manners and seemed to be of royal lineage.

He obliged by answering, "Good day kind sir, my name is Bourdicca. I am the captain of the troops at the fort in Kalmar. I hail from south of Londinium."

Torrin nodded and wondered to himself, what is, or where is, a Londinium? Now it was apparent that Bourdicca, Ancropolis and Torrin had been left to care for the horses. Ancropolis had been exploring the area to locate a stable or something to aid in this task. He returned and reported he'd spied a bit of a trail to the side of the place and figured they would find a stable there or somewhere to at least tie up all the horses.

As the three of them gathered reins and were ready to leave, a huge man emerged from the tall doors and said, "Bring them jolly mounts right in ere and we'll get 'em taken care of, in the proper manner due such fine steeds."

Ancropolis looked at the big man and exclaimed, "I ave heard of giants in the forest, you must be one of them."

The big man grinned and replied, "Welcome, I am Zachariah, keeper of the Center. Please call me Zach. I have lost me manners; you fine gentlemen be?"

Ancropolis answered first, "Me family named me Ancropolis. Chrisholm and I run the tavern named Eskil at Kalmar."

"Ah," exclaimed Zach with a smile. "We've been looking forward to you both visiting us here." Zach then looked at Bourdicca.

"I am known as Bourdicca and am captain of the guard at the fort in Kalmar." said Bourdicca, rather proudly.

"Welcome my good man," said Zach, who then turned his attention to Torrin and asked, "You must be Mr. Torrin, you arrived with the famous Dessa?"

"Yes sir," replied a bit of a befuddled Torrin. "I dunno how she be famous, but I'm sure we'll find out."

"Yes, tonight will be a great celebration of all the possibilities," said Zach with a smile. "Please, follow me inside and let's get those mighty animals taken care of for the night."

With that, Zach turned on his heel and headed towards the big doors.

As the rest followed, horse reins in hand, Torrin wondered, 'Center? Famous?' He shook his head and thought, there is something going on that always seems to be one step ahead of me.

63 Livery

Torrin led Samoot through the huge double doors, Uta and Calandra followed along, as was their custom. His eyes spun up to the ceiling as he surveyed the massive room. The equally massive man who had beckoned them to enter with the horses through the front doors (never done that before!), motioned for Torrin to bear to the right and follow.

As they passed through the entrance, the Völva (or now, we know, she is Ipi), Chrisholm, Dessa and Gustav were all talking at once in a tight knit group off to the side. Torrin noticed that Ipi had a goblet full of a dark red liquid. The goblet was made of clear glass, which was the first time he had ever encountered such a thing.

The eight horses that had raced the riders through the woods, led by the men filed into a huge stable. Carefully oiled, master saddler-built tack of all kinds and styles hung on stout wooden pegs along walls between stalls. They passed the door of a sizable feed room filled with bags of oats and barley along with tied bundles of hay, stacked high to the ceiling. A large platter of clean fresh carrots and apples sat on a bench just inside the feed room entrance.

Torrin heard Uta give a wet whinny and Samoot seemed to answer back as they passed the feed room. He did wish he could communicate with these animals like Dessa. And was sure these two were having quite the chat at this point. Maybe it was the carrots and apples?

The massive man opened stall doors and each of the horses found themselves in an airy, clean stall with fresh water and a full hayrack. All four men took to the caring of these hardy steeds who'd run hard through the woods. Furthermore, Uta, Samoot and Calandra had been on the trail for days and were enjoying the idea of a good brushing, a warm rest inside, with full bellies!

It took a fair amount of work and time to unsaddle, brush and pile bedding for the horses. But these men had grown up with this sort of labor, and they made quick work of the tasks. Especially since there seemed to be a dinner, and hopefully more, waiting for them afterwords.

Torrin called out the question asking if the carrots and apples were fair game? The answer came from the big man who was attending to Calandra, that yes, it was all available to share and please help yourself. Torrin made sure their horses had a treat to enjoy.

Soon, the stall doors were closed, the horses tucked in warmly with blankets and the happy sound of knarfing hay was heard throughout the stalls.

* * *

Torrin walked up to the massive man and introduced himself, "Evening, sir, I am Torrin McKenna, son of..." and Zach interrupted him.

"Aye, I know all about ye. Where ye hail from, yer past, yer goings on, and all that. I am verra sorry about your athair. That man Garwen was about as mean and nasty as dey come. Appreciate you and da misses offing him the way you did. Made quite da story round here."

Torrin, not usually at a loss for words just stopped and stared. Finally, he found himself saying, "How do ye know about us? Is ye a wizard or somethin?"

Zach chuckled, "Ah me friend, we'll explain it all at the supper, which we should get ta after 'n we wash this horse scrabble off. Call me by me name, that being Zach. Zachariah, ifn I happen to be in trouble or we is bein' formal." The big man smiled and held out his hand in a gracious gesture.

Torrin accepted the proffered hand and warmly shook it. The strength of Zach's grip was at once scary, and immediately Torrin thought, I'm glad he's on our side. Then he thought, well, I hope he's on our side!

Bourdicca and Ancropolis walked up, and introductions were shared all around. Zach made sure every one of the horses had gotten plenty of well-dried hay and some of the apples and carrots. Since all looked good, he led the men to the washroom where an astounding sight greeted them.

A hollowed-out log protruded through the wall about chest height for

Torrin. Underneath stood a basin of solid wood, a smooth bowl carved cleanly in the center. At the back, a drain flowed through the wall near the floor. The bowl was almost big enough for a full-grown man to get in and comfortably sit down. Zach turned a chunk of wood sticking out of the hollowed log and clear water began to pour from the log protruding through the wall.

Zach said, "Ah me boys, wait a moment, and then enjoy gettn' yerself clean in the most wonderful way." Zach passed around bits of freshly scented soap and then the water flowing from the log began to warm. And then, a wonderful thing happened, the water became hot! Never before had any of them experienced such a thing. It was a wonderful treat to wash up with warm water, and they all enjoyed the luxury as a smiling group.

As they dried their hands on clean, soft towels, Torrin asked, "If I may be so bold ta ask, how do ye heat the water? It's really wonderful!"

Zach smiled, and said, with obvious pride, "Ah, we discovered a hot spring up the hill just a short way from the whole place. Usually, them hot springs stink to the hills of rotten eggs. But no, this time, we got lucky, and this one runs clean and pure. So, we hollowed out logs to make pipes and ran the pipe to the center. There is a split, where one pipe goes to the house and the kitchen, and this one comes inna here."

Gustav asked, "Don't the pipes freeze up and then break apart in the winter with the damnú' cold?"

Zach answered, "Good point, we ad to deal with that the first winter, then figured out, just let the waters run and keep running all through da coldest of the winter. The hot spring, she never stops, so it's not like we is wastin the heat. The waters warm the kitchen area nice when the fires are not goin for da cookin, and the stables here stays pretty nice too. Even in the fiercest of snows and storms. Makes for a comfy respite when the wild things come in to get out of the cold. Ya know, when they need a break. Especially when they have the youngins who would not make it through the worst of the freezn' times of winter if dey dinna have but a place to warm up."

Ancropolis said, "You have found a fine spot to build here. The place is amazing."

Zach simply nodded.

Torrin had been thinking about what Zach said. The wild things? Dessa and her link to nature? Ipi and her link to wisdom? This monstrous place in the dark forest with nothing around? What is going on here? What for that matter was this place?

Before Torrin could form the words for all the questions racing through his head, Zach motioned for them all to follow him back inside. He followed along and noticed that the hair on the back of his neck was not standing up. He was concerned, but certainly not threatened.

64 Decided?

The four men left the stables and filed into the great entryway of the building. All of them were commenting on the enormity of the structure, as well as the craftsmanship that had gone into the construction of the space. Everywhere you turned, the work was large, heavy and exquisite.

Zach led them through stout doors toward the inside. Along with being heavy, these doors were tall enough to let the big man walk through without ducking his head. They traversed a hallway adorned with lit sconces that flickered warmly in the chill air of the evening. Zach called out the purpose of rooms as they passed by, ever deeper into the large structure.

"This be our library where we keep the books, maps, correspondence from others and our family history. That history goes a long way back." Each man peered into a dark room. A few manuscripts were neatly stacked on shelves. Rolled maps adorned a higher shelf, their long rolls hanging over the edges. These maps were bound with various colored cording. The biggest maps had gold cords, where the smaller were adorned with green cords, looking brilliant and shiny like silk. Various papers were stacked around on shelves as were small carvings of what looked to be animals from other lands.

Torrin thought to himself that this place was a bastion of an enigmatic glimpse into the future. Ipi had introduced them to the ideas of writing, paper, and pen at the Journey Inn last winter. He'd never imagined such a thing would exist en masse. He decided to ask Zach to show him the contents of the library after supper. Maybe he and Dessa would be able to stay for a time and learn more about these curious and obviously forward-thinking mysteries.

"This ere is the smoking room," said Zach walking down the big hall. We may retire ere after supper and maybe enjoy a dram or more of my private scotches. I am happy to share. And am sure you will enjoy the experience."

"And now we enter the refectory. This be me pride and joy. Well almost. I do enjoy the kitchen, bein the center of me cookin and good food of course."

The three men entered the hall where they would take their supper and again stopped to gape.

An extensively long, finely crafted dining table made of oak highlighted the center of the room. Its wood shone smartly in the bright blaze of firelight emitting from three massive stone fireplaces. Each side of the table held more chairs than Torrin had fingers. He knew it was a great many chairs and was amazed at their opulence. Finely tooled scenes of the forest adorned the back of each chair. The brown fabric seat cushions looked comfortable and hardly worn. Candles were spaced out in the center of the table in a neat row, adding a gentle ambient light to each carefully set place setting.

Along one wall, a row of silver platters displayed an astounding array of foods with a few candles on tall brass holders for light. Fresh fruits and vegetables of all colors and sizes were heaped on each platter. Food Torrin had never seen or eaten, let alone heard of, was piled high and plentiful. And fresh! This late in the fall season, fresh foods like this are wishful desires. The fare in most kitchens came from pots stored in root cellars. Root vegetables were dug from the field, or meats smoked and hung for winter. By this time of the year, most people were consuming their stores until spring could provide more options and variety.

The one treat always available year-round is cheese. Generally made from goat or sheep milk. Yes, fresh cheese was a staple found in many homes. In this room, three platters sported a variety of cheeses; soft, hard, yellow, white and a curious one, it had blue streaks?

Long, soft, crusted loaves of bread showing a slightly toasted finish, warm from the oven were stationed on a cutting board. A knife of lengthy proportions sat waiting to slice the carefully stacked loaves into delectable additions to what looked to be a fine meal. A marvelously crafted and chilled butter crock stood at the ready to be upended and the soft contents spread on the still warm bread. The smell rising from the bread was overwhelmingly delightful.

Torrin scanned the room, trying to take in the grandeur and all the elements. One thing he did notice was that along one wall there were various rugs and pillows. These were neatly stacked in piles. All sizes, various shapes and colors as well as textures. Interesting, he thought. The place was endless in curiosities.

As some of the men were looking at the food, Ipi stood on a chair at one end of the table and announced, "My dear friends, and we will all be friends after this time together, let us now partake of the wonderful meal my little deartháir has supplied for us from the incredible kitchen of this place." Soft murmurs of gratitude were heard in the room.

Ipi continued, "I ask you now to join me in a moment of quiet reflection as we rejoice in the gift of nature's bounty spread before us and we give thanks for our safe arrival." With that, she gently brought her hands together, bowed her head and was still. Torrin and Dessa did the same, as did Chrisholm. The others looked around, a bit confused and then followed suit.

After a few heartbeats, Ipi unclasped her hands, brought up her head and said, "Welcome to the Spiritual Essence Center of Nature. Let's eat! Please help yourself to a plate from the table. Tonight, we enjoy a self-serve buffet, since Zach and I preferred to not employ any assistance this evening, nor are we playing the role of servant. We are all in this together."

Ipi jumped down from the chair, pushed it in, and went to grab a plate. She looked up and saw that no one was moving. Not a soul. Six sets of eyes were staring at her, and none of the faces holding the eyes were smiling.

The only sounds to be heard in the huge refectory were the crackling of the warm fires in the massive hearths, and the gentle hissing of candles on the opulent dinner table and buffet.

Glances between the folks were shared as everyone waited for someone to speak and ask the question on every 'friends' mind.

From the corner of the room, away from the food and the knot of people that had formed near Ipi came the sound of someone clearing their throat. It was Ancropolis. He pursed his lips together, glanced around and said, a bit haltingly, but anyway, said, "Ifn ya don mind. Could ye and yer deartháir maybe shed some light on why or what we all be don' ere in this grand place? We appreciate the ospitality, really, but what be da deamhan goin on?"

Ancropolis was certainly happy to hear accompanying sounds of agreement emanating from the group, such as, 'Yes. Right. Please.' and more.

"My dear Ancropolis. Well, everyone really!" Ipi seemed a bit taken aback by the question. However, as we know, Ipi is never really taken off guard for long. "Please forgive me. I guess, forgive Zach and myself. Yes! We will explain all of this. Yes, all of this in great detail, after we enjoy our supper. Now please enjoy this meal while it is still fresh."

Everyone looked at each other with puzzled faces and it was clear none of them really understood what was happening. Ancropolis shrugged his shoulders as if acquiescing to the moment.

Bourdicca, who never needed to be asked twice to enjoy a wonderful feast, picked up a plate and headed toward the buffet. Ancropolis grabbed two plates, handed one to Chrisholm and beckoned her to lead him towards the food. Gustav had been standing next to Torrin, chatting about the tooling on the back of the chairs. Gustav motioned for Torrin to go ahead with Dessa, following Ancropolis' lead.

Gustav stood next to Zach, watching everyone with curiosity. Neither had yet said a word. As the line at the buffet grew, Gustav turned to Zach and said, "It is a pleasure to meet you again. I had no idea this building was so immense."

Zach responded with a smile and said, "Am glad you returned. We did not know if you would return or how things might work out, but you are here and let us make the most of a grand and glorious evening where so much is to be disclosed. Please understand, not even I know all the details yet."

Gustav looked at Zach for a moment and then said gently, with an undertone of seriousness, "What do you mean sir? How things might work out?"

Zach said, "In due course sir. In due course. And it will not be long. You will know everything, and everyone shall hear it together. As I said, I am not privy to all that has been decided, or maybe not yet be decided. For I am here to serve and listen. So, stay alert and pay attention as the plan unfolds. I do know though, I am as hungry as a spring bear and the line at the food has abated."

With that, Zach made tracks toward the food.

Gustav thought, what plan? What has been decided? What needs to be decided? Who is this group? Why were they wondering if I would return? Most importantly, who are 'they?'

Zach headed toward the buffet with Ipi. Gustav took off his pack and carefully set the pack against the wall. Then, since he too was hungry, he went, without too much apprehension, to enjoy the buffet.

As he stood there waiting his turn at the long table of carefully prepared foods, he noticed one plate left on the table. It was alone at the head seat. A large clear glass goblet sat alone by the top of the plate. It looked for all the world to be full of dark amber scotches?

65 Music

On this same night Torrin, Dessa and the others were together with Zach, Ol Dogger sat for a while by himself next to the recently completed, huge blazing hearth of the new Journey Inn. Nicely sculpted seats had been built on each side of this amazing pristine fireplace. The designer had explained many practical uses for these areas of repose to Ol Dogger one evening.

First, these seats would be warm for anyone who needed to get de-iced during the long cold winter days. Then, what a great place to remove boots that are wet and cold. You are near the fire and near the new boot rack for drying wet soles. Then, sometimes, like tonight, people need a quiet place to sit and sometimes ponder their thoughts.

Tonight, Ol Dogger was pondering. He just needed a bit of time to himself to close his eyes. Close his eyes and let his brain catch up with all the thoughts and topics cluttering his mind.

Dogger had been very busy, ever since he'd gotten enough strength to help, in the rebuilding of Journey. He did not always understand all the fancy goings on, or reasons for some of the amazing architecture growing around the new entity. But he knew in his heart, the people working here had nothing but love in their hearts. And for the most part, he figured it would all work out.

There was only one problem for Ol Dogger! It was a perplexing issue he had been facing all his life. But since last winter, its head had raised itself anew and would not go away.

He missed her. He actually missed her a lot! As well as Dessa, Torrin and Quillan. They had all become such a wonderful part of his long life.

So many people had come and gone for him. So many he could not remember but a few. And for the most part, they were good folks. But not a one had made his heart turn a flutter like Ipi. Oh yes, he enjoyed her warmth in a comfortable bed. He certainly did enjoy all the carrying on under the covers. But it was just the presence of her company that made his days a bit brighter.

He was trying to not let her being gone away bring him down.

So, he sat quietly, trying to count his blessings, thinking about all the goodness surrounding himself and everyone here. Again they had a sturdy roof over their heads, a half-finished kitchen, stables that were done to the point to keep a horse for a night or two and good people all around. Good people, coming. Going. Staying. Like Journey was meant to be.

So just as she had taught him, he took a few deep long breaths. He focused on the sound of the air as it passed through his old and withered nose. He concentrated on how his cheeks puffed out as he exhaled. And he was able to relax a bit and let the stress of his loneliness fade.

And then, from nowhere, her small, gentle, familiar voice said in his head, 'Please. Just relax, soon, we will be where we are meant to be.'

Dogger stood up and said loudly, "We need som music tonight!"

66 Supper

Gustav was the final person in the group to take advantage of the buffet in this remarkable room called a refectory. He took note, there was plenty of food still waiting on the various platters and in the large bowls. More than enough really. It truly was an amazing feast. As he moved along, selecting various fruits and vegetables, he encountered items he had never seen, nor heard of before. An orange ball the size of his fist? He asked Zach about these and was informed they were called oranges. Zach showed him how to peel the skin and eat just the inside.

Curious thought Gustav as he sat down with his plate full. He first tried the orange. A smile emerged from his face as he found the new fruit quite tasty.

Torrin asked Zach, "I verra much appreciate all this wonderful food, but I can't help but notice there is no presentation of any meats. Is that on purpose or have ye had no luck on the hunt as of late?"

Zach wiped his mouth on the back of his sleeve. He had been consuming a rather large share of the dark red wine that filled everyone's goblets. Sitting back, he smiled, "Well, my friend, I guess ye might say the lack of meat on our table be on purpose. You see, here at the center, we only consume food created from meat when it's given to us, or presented to us in a way that does no damage to a viable animal of the forest.

"Are ye telling me that ye don't consume meats because it harms the animal and that be a bad thing?" Torrin was intrigued.

Zach was quiet for a moment to gather his thoughts. He didn't usually have to explain the menu approach of the Essence Center. He also knew it was different behavior than most people practiced. "Yes, that be it," answered Zach. "If an animal be injured, we will consume that beast to put it out of its misery. And, periodically, when we need some meats, we'll head off to the coast for the fishes in the ocean. Besides that, though, we get plenty of meat-like food from the eggs of our chickens, the heavy creamy milk from our sheep, goats and both our cows."

Torrin was a bit speechless as he considered the mathan back along the trail. It struck him now, how he had approached eating all his life was now challenged. His face must have taken on a solemn look, because Zach added more to the story.

"We know that how we eat and look at the animals be a bit different than most folks. But we is in service to the critters of the forest here, and eating them just sort of puts us at odds with what we do."

"So do you find angst in yer hearts over most people eating meats of some sort, so verra often?" inquired the now very curious Torrin.

"It be a way of life that we understand," sighed Zach. "We hold no ill will toward the people. We do want folks to raise more livestock and chickens and use the generous gifts of them critters, like creams and milk and cheese for foodstuffs over time instead of taking their lives."

"Yev given me much to ponder," replied the still inquisitive Torrin. "Thank you." He turned his attention back to the huge table and the others.

Ipi was having an animated discussion with the people at her end of the table, and he found himself entreated by her logic. This was a verra different person than the one who had been living in that nice upstairs room at Journey last winter. He listened carefully…

"It's a grand time to be alive you see," said Ipi. "As I said, things are changing, and we at this table know this to be a verra essential truth. It's why we are here tonight, to enable movement forward. You see, almost everything we humans believe as undeniable truths, is shall we say, fundamentally wrong. We, all of us, are beginning to see the emergence of a real and true human spirit that is so much different, and more powerful than we have ever encountered. Ever! Ever since the beginnings of the human race."

Gustav piped in, "My lady, could you expand on this idea of these undeniable truths are ye be talkin of?

"Certainly," replied Ipi. "Take for example having a king who reigns supreme over all the people of a land. Some people feel this is the only way a society must operate."

Ipi now stood, talking excitedly, animated and waving her hands. "That king collects taxes and the people have no say in the laws or rules they must endure. They are simply subjects of the king and his will and his tyranny."

Ipi stopped to take a breath, and as she did so, she looked at the faces of everyone seated at the table. She knew she had a captive audience, at least for the moment. She also knew that talking about upsetting the royal order would be deemed dangerous by most everyone listening. "We have discovered, when people have a say in their future, in their life, in their work, in their laws, they are happier, more creative, curious, work harder and create a better world."

Chrisholm replied, "I am not disagreeing with you, but I don't really understand what all ye are saying, and how this theory of yours applies to any of us seated here tonight?"

"Oh yes you do my dear," said a new soft voice from the head of the table. "You just have not come to understand the enormity, nor the repercussions of, and consequences of this reality, yet."

All heads turned with curiosity to take in this new voice.

There had been no-one in that seat, just a heartbeat before. But now, a tall woman, with flowing blond hair, dressed in a beautiful blue gown sat comfortably in the head chair. She held the clear glass goblet Gustav had noticed in one hand and was sipping the contents, which she seemed to enjoy immensely.

"Oh my, you have arrived!" exclaimed Ipi happily as she sat down. "Now we can truly get this party under way. And for all it's really meant to be!"

67 Next Course

"Good evening, Marjie," Dessa said with quizzical tones, purposefully introducing this curious character's name to everyone. "Figured you would show up sooner or later. Surprised you didn't make more of an entrance?"

Marjie pondered for a moment before calmy replying, "I make my entrances the way I do, to get my point across. Just as Ipi here gloriously played the wild role of Völva to help our friends see her link to the spirit world. I will do what I must, to help anyone see, feel and understand the only true power. That being the power of nature."

Ipi raised her glass as a positive response to Marjie's kind words. And as she did so, she looked at Gustav and winked.

Gustav sat quietly, lips a bit pressed together. He seemed to be deep in thought.

Dessa nodded. Everyone else looked on to see if this new aspect of the evening would be formally introduced. Also, with some explanation of who, or what she was. And how did she arrive at the table without being seen?

Zach, recognizing the need for introductions stood up and announced, "Everyone, I am pleased to introduce to you earth's agent of nature. We used to call her 'Nature,' but she was verra firm in helping us understand, that name was boring, so for some reason we settled on Marjie. Really don't remember how or why, and it doesn't especially matter. Anyway, Marjie here, when she is on earth, is a spryte. She can take on any form, she can do most anything and I verra much would advise ye, to stay on her good side."

"Thank you, Zachariah," said Marjie. "I guess, for those of you who have not met me before this evening, I should give you a little demonstration of what he meant." With that, Marjie shrunk herself to the size of the glass goblet she had been holding and popped herself up onto the table from her chair. Now she was tossing sparks just as she had for Dessa on their first meeting at the side of the mathan.

Marjie then flew up into the rafters and long beams of the refectory, did a pirouette, showering everything and everyone with tiny sparks. She then flew, sparks flying, under the buffet table lifting it halfway up the wall with one hand. She didn't spill a drop. Setting the buffet down, she retired back to her chair at the dining table re-emerging as a full-grown adult. Then, throwing smiles at everyone, she calmly picked up her glass goblet and took a drink.

68 What

"Agent of nature?" quired a puzzled Gustav, "Verra interesting, however, please regale us with some words of wisdom on what is really meant by a fancy title like that. And truly, I ask, and I ask also for everyone else in the room, based on their curious looks; why are you here, with us? Better yet, why, this fine evening, are we here with you?"

Marjie winked at Gustav and gave him a smile. It almost looked like she was flirting. "My good man, nature is everything. We are all part of nature. This earth, where we live, is nature at its most wonderful and finest. We have air to breathe, water to drink. The ground, with the help of the air, the water and the sun bring forth food for us to eat. You see, it's a big co-dependent system of cycles. And for all the issues we must endure, in the end, the whole thing has worked fairly well."

Ancropolis asked, "You mean all of us are part of nature? I thought the trees and the birds; they be of nature. We are humans. Not part of the forest?"

Marjie took a sip of her beverage. She glanced not at Ancropolis, but at Chrisholm, tilted her head and then gave that same small smile she shared with Gustav, before saying, "My dear Ancropolis, what may I ask, if anything, would you take away from nature and it would not make your life miserable?"

Ancropolis thought for a moment and said, "Well I would guess, take away winter. Take away all them cold harsh months where we are near to freezn' and struggling and trapped inside by our fire to be warm."

Sounds of agreement came from most of the folks at the table. The idea of no winter had its merit in everyone's mind.

Marjie smiled, "Ah, the idea has been bantered about in nature for, well, since time began. But our cycles and the shear need for balance dictate winter and a change of seasons. Winter, or the change of seasons is rather essential."

Ancropolis looked around and was glad to know he was not alone in having a verra hard time understanding what the pretty lady had just proclaimed. He asked, "Could ye please explain what ye mean by them words?"

Zach made a heavy sigh and sat back in his chair. Ipi giggled a bit and refilled her goblet, right to the top. Everyone else waited.

Marjie began, "As I said, all this is a co-dependent cycle. Change one part, such as remove winter, and the delicate balance falls apart. For example, far, far, far south of here, there is no winter. Well, winter as ye know it in these parts of the world. The water in the oceans, lakes and streams runs warm. During part of the year, lakes will dry up. Streams and even rivers will run dry because it is so hot most all the time."

"So why must we endure winter?" asked Bourdicca.

"Have ye ever noticed steam rising from a pot when it is cooking over a fire?" asked Marjie.

"Yes, of course," answered Bourdicca.

"In the far south, much water rises into the sky because the land is so warm. The land is warmer because days are longer, the sun is hotter. Since the weather is warmer, large amounts of water move up into the air from the rivers, lakes, streams and oceans as a vapor. Think of the sun as a fire, slowly boiling the water from the earth. You all see this vapor in the air as clouds."

Marjie continued, "Please understand, the world be a verra, verra big place. All that water vapor needs to cool so it can fall back to earth. If it did not cool, there be no rain. No rain, no forest. No forest, no animals, no habitat fit for humans. Winter was put into place to cool the earth, so it does not become one hot, scorched desert with no bit of life. It's all bigger than most anyone can understand. The short story, please believe me, if we did not have winter, all the forests would disappear. There would be no trees for logs, no green grasses for the animals and no farming, as you know it for the food you eat."

"I'm seeing this is complicated, so for now, I'll say, it makes sense, as much as I can understand" said Bourdicca. "But what are we, this group of everyday humans doing here? Tonight."

"Just listen big guy," said Marjie, with a hint of sarcasm. "The human race was progressing well, so about 10,000 years ago, we..."

Torrin interrupted, "What is a 10,000, and what is a year?"

"Oh my," quipped Marjie, "Back to basics. Maybe we should have had Ipi stay at Journey a few more seasons." She smiled and continued, "A year is one round of the seasons, spring, summer, fall, and winter. And, 10,000 is...? Let's see, that might be the number of footsteps from here, back to the fort at Kalmar. It's that counting stuff Ipi showed you last winter."

"Ah," Torrin said with a smile. "So, 10,000 years is a great many years ago. Well in our saying, a great many winters ago. Am I close?"

"I would say, you are!" exclaimed Marjie, "Let me continue. 10,000 years ago, we gave humanity the ability to use fire. Fire was not as big as the wheel, but it was big. From fire came many improvements in life for humans. Cooking meat makes for healthier people. And of course, when items get verra hot, they melt. So, humans, being curious, and growing smarter, figured out how to make metals from melting rocks. How to bake concrete and clay for building better structures as well as firing pottery to safely store and transport food. And just a 1,000 or so years ago, glass. All these fine inventions allow people to build tools, improve life and one other important aspect."

Not a person at the table moved, wondering what was coming next.

Marjie continued, enjoying the fact she had an audience sitting on pins and needles, waiting for her to carry on. She did, "These tools mean you don't have to spend your entire day working to survive. You can think, create, share ideas and build improvements. One example is the wheel. You came up with that about 5,000 years ago. The wheel, combined with fire, gave humanity a lot to work with and create. Humans grew and progressed well, until some got too smart and decided to take control of other humans. That is where people, the human race, got off track. And, its where we are now. These nasty kings and queens are ruling harshly over folks. They are taking advantage of them. Keeping them under their thumb. The framework does not enable humanity to grow at its best."

"Wait just a moment," said an excited Dessa. "My athair is a king and he never held his people back from growing." Dessa was a bit red in the face and her eyes were dark turquoise.

Marjie looked hard at the girl with red hair. Small trails of sparks emitted from her fingers. She grasped her goblet and took a healthy mouthful. Beginning again, she spoke slowly, "Benevolent rule is still a régime. A régime, not elected by the free will of the participating humans. These ruled humans are working, in the long run, for the success of the ruler, not themselves and their families. And, the people ruled have no say in their future, denying them happiness and purpose. It leaves them devoid of their true humanity."

Marjie sighed and continued, "We ran a test. We ran a test with the people of the northern valley. They live free. They are happy. They have no ruler. They answer to themselves. This method of unleashing free will only works to a point though. As a group gets larger, there must be a center of command to coordinate the larger ventures that are for the good of everyone, like building roads. So, like a kingdom, the only difference, the people decide who is in charge. Not some family who bludgeoned others and then gets to take over and run good people into the ground for a thousand years. Our next step is to enable humans to decide who rules them. We call it a democracy."

Bourdicca again found his voice, "This all sounds interesting, a bit of a fairy tale,"

Marjie frowned at the 'fairy' word.

Bourdicca pressed on, "But what do we folks, who really have just met, have to do with your far-fetched idea of having the common folk rule themselves? Which, by the way, I find somewhat of a ridiculous idea."

Marjie toyed with her beverage. Her eyes scanned the folks at the table, and for a few moments, the only sounds in the room came from the crackling of the fires and soft hiss of candle flames.

Straightening in her chair, Marjie then she stated, in a voice that did not beg a question, only a statement, "You are the ones to take the idea of democracy to the human race and make it a reality for all people of the world."

The room became very quiet again. This spryte, whatever it was, and it seemed powerful and knowledgeable had just, shall we say, 'dropped the penny' on the assembled group.

Facing a mighty spryte like Marjie and hearing the plan was for them to depose the ruling class of the world had a bit of an unnerving effect on most everyone. Especially unnerving since it seemed each of the newcomers at the table were to do the dirty work of upsetting the ruling class.

Gustav stood and said, "Well, I'm thinking we all share a hardy beverage and chat a bit." He produced an amber colored bottle from his pack saying, "I have brought my best scotch to share, and I hope you will all take advantage."

Bourdicca held up a hand and said, "But, we need to…"

Gustav quickly looked at his second in command and sternly barked, "Later Bourdicca," and then a bit softer, "Just later."

Zach commented, "That my friend looks like a fine article to share and is something for the smoking room! Please everyone, let us adjourn to the comfortable seats of that delightful room. I'm getting the feeling this session has lasted long enough."

Everyone eagerly followed.

Except Marjie.

69 Dram

As the group followed Zach to the smoking room, Torrin had his eye on the room next door. The room Zach had named the library. Torrin hoped to have a tour later and experience more of the written word, and these interestingly rolled things called maps.

The smoking room had enough chairs for everyone to take a seat. The whole group was present. That is, except for Marjie.

Bourdicca asked, "Where be the spryte lady? She should join us for some time to chat and relax after this long day. Actually, it has been a lot of long days since the Völva arrived."

Ipi blushed and said, "I can explain. You see…"

Zach interrupted by clearing his throat and interjecting, "My dear deirfiúr, I do feel that I should share a dram with these fine folks before we, or you, embroil ourselves into discussions. My apologies for interrupting you."

Ipi sat herself on a sturdy wooden chair; it sported fine tooling as did all the other chairs in this room and the refectory. She nodded and said, "No bother my dear dearthair, where are my manners?" She stood up and began to distribute beautifully decorated, small, clear glass cups from a side cupboard.

As Ipi did so, Zach removed three amber bottles of good size from another cupboard. One bottle sported a white muslin top, secured with twine around the neck. Wax had been fashioned around the top across the muslin. He explained that the wax created a seal, keeping air out and the spirits in.

The second bottle had a gentle brown covering that looked like leather. It too was tied with twine. Zach explained the leather would seal on its own.

A third bottle was covered with jet black silk, with twine and wax seal.

Zach towered above his guests, a gentle smile upon his rugged face, and he held the first bottle, the one with the white top in his massive hand. He spoke with gentleness and caring, such as a teacher would speak when introducing a new topic, one near and dear to their heart.

"We have three fine scotches to encounter this evening. Starting with the lightest and ending with the most powerful and aromatic. Since these are verra powerful in nature, I be sharin just a wee dram of each. An, ifn ye are not fond of the stuff, and many are not fond, fer good reason, feel free to pass or offer yer portion to someone else. Sweet Ipi has some fresh sheep's milk if'n ye like. And I did grind some fresh cinnamon for ye te enjoy with the milk if ye like to go on an alternative adventure."

Everyone except Dessa was keen to try Zach's scotch. Dessa desired to only take a long whiff of Torrin's, to experience the flavor. She said her insides had been a bit jumpy of late and felt fresh milk would suit her more favorably.

Ipi fetched the pitcher of milk and a bowl of cinnamon. She filled Dessa's cup and set the cinnamon to the side so Dessa could add some to her own liking.

As Zach poured Ipi's dram, she wound her fingers around his wrist as far as her small hands would allow, and coaxed a bit more from the bottle into her glass. She looked up at him and warmly smiled.

When finished pouring, Zach took his seat and said to the assembled group, "Slàinte Mhath," and held his glass high. Everyone replied with the same 'Slàinte Mhath.'

Ancropolis took a sip and said, "Oh my."

Chrisholm tried a sip, tilted her head, nodded with a humm, "Verra nice."

After offering Dessa a whiff, Torrin took a hefty taste and said with an amazed look on his face, "That take the hair offn most anything."

Gustav and Bourdicca, took their time. After inhaling a full breath of vapors radiating off their cups, each took a very small sip and let the liquid vaporize into their mouths. With eyes closed, each nodded a 'Yes' with their heads, both appearing to enjoy the gift.

With the first round of sharing underway, Gustav turned to Ipi and asked, "Please now dear lady," he paused and then continued, "ye are so different than what has been beguiling me and my men for the last days. Could you give us a glimpse into the reasons for yer, ere, exotic behavior?"

"Certainly my dear," came her gentle reply. "You see, a Völva, to be taken seriously must perform ritual magic such as seidr to tie themselves to the spiritual realm. If I had simply arrived at your fort, and said in a kind way, 'Hello, I am your Völva,' ye may not have taken me so seriously. So, I had to put on a bit of, drama to secure my place in yer hearts and minds as a magical lady of the spirit world. That was one part. The other part being, Dessa and Torrin were still enroute and we needed them, along with the rest of us. So, I had to keep everyone entertained and wondering for a few days to give them time to arrive in Kalmar and join us."

Gustav nodded his head and replied with his glass raised, "I do understand, an ye did a fine job. If I ever need a Völva again, you'll be the one I summon. I do however need to explain to the men of the garrison something. Just not sure what to explain as of yet."

Ipi nodded a thank you and raised her glass as well.

The next round of scotch was a bit darker, more flavorful and as would be the case, a wee bit more powerful. With this sort of beverage sharing, as one might expect, the room was getting relaxed and felt warmer.

Before Zach could bring out his third bottle, Gustav produced the bottle he had brought along. Everyone who was trying the scotches enjoyed a dram from this treasure. Although Gustav's bottle was better than most, it was no match for the wonders of Zach's private stash. Everyone agreed though, the shared dram was wonderful and were profusely thankful.

Zach's last bottle poured out with a bit of thickness, none like anyone had experienced, well, maybe. Chrisholm's eyes went wide as she witnessed the pour. The thick amber fluid had an aroma of scotch, a burst of cloves, honey, almonds and vanilla. There were yet more flavors. They were hard to discern.

Chrisholm asked, "How, or where did you create this fine beverage?

It is akin to what I have been working about at Eskil for an eternity. This is an absolutely marvelous buidheach."

Zach replied, "It is the magic of me dear deirfiúr. She be a taken a hefty portion of my latest batch and disappeared to the kitchen for days at a time, addn flavors and mixes and such. She was lookn' for the charmed mix of flavors, and I day say, she found it. Maybe she takes ye to the kitchen in the morning and show ye around."

"Happy to my dear," said Ipi, now in a very relaxed state.

The room was currently relaxed with everyone enjoying a more calmed state of mind and body. Torrin asked, "Zach, could ye show me around the library? I am most interested in exploring the writings and those things you call maps. It's all verra new to me. And, as Marjie said, we humans are curious."

"Happy to," replied the big man, now also very relaxed. Both of them stood up and were almost blinded when the room was filled with the bright energy of fiery pixie dust suddenly swirling around in the air.

Marjie appeared, glass in hand, sitting on the arm of Ipi's chair. "Before ye go, please fill me up with yer last taste, the dark one. I hav' to get me head around what I am going to tell these folks at breakfast."

70 Library

Books of various sizes, bound in stiff muslin covers, adorned in assorted colors, stood at attention along one shelf. Thick older volumes with cracked leather bindings inhabited another. These older works might be considered tomes since they seemed to radiate wisdom and knowledge. Their corners were bent and frayed from use and age. They looked like they were as old as the earth itself. Large volumes packed with painted pictures, showing massive rooms of bright colors and people in all sorts of costumes, lay on one shelf.

Torrin gently opened one tome after another, looking at the strange characters. The stick figures, swirls and ornate twirls of the characters made not one bit of sense to him. He did remember Ipi had shown the group at Journey some simple writing during the previous winter. However he had not enough experience to know what he was exploring just now.

"Ye look like a child who just received a surprise present from a dear friend," said Zach, chuckling a bit.

"This is writing!" exclaimed Torrin. "I canno make sense of any of it, but if this is a gathering of words and thoughts and dreams of people over many winters," he paused to take a breath, "It be like we talk to each other over time and space and share thoughts." He looked up at Zach, "This jus be a marvel!"

'Ah me lad, this is just the start!" smiled Zach. "Look at this!" Zach unrolled a large map of the coastal area, including the North Sea heading all the way down to southern Britannia.

"What be this?" inquired Torrin.

"This me boy is a map. Used by the sea going ships that land to Kalmar. They use the stars to guide them and pages like this to help them know where they be when out on the water. Did ye see the ships tied up at Kalmar?"

"Yes, we did!" exclaimed Torrin, remembering the exciting view of the huge, masted schooners tied to the wharf. All this was spinning around in his head. The world was so much larger and complicated and organized and bigger than he had ever imagined. "It's just a lot to take in," he said to Zach.

"Yes, it is, and now we are going to change every last piece that be broke."

Dessa had been quietly perusing the interesting objects in the library. She was just as interested as Torrin, but he was having a good time voicing his curiosities, so she let him ramble on and ask questions. She was simply intrigued with this whole idea of writing.

A large book with ornate bronze hinges attached to its leather cover caught her eye. Something spoke to her in the details of the bronze. What though?

She kept exploring book covers, until she found the pattern. It was right there, hidden in plain sight and once she saw it, she couldn't let it go.

Book after book, cover after cover. The overall images were different, yet they all isplayed a recurring subject. The repetition was clear.

One cover, was carefully painted with rich colors. A dark mountain on the left and another on the right. Yet in the center was a small light. Maybe a candle, or an oil lamp. It represented light though. Everywhere, light?

She went back to the bronze hinge. The detail that had intrigued her now jumped out. A small single flame was embossed on each hinge.

The room was calm as Torrin leafed through a colorful tome. Zachariah sat quietly reading, a smile perched on his face.

Dessa softly cleared her throat, then spoke, "I'm noticing a theme. Many covers have a flame, or a candle or some sort of light. It's repeated again and again."

Zach's eyebrows perked up a bit and he commented, "You are verra perceptive. I am impressed you noticed. Yes, light or a flame is a common theme in books and stories."

Dessa licked her lips, pondering, "What's the meaning behind so much stress, or repetition of this, this idea? The flame, the light, its everywhere."

Zachariah, placed a small white feather in the book he'd been reading and gently closed the cover. Looking at Dessa, he softly said, "For humans to move forward, we must be curious, learn and invent. Most of us do not live long enough to discover all we need in order to be the most we might be. Stories told together around the table or the fire have long been used to teach others. To teach, discuss ideas, hope and dreams. For thousands of years, those stories were the backbone of the human race growing in knowledge and sharing wisdom.

Dessa looked at Zach and said, "The stories we tell each other are important, but now we have another tool. Books. Books bring knowledge further than our own circle. Books and all the thoughts they hold travel long distances. Knowledge is symbolized by the light of the flame. It really represents the power of sharing knowledge, ideas and all that is good in humans."

Dessa looked at the man and then said, in a very matter of fact way, "You set up the cave."

Zach stretched a bit and simply said, "Yes of course. It took a while to cut all that wood. I hope you enjoyed it."

"We did," answered Dessa, nodding politely. "And we appreciate your efforts. But that cave? All that darkness and then the wee candle? What did it mean?"

"Only light can defeat darkness. Darkness, cannot defeat light."

71 Night

All good evenings should end this way. A slow walk up a wide staircase, to a nicely appointed room. The group marveled at large well-crafted paintings, sculptures and carvings adorning the walls along the staircase and upstairs hallway. Zach ushered each person, or couple, to their respective rooms with quiet directions to bathing accommodations at each end of the hall. There were four bathrooms for attending to personal needs.

All four of these bathrooms included hot running water! Such luxury, no one had ever experienced before. Truly amazing!

Dessa and Torrin were ushered into a room near the end of the hall just outside one of the wonderful bathrooms. Dessa stopped when she entered the room and Torrin, not paying attention, resoundly bumped into her, almost sending her flying face first to the broad floor.

"Me bràmair, I am so sorry, I di not see ye standin there, I..." exclaimed the startled young man.

She did not let him finish, "Look!" said Dessa excitedly, pointing.

Torrin looked up to where she was pointing and saw what had stopped her cold upon entering the room. In the flickering light of a few candles was a huge, gleaming iron domed bed. Just like the one they had spent so many safe nights in at Journey.

The top of the dome had been raised up by ropes and pulleys fastened to the rafters above. Underneath, just as at Journey, the bed was full of soft white sand.

Dessa and Torrin had lamented the loss of their bed at Journey. Their iron domed bed was, other than in a creek or some body of water, the only safe place to share a long deep kiss. The blue electric sparks they created were dangerous most everywhere else.

Dessa skipped over and scooped up the sand in her hand. The fine white crystals slid gently and evenly through the small spaces between her fingers. The sand was as soft as goose down. It had been carefully raked even and clean.

"Now look at this!" declared Torrin. He held a door open to their very own private bathroom. Soft towels lay on a low stool. The bark had been cleaned from the stout wooden legs and the image of a fawn expertly carved in the top. A small sink stood in one corner, and of all the things they had never come across, there was a bathtub!

Torrin walked over and removed a block in the pipe protruding from the wall, just as Zach had done in the stables. Clear water coursed through the pipe, and he said to Dessa, "Wait a moment, ye are not goin' ta believe this!"

Soon, soft steam vapors swirled off the water flowing from the pipe. Torrin figured out how to affix a plug into a drain at the bottom of the tub and it soon began to fill with hot clean water.

"It's. It's just amazing," said Dessa. She was letting the warm water run over her hand. Her mouth was almost hanging open. "I don't think I ever want to leave."

Torrin laughed, and said, "Ifn ye want to stay, I'm okay with that. But home is where home is. Anyway, we'll enjoy tonight. And it do give us ideas for Journey when we get back to the place."

He looked at Dessa, tilted his head and asked, "Me lady. May I wash yer hair for ye?"

She looked as though she was going to cry. After she dropped the belongings she was carrying, she walked over to him, hugged him tightly and let the tears flow. He held her close and let the stress of everything melt away, as clear rivulets coursed down her beautiful cheeks.

That is, until the tub was full of beautiful warm, clear water.

Torrin let go of Dessa, secured the block in the pipe and returned his attention to his love.

First he loosened the tie behind the neck of her shirt and lifted it off her body. Actually, it was more like he had to slowly peel it off, she was in such need of a bath and the shirt was in need of a good washing. He could see bits of dirt, leaves and remnants of the trail stuck to her skin.

He figured he was probably sporting the same bits of chaff and looked forward to losing it. Losing it in hot water. With her!

And of all things, it was water they did not need to heat themselves.

Oh the joy of it was exhilarating.

Boots, shirts, pants. All of the things one wears ended up scattered upon the wooden planks of this tremendous room.

A generous lump of freshly scented soap sat on a small shelf near the tub. The two of them used up the entire quantity that had been supplied. But it took them emptying and filling the tub three times to do it.

After they were both more truly clean than they'd been in quite a while, Dessa brushed out her long red curls to a smooth sheen. Her fear was if her hair would be in such a knot, she would have to shave her head in the morning. While Dessa brushed, Torrin took to washing breeches and shirts and other clothing items, long in need of a good cleaning. These he hung up on pegs scattered in good supply across the walls. As he worked away, he commented that these people had thought of everything!

He stopped working when he noticed her pale body, resting on her side, naked upon the white sand. Yellow candlelight flittering across all her soft parts. As her head was perched upon her left hand, red curls flowed down to the sand from her smiling face. Her right foot slid up her leg to her knee and her right hand slowly traced a line from her thigh to her lips. She made a kissing motion upon her fingertips and then beckoned him to join her.

She did not need to repeat the invitation.

Torrin entered the big iron bed and thenslowly dropped the metal dome over their entirely naked selves. They found themselves in an almost familiar environment. Where the great iron bed of Journey had been pitch black inside, unless they lit a wee candle, this one had some light.

Neither noticed the light until the sparks had subsided. Torrin had been exploring Dessa's soft skin, from ankle to forehead with his lips. As always, he was marveling at her smoothness and the warmth of her skin. He also enjoyed her little moans when he toyed with her oh so delicate parts.

He lay back since she had indicated, she was to have some fun exploring him, when he said, "O' dhìol, how did they do this? The light of the candles is coming through the metal!"

Dessa looked up and ran her fingers over the area where the light seemed to be coming through the heavy metal that kept their sparks from engulfing the room in deadly fire. "Is nothing but some sort of dark window."

She looked at him and said, "Just lay down yer head, close yer eyes, relax and we'll explore more in the morning. Right now, I am going to explore what I am wanting right here."

Her ministrations both aroused and relaxed his entire being. He lay back and let the warm sensations of her care upon his most sensitive parts fill him with pleasure. The evening was neither rushed nor slow, as these things should be. And repetition was made, until more became impossible.

It was a while before either slept.

72 Breakfast

Bells? Am I dreaming? Dessa opened her eyes, and it took a moment to remember where she was. For an instant, she was frightened. She figured it was morning, but it was so dark!

And then she remembered the bed, the building, the craziness of everything going on. Turning toward Torrin, she ran her hand from his shoulder to his hip. She used just a bit of pressure with the tip of her fingernail to get this attention.

Torrin softly moaned and said, "Now it's me own turn to not want to wake up and leave a warm bed."

She replied, "You can stay here as long as you want, but I need to get up and enjoy a quick bath before we go downstairs."

Then they both heard the voice of Zach and bells ringing. He was announcing from the hallway that breakfast was ready for anyone who would like to partake, and they should make tracks to get to the refectory.

Torrin raised the top of the bed and they both got out, dusting off a bit of sand and relishing their feelings from the night before. Dessa headed straight to the tub and got it filling quickly.

Torrin left the room to find Zach. When he returned, he had a new lump of that wonderfully scented soap in his hand. He shared it with Dessa who was now sitting happily in hot water up to her neck.

As Torrin dressed, he noticed his clothes were almost dry, but they felt so much better, being clean. Same as he felt about himself. His thoughts turned to the steeds, hoping the horses were well rested and ready for the next part of this adventure. Although, he wondered how they would fair riding in one of those massive ships they had seen, tied to the wharf near Eskil? Oh well, he decided, I'm sure has ridden a ship before. And if they were to keep going forward with spreading this idea of democracy, they would have to eventually take a ship far out across the waters and visit distant lands.

Dessa emerged from the bathroom and began dressing. Torrin sat on a stool and admired her as she dressed. Dessa blushed just a bit and said, "What are ye starin at?"

Torrin grinned and remarked, "I just never tire of lookin at ye."

She smiled.

* * *

Tables in the refectory had been set into a large U shape. Chairs occupied one side of the tables. It looked as though a discussion was planned to ensue.

Where the large buffet had been set up last evening, now there was only one table. Fresh bread, a variety of cheeses, sweet milk and a plate of fruit were displayed in a nice arrangement.

Most of the others who had arrived in the group were already in the room, standing by the only fireplace holding a fire. The morning had arrived with a chill to the air, and being by the fire was a good way to chase those chills away.

As Dessa walked toward the fire, she could sense Torrin following behind. She looked forward to the warmth of the flames on her face and becoming involved in whatever discussion was in progress. As they walked, she felt Torrin nudge her hand, as if he wanted to walk with her and hold hands. She instantly flashed in her mind the idea that she was so lucky to be with a romantic man. Someone who cared and someone who…?

Who had wet hands?

She turned to look at Torrin, but he was back by the doorway, immersed in conversation with Bourdicca. She looked down, and tears promptly filled her eyes as she looked into the strong blue eyes of Praritor.

Dessa gasped as she knelt down and wrapped her arms around the big shaggy neck of her favorite wolf. And then she heard in her head, "I've missed ye so, and it is good to see ye."

And then the side of her face was wet as something warm, damp and rough licked her and she heard, "Ye always liked him better." Dessa turned and looked into the deep yellow eyes of the cougar, Ailis the Fergal. Her arms wrapped around his big neck, and she buried her face into his course yellow fur, enjoying his natural smell and the feel of his pure muscle.

Dessa said to them both, "How? Why? I don't understand, ye were gone. I'm so glad ye are back! But what? I don't understand. Oh my." And she did her best to wrap herself around the two of them. Which of course was impossible, given their size.

Dessa took a deep breath, sat back on her heels and noticed the faces in the room. There was mostly silence and looks of amazement from just about everyone. Zach, Chrisholm and Torrin were smiling. Ancropolis, Bourdicca and Gustav looked as though they needed a way to climb the walls and Ipi was quietly eating some cheese.

Standing up next to her furry friends, Dessa said to the room, "May I introduce you to two of my favorites, shall we say, characters of the forest. Praritor the most alpha of the wolves and Ailis the Fergal, the most fearless of the cougars. They have each been our saviors in many a time of my troubles, and that of Torrin. I just don't know what they are doing here?" She looked at Ipi, for some explanation and Ipi just put some jam on a chuck of bread.

Looking down at Ailis, Dessa asked, "What are you doing here?"

In her head, Dessa could hear Ailis begin to speak, "We was called by…" And then everyone heard the commanding voice of Marjie say, "Me, my dear. Me. I summoned our friends for a special adventure, which we will now discuss. Pay no mind to either of them, they are gentle as kittens in this place."

Marjie had suddenly appeared at the entrance to the refectory. She was dressed in her usual blue shimming gown; her hair was perfect, as customary. She carried an air of authority about her that belied any joviality.

Marjie clapped her hands together to make sure everyone was listening and said, with a commanding tone, "If everyone would please help yourselves to some food and take a seat, we will get started, this will not take long."

Usually, Marjie is right.

* * *

Eventually everyone was settled at the tables, and it really was nice to be able to see each other as a group. The seating Torrin mused was a cozy arrangement. Praritor and Ailis lounged on large blankets on either side of Marjie at the front of the big U. The warm fireplace behind them burned brightly, and they were obviously enjoying the warmth. Marjie sat a bit regally upon a chair, all by herself, only a clear goblet in her hand, and it looked very much like it was full of a dark amber beverage.

Breakfast plates on the tables showed the last of the morning's eating. Mostly crumbs to remind folks of the gracious hospitality they had enjoyed.

Marjie cleared her throat and began to speak. "Thank you all for being here again this morning. As we discussed last evening, nature has decided the human race is to progress and become more valuable upon the earth. If we are to move forward, this is our only option. We have tried with the forest animals, but their root intelligence is limited, as well as their ability to hold things in their paws since they lack a thumb.

Both Praritor and Ailis growled a bit, looking up at Marjie. She smiled, eyed them both and said, "Relax, we are not disparaging you, it's just the truth. We need you as part of the whole system going forward. It just is, what it is. Also, you don't seem to organize well into groups. Humans finally figured that one out."

Both animals lay back down with a sigh. Ailis turned onto his back to let the warmth of the fire flow over his belly. Dessa could hear a muffled groan with words that sounded like, 'Cats, so uncouth' coming from Praritor.

Marjie focused on the humans at the table and continued, "We need to move forward with the cause to change ruling from the entitled, to the elected."

Bourdicca commented, "If I may, it's a fine idea, but no king is going to just step down and let the peasants or the barons take over rule in their kingdom."

"Oh sir, we know that for certain," answered Marjie. "So, we had been grooming Dessa and Torrin to take this verra disruptive message to the world and work it out with humanity for the next thousand years or so. Whatever it takes. But we made a mistake. We thought a spoiled brat princess would learn to appreciate a free life so much, she could take the message forward. And we thought that a well-raised boy might be a good second for the girl."

"Spoiled?" exclaimed Dessa, rising to her feet. She looked around the room for support. She only saw looks of amazement and question. All this was still a lot for everyone to swallow.

Torrin bit his lip and thought to himself, 'Second?'

"Get over it dear," said Marjie to Dessa. "You have done just fine. We didn't know you could get pregnant, and having a child, on the move, given the task ahead was not going to work. Not for the long run. You two will go back to the Journey Inn and run the first election, create the first democracy and help determine how to best operate such a new concept among a growing population of humans. That will be an interesting experiment, especially now with all these people traveling north to live in the free valley."

Marjie now looked at Gustav, "What we have discovered is we need someone who understands the thinking of a king, the ways of politics and is not shy to have a candid conversation with a mighty ruler. And we needed him to have a second who is wily enough to keep her wits about her on any occasion. So, we have chosen Gustav and Chrisholm to go from here and take the idea of democracy and free elections to the world."

Ancropolis looked stricken. He turned to Chrisholm and muttered, his voice hardly above a whisper, "Is this true?"

Chrisholm sat up tall in her chair, turned to her lover and softly said, "I told you, that in my dreams, there were far off places and people that beckoned me to them. I always went to those places from this building. What I did not tell you was," she gulped, "I was never with you."

"Were you with him?" Ancropolis asked as he stood up, his fists in a ball and the color continuing to rise in his cheeks.

"No, I was with her," Chrisholm pointed to Marjie. Ancropolis left the table and stormed toward the hallway.

Marjie continued, "Let him go, he will be alright, he just needs some time to settle down." Marjie now turned to Torrin and Dessa, "Torrin and

Dessa, you need good people to help run the new Journey Inn. Your old system of barter will no longer work since the place is now much larger and will become too busy. Take Ancropolis with you to run the tavern. He will love it and has the experience of successfully operating Eskil."

"Aye, but I dinna know we was havn a Tavern," said Torrin, a bit muted.

Marjie answered, "It's in the works. Your friends that you liberated from the evils of Garwen have been adding it to the side of the Journey Inn that overlooks the creek and waterfall. It's coming along very nicely."

Gustav commented, "My regards to you for feeling I can move these conversations forward, but I am at a loss on how to do so?"

Marjie turned and addressed Zach, "Did you check to see if all is in order?"

Zach stood, looked at Gustav and said, "Did you bring it?"

Gustav rose from his chair, walked over to his pack and carried it over to the table. He opened the drawstring and produced the silver platter he and Zach had pounded out many days before. Picking it up, he looked at Zach before walking over to Marjie. He set the platter onto her outstretch hand.

Marjie looked from the platter to Gustav and said bluntly, "Say it."

Gustav looked around the room at the assembled group. He did not miss a beat and began to chant,

"May my deeds be the hammer to shape not only my future,
but that of generations to come.

May the forge of my heart craft this world
into a place worth living.

May my fire stoke yours.

May my resolve remain stalwart in the face of adversity,
and serve to embolden the weary.

May my hands be stayed in anger,
but never idle toward peace.

May the song of my heart be that which I sing the loudest.

May you find respite, in my presence."

Marjie looked intently at Gustav while she fired a question to Zach, she simply said, "Zachariah?"

The big man had been standing like a statue while Gustav spoke the lines of the mantra. Now with the question in the air, he took a deep breath and simply said, "Aye."

"Then," said Marjie, "It is settled. Gustav and Chrisholm, you will be successful. Remember, we will be there to help you when you need it. Your mission will be in conflict with most everything humans believe about the idea of rule. Free choice flies in the face of the powerful religious leaders, all the ruling families and despots who are crushing the spirit, purpose and resolve of the human race.

Chrisholm cleared her throat and said, a bit demurely, but with growing conviction, "Here. Here in this room, with tame beasts of the forest," she looked at Marjie, "you, a seeming master of all that there is, with our belly's full and a warm fire, this all sounds so wonderful and inviting. But I canna begin to think of what transpires to make such a thing begin to come true. Nor my role."

"Aye," agreed Gustav. "What the lass says be true. I feel it in my heart, and I can understand the ideas of it all, even if it is making my head hurt. But Chrisholm and I only know each other from a tavern. What is my role too?" He looked at Chrisholm with questions on his face and shrugged his shoulders.

Marjie smiled, tapped her long fingernails on the side of her glass and she began, "Chrisholm, you are the voice of heart and the higher road to Gustav. What is meant by that is; you bring a softness that is necessary when the times are harsh. You will forever have the power to summon nature to your side to help. You will help Gustav see the ideals behind the logic of the moments that face you. Together, you will find the necessary wisdom amongst the turmoil to move ever forward toward success."

Marjie turned to Gustav, "I have watched you work the myriad maze of Barrons, landowners and ultimately your king. I have listened to you speak truths in order to serve the men of your garrison. You know the ways of the powerful. You know how to earn their ear, their thoughts and their respect. We need your thinking to advance this ideal of freedom, the power of democracy, and the growth of the human race."

"And, you are I must admit, a man. As disheartening as it is, the reality of present time is, officials will not listen to most women. The only women in power are within the family, and that power is not certain. We experience this too often."

Marjie turned her attention back to the whole group, "All of nature knows we cannot dominate over the ruling classes in order to achieve success. They have too much material power. They will fight until everything is completely ruined."

She took a rather large sip, sighed and continued, "We also know we cannot compromise with hierarchical rulers who rule by what they term 'divine right.' Attempts to compromise have been and are futile. These despots will lie and break promises. Power eats at the heart and soul of most men," She looked at Zach, smiled a smirky smile and finished with, "not all men, thank goodness."

Marjie put one hand down on Praritor' s head and scratched him between the ears while she spoke, "You will integrate the idea of freedom into the hearts of humans. It is the only way for this to work in a sustainable fashion. This process and integration will try your patience and create chaos for many. However, chaos of the present time is needed for a new order to emerge."

As she took her hand from Praritor' s ears, he sighed and lay his head between his huge paws and she concluded, "Dominate, compromise or integrate. Integration is the only way. And you start with the common folk."

Marjie looked around the room. Not a face twitched as they absorbed the message. A message bigger than anyone really could comprehend.

Marjie concluded with, "Trust me, the effort will be worth it, and will take a verra, long, time."

73 North...

"What the deamhan did you say to that man to get him so eager to join us and come to Journey?" asked Dessa to Torrin as they rode north, away from Kalmar, away from the Essence Center towards Journey.

"Well, if I must be honest, I did not have to say much," said Torrin in a bit of a hushed voice. "He told me he had always been a bit anxious of Chrisholm because she was so strong and smart. He confided he felt a bit second-rate with her bein so close to nature and with her visions. After the shock of breaking up wore off, he decided he was better off this way.

"I see," said Dessa. "How do you feel about me?" she asked. "Are you feeling like I overwhelm ye and yer second rate?"

Torrin laughed, "Oh no me dear. You are just fine. You do your thing, I do mine and we meet nicely in the middle. Guess it's like Marjie said, it's not dominance or compromise, we integrate."

"I'll agree with you on that!" remarked Dessa, and she smiled at him in a way that made him tingle a bit inside.

Dessa pondered for a moment and then asked, "Did ye get good ideas from Zach for the new Journey Inn during the last night we stayed in that magnificent building?"

"Oh aye, yes, so many," said Torrin. "I do want to build a library and have a place where we can ave Ipi teach people reading and math. The reading thing, it just opens up a world of possibilities." He thought for a moment and then added, "No, really, it delivers a world of possibilities to the reader and is just overwhelming fun! It's like climbing into someone's brain and figuring out what they is thinking."

"Seems like the whole idea has got ye thinking about a lot of ideas," said Dessa.

"Yes! The man read to me writings from a traveler who had

adventured over verra tall mountains. The reading was like I was there. I could close me eyes and picture the snow, the cold wind and the wide snow-drifted landscape."

"I agree, it's something to teach the folks of the valley," added Dessa.

"But, with all these possibilities for the future, there is one thing though," said Torrin. Dessa turned to look at him, waiting for the one thing. He cleared his throat and said, "Could ye teach me to talk with the animals? Even jus a wee bit?"

"Oh, my dear, if I knew how to show you, I would. I have no idea how it's done or how it even comes about. I just know it's there." Uta gave a wet whinny and Torrin was sure she was talking about him.

Ipi and Ancropolis rode back a bit to stay out of the dust. They engaged in long, upbeat heartfelt conversations about the future of running a tavern in the north. A place where more and more people were settling every year and the thought of a formal gathering place for food and drink open to the public was a very new and probably wonderful idea.

Periodically, Dessa could see, or maybe more feel the sensation someone was travelling alongside the trail just inside the woods. She knew it was the big gray wolf Praritor, and the tawney cougar, Ailis the Fergal.

She did love the presence of the two of them when they made their evening camps. The big animals would stroll into the area, generally Ailis in the lead followed by the big gray wolf. The two partners would nuzzle each of the humans, give their regards to Dessa and then lie down near the fire. They both certainly did enjoy the warmth of a good blaze and avoiding the chill of the night air.

For Dessa, Torrin, Ipi and Ancropolis, their travels north, their venture to the big valley went without issue or trouble. On the final night of camp, before arriving at Journey, the enigmatic virtues of human nature reasserted itself wonderfully.

The four humans had been invited to a large camp of voyagers heading north. Voyagers heading north to freedom, to possibilities. To adventures of their own choosing. Ipi and Ancropolis readily joined the group. Dessa and Torrin politely declined, saying they wanted one last quiet evening, alone in the forest before they were with the large group again.

Privately, they both wanted to share one last evening with Praritor and Ailis. Dessa was concerned that her ability to communicate with them might end with their arrival at Journey. She was verra sure the wolf and the cougar would not be keen on sharing the evening with a large group.

They found a small clearing under a tall tree. They set up their site, gathered some wood and started a fire. It was not long before Torrin had bright yellow flames sending warmth across their little camp. The evening had the feeling of rain in the air, so the two of them had quickly pitched their small tent to avoid getting wet on their last evening on the trail.

Shallots, potatoes, beans and spices simmered in the big pan over the flickering flames and bright orange coals. Before long the wolf and cougar arrived and lay down on the leaves across from the humans, their big eyes blinking in the firelight.

Dessa said out loud to her furry friends, so Torrin could at least hear half the conversation, "Does our time with ye, end when we arrive at Journey?"

Praritor looked at Ailis in a way to indicate the cat should speak. Ailis took a deep breath and slowly said, "Aye. We understand we can return if needed to do the bidding of nature, if it be necessary. But for now, ye need to be moving forward on yer own."

Dessa said, "I see. And I will miss ye. Miss ye so much, like afore."

Praritor rumbled in his deep base voice, "Ailis said it before, we are honored to have helped ye. And it's still true. We did not know another chance would come so soon. It's been joyful. Although, it will be good to get back to the family. The pups are about ready to set out on their own."

Ailis hissed a long, "Yes."

"When do we part, or rather, when does this end?" asked Dessa.

Before any answers could be given, sparks swirled over the fire and Marjie materialized. She was just tiny in the gathering darkness but seemed to be briming with happiness. She sat upon a stone near the fire, smiled at everyone and said, "Top of the evening to you all!"

"Ye are always a surprise, aren't ye?" said Torrin.

"More than that me lad," said Marjie. And she tossed what looked like a million tiny sparks towards Torrin. The sparks dissipated with no harm or fire.

Torrin looked at his arms and hands and said, "Now was that necessary?"

Marjie smiled, she looked up at Torrin and just made a bit of a humming sound. Then, as if by magic, Torrin heard the deep base voice of Praritor talking in his head, "Ye are a mighty spryte, and ye do earn that badge of mischief people put upon yer name."

Torrin looked at Praritor, looked at Marjie and said to Dessa, "I heard that! I just heard what that wolf said to you!"

Dessa replied with a simple, "Oh my."

Marjie spoke, "Yes, I know, you being able to talk to these wily beasts came with those sparks. I would hate to leave company with you, for now, with you thinking I have no joy to share with others. This is only until you arrive at the top of that hill and come within sight of the Journey Inn. I figured you should know what your sweet lady has experienced."

Torrin replied, "Tis amazing. And, I guess, I will jus say, Thank You."

"Well, I did not want you to miss out on the experience, entirely," said Marjie, the look of mischief bright in her eyes.

Marjie looked towards the dark forest and then everyone heard the footsteps. The soft padded footsteps of a mathan cub entering the clearing. Dessa knew right away who it was. The cub gave a nuzzle to both Praritor and Ailis before lumbering over to Dessa. She put her arms around the brown fuzzy neck and gave as big a hug as was possible. Dessa was amazed at how much the young mathan had grown in the short time since they had crossed paths on that fateful evening.

The cub looked at Dessa. She and Torrin could hear these halting words, spoken in their heads, "I know what you did was hard. I know I miss my mháthair with me whole heart. But I also know, what had to happen you could not change. So, I thank you for all the kindness and love ye gave. Safe travels to ye, and I wish ye nothing but happiness."

The cub sighed, turned and ambled away into the darkening forest, along the way she had arrived.

Dessa turned to Marjie and asked, "Is there always this much sadness among the animals?"

Marjie replied, "No, they do not share more troubles than you humans. All in nature share their joys and struggles fairly. Until we meet again!"

With that said, Marjie disappeared in a flash of fire and millions of sparks.

Torrin looked at Ailis and Praritor. He was not sure what to say, or for that matter, how to say it. So, he just started to talk. "I am not used to talking to animals. And you both are magnificent creatures and such a friend to the both of us. Where do I begin?"

Dessa was simply listening and enjoying watching Torrin struggle with the whole idea of talking to these two. She was remembering what it had been like to first know she could communicate with them.

The conversation went on for a while and then, as the night gradually darkened, and the forest rested, the words fell away.

Eventually, Ailis and Praritor went to sleep.

Dessa turned to Torrin and said, "Let's eat one last quiet meal, its already cooked. " She noticed, this time, the tears were in his eyes.

74 Direction

Gustav and Chrisholm had departed from Kalmar on a three-masted schooner that rode light in the water since its cargo had unloaded at the port. The north seas are traditionally a bit rough, and today was no exception.

To stay upright on the pitching ship, Gustav had to hold tight to a long rope secured to the deck. "Can ye show me how ye know we are heading in the right direction?" inquired Gustav of the navigator who was standing over a large chart surrounded by impressive brass navigational equipment.

"Well mate," said the sailor, "We knows today's date, so I look on the antikythera's dials to tell me where the stable and the movable objects are in the stars above. Or during the day, use the sun. Then I takes me astrolabe, sight the position of a stable body and that tells us the angle. The angle gives me a pretty good idea of where we are on the map."

Gustav was a bit in awe and replied, "Really good sir, that is amazing."

"Nah, learned it from me grampy. He was a sailor all his life, jus took a bit to figure out all the variables and de math parts. Of course, since we sail further and further now, I'm always a learnin."

"So where did such wonderful inventions such as this antikythera and astrolabe come from?" said Gustav.

"Aye, da Greeks. Those guys, an impressive bunch of inventors if ya ask me," said the sailor. "Da captain, he won this gadget (indicating the antikythera) in a poker game. At the fair port of Athens. I daresay, the mate who be losin it might a got keelhauled. But it do come in handy." The sailor spit over the side of the ship and finished with, "As long as we can see the stars and moon from time to time then I can pretty much figure out where on the water we is located."

Gustav thanked the man and returned to his cabin. He told Chrisholm, "It's true, I see it time and again, people left to their own wits will create amazing things," and he told her all about what he had heard about sailing navigation.

Chrisholm said to him as she rocked with the boat, enjoying the rhythm of the sea, "I sense ye is beginning to take hold of this idea of purpose and the might of free will in yer mind."

Gustav smiled at her and said quietly, "Yes, it's amazing what a person can see, when they open their eyes and being looking around."

Their trip south was uneventful. Eventually they landed at the big port of Londinium with the wide river Thames flowing by. Huge warehouses serviced the ships tied to the massive docks.

"Where do we go to get started?" asked Chrisholm as she stood on firm ground, swaying a bit on her sea legs for the first time in many days.

"Ah my dear," said Gustav. "Where all good conversations start. A pub."

75. Well?

The two of them sat in the smoking room of the Nature Center on comfortable chairs. No sounds present, except the periodic sharp snap of the burning fire in the small hearth. He loved the quiet, almost more than the busy times of hosting the periodic sessions of the Center. But he knew in his heart, all that noise made these contemplative quiet times so much more precious. When the Center was full the place was a cacophony of sound, unbridled energy and a pursuit of a better future for everyone and everything in nature.

Right now, though, it was time to let his mind catch up to the present. And again, he muddled in his thoughts; why is it so relaxing to just watch the flames of the fire?

Soon enough though, the silence was broken. Broken by Marjie, as she sat in the other chair, holding her favorite glass of scotch, pondering the same firelight. She quietly asked Zachariah a simple question, "Well?"

He did not answer right away. Just as when she had requested him to gather Gustav from the forest, he paused, set his teeth tight and had pondered. He knew an answer too quickly might not come across well or simply not truly thought out. And there was no need to hurry an answer anyway. The plan they had been working on, since the miserable fall of his beloved city of Troy, was now just underway.

Finally, after he added more logs to the fire and set things right with the hearth, he leisurely responded to what he knew was a verra deep and personal question for the spryte. She never, never asked his opinion unless the question was haunting her soul (if she had a soul, which was a question he knew he would never be able to really ask her).

So, a careful response was in order.

"I must admire what you did. Really, from a number of turns of the wheel, or was it fate that held us some luck. Does not matter, the stage had been set and the wheel was in motion. We had settled on the boy and the girl a while ago, and it all seemed right. But then, as they do, things change, with the baby and all. But yer thoughts about the redhead not being heard, that rang painfully true. And the boy, Torrin, well, he did not like what transpired, with his family's kingdom being overrun and all. There is not a one among us humans that can go forward for a long time and not get tired of carrying a burden. That burden will always come out. Especially in the worst of times. Sad powerful burdens eat at the heart of humans. After what you told me he said to you in the forest, I was concerned that he might crumble when the going get tough on the journey to freedom."

"Thank you Zach, I agree," said Marjie. "Sometimes I can be open to every idea and possibility, and that makes me blind to what must be done. It is a verra grand plan. I don't even know if it's possible. But I do feel in my heart, we have to take the risk of moving forward. There is so much at stake. The humans must progress. At the rate they are having babies worldwide, they will have consumed all the forests, killed the air you all breathe and spoiled the water you all drink. And then everything must start over again. And that was no fun. That last time we had to make it all a fresh start, from scratch. That meteor made such a mess of things. For so verra, verra long."

Zach chuckled and said with a smirk, "You Miss Marjie are a true, and true to form spryte. I sometimes wonder if you have not a heart."

"Someday, when you are not looking, I will make you pay for that comment," replied the smiling spryte. "I do have a heart, and it's for a better future for everything, not just the humans. But they, they are our last hope. If they cannot build a clean, free environment, then I will do what I must. The natural order of the earth is the only end game."

She held out her glass and he refilled it, this for the third time. As he set the amber bottle down, he asked, "I know yer body is just temporary, how do ye drink anything? I always wanted to ask. I figure the scotch should just flow through you to the floor."

Marjie laughed and said, "I do like to keep ye guessing, ye big lout. I like to keep ye guessing as much as I like drinking yer finest scotch." She looked at him and smirked, "Haven't ye figured it out? I can do just about anything I want to do."

"Oh!" he replied.

"Yes, I can do anything I want to do, except be human. And that eats at my soul. It has for over a million years."

He sighed as he thought of the depth of her answer and then looked at her. For the first time ever, he noticed the flames of the fire did not reflect in her face.

It was a wee bit unnerving.

76 Home

Five horses and four riders paused at the bottom of the long gradual hill that led up to the site of the new Journey Inn. Today had greeted them as one of those special rare endearing days of fall. The air was crystal clear, but not too cold. The sunshine was bright and warming in the crisp air, not harsh like the mid-summer sun's heat.

Fall's pinnacle in the valley was always special. Earlier each fall, bright yellows mixed with the amber browns of birch and rowan leaves' blazing color in the low angle of the sun is almost blinding. The steady plucsh of falling leaves had now departed, since it was later in the season. Most of the color had also departed. Today however, was one of those special days where the threat of winter's cold and heavy snow seemed far off.

Red squirrels with long tufted ears darted through the woods and across the trail. Their little bodies made a mini-dust line as they zoomed across, presumably playing a whimsical game of tag. They chased and chattered on, seeming to pay no mind to the humans or the horses. They also, for some reason that was not to be understood, did not worry about the cougar and wolf traversing the woods nearby.

Dessa looked up the long sloping hill and sighed. She knew they had arrived at another point of change, another transformation. Many of the transformations she and Torrin had encountered came upon them, and they had to basically discover the difference. She knew though, at the top of the hill, this change, they would go through verra consciously and purposefully. And she hoped, they would continue to change as they needed, it was just life, she mused.

She wondered for a moment why she and Torrin had not tried to stay on their quest? Why had they let go so easily? Then she absentmindedly put her hand over her belly and took in a breath.

Torrin dismounted from Samoot, boots kicking up small clouds of dust as he landed. Dessa sat warmly in the saddle of Uta, watching him. She knew it would be a moment for him and herself that would never leave their memories. She hopped down.

Dessa started with Calandra, and with each horse, took a moment, as did Torrin. They were saying their goodbyes. They all knew, at the top of this hill, once the new Journey Inn came into sight, everything would be different.

Everything would be as it was, so long ago. Was it just two winters? So much had happened, so much was still yet to occur.

So much was yet, well, unknown.

Still perched upon their mounts, all Ancropolis and Ipi could hear were many wet whinnies, and soft goodbye murmurings from the humans. Although these two knew what was going on, speaking with the animals for them was pretty much an unsolved mystery.

Samoot ended the conversation with these words to Torrin, "I enjoy ye as a rider. You is kind, you is patient. All of which I appreciate. However, what you have given me is the greatest gift. A better future, or at least the possibility of a better future for my offspring. You and Dessa, your hearts are bigger than all of us."

Dessa and Torrin took a turn for each other. They hugged, and for one last time, kissed. They kissed and let the heat and sparks fly. Standing on the dusty trail, there was no worry of the spread of fire. They wanted to enjoy this one last special moment. Although they knew in their hearts, all moments like these always would be special for all their lives, in their hearts.

Then, without a word, they mounted up and urged Samoot and Uta to gallop up the hill as fast as possible. Ancropolis and Ipi followed close behind, trying to avoid the dust from the thundering hooves in front of them.

When they rounded the corner, the very sight of the place took their collective breaths away and brought tears of joy to their travel weary eyes.

It was, in a word, beautiful. Long lines of well-hewn logs, sparkling glass windows, large chimneys and an inviting front porch with broad open and pleasing doors made the first impression. The new Journey Inn was magnificent in all regards and was a testament to love with purpose.

He came running out the doors as fast as his old legs would carry him and Ipi jumped into his arms. After a spin and a big hug, Ol Dogger set her down, looked her in the eye and said, "Will ye stay with me now and never leave?"

Ipi smirked and said, "Unless nature calls, I'm here for the rest of time. But we do need to visit my deartháir at least twice a year."

Ol Dogger whooped in glee and agreed, without hesitation.

Dessa slowly dismounted from Uta, her face shining as she took in the amazing sight of the new Journey Inn. Turning to Torrin with a loving smile, she said, "Looks like we are home, and this is a fine place to raise a family."

77 Postlude

It's interesting how such a large flow of water in a mighty river can pass by and make hardly a sound. So quiet, yet so much power in the running water of that river! Just like all the power, now quiet, of the barons and noblemen standing around waiting for King John to arrive. Chrisholm cleared her throat and brought Gustav's attention back to the matters at hand. It was a cool spring day by the River Thames, in the serene fields of Runnymede.

Gustav and Chrisholm had been posturing the ideas of freedom for just over 1200 years now. Yes, it had taken a very long time.

The fiercest of debates had raged on for a good month now among the nobles. The Barons had seized the idea of putting the king at their level of the law with a fervor neither Gustav nor Chrisholm had ever experienced. Now the date was set, all had agreed on the long manuscript, and only one thing was left to do.

And that was to put King John's seal on the document. The king had agreed to sign, forcing a few of his own ideas onto the document.

By noon, all had been signed, sealed and accomplished. Runners were sent to all the towns to read the proclamation of the newly installed Magna Carta. Joy was palatable in the air as the reign of John's terror of imprisonment for no reason, taxation on a whim and other tyrannical absurdities was now over. Through agreement and much compromise, the monarch was not above the law, he had limited royal power, and the rights of the barons was protected.

By evening, Gustav and Chrisholm sat alone in their little apartment. They were celebrating. Celebrating almost 1,500 years of work. Years of cajoling, talking, debating and being politically careful. The talk they were spreading was considered a heretical doctrine by any King or Queen of the time. They'd been cautious, and through their patient efforts, now the time seemed to be right.

Free people, free will, no one above the law, not even the king. No more government thievery, conviction or jail without cause.

As the two of them shared their bottle of wine and a nice supper, Marjie materialized on a stool next to the door. "Congratulations on getting the first step out the door, so to speak," said Marjie.

"First step? This is fantastic," exclaimed an excited Gustav.

"We'll see," replied the spryte. "If anything, you have people talking about freedom. If they don't participate, it can't happen. When they own it, it works. Don't worry, these things take a verra long time."

And now you know,

you are,

and,

have been,

part of the journey,

all along.

The end...

Or just the beginning of your real journey...

Always life to your fullest purpose, it feeds yer soul!

78. Afterlude

The Magna Carta was the first attempt to put royalty at the same level as the people. Although, as history proves, King John would welch on his agreement in a short time. Thus, proving compromise does not work in these matters.

However, the ideas, the wording and the seeds of freedom had been sown among the masses and embraced by the Lords and Ladies of the land. So to speak, the middle and lower classes were beginning to form to the idea of owning their own future.

The language of the Magna Carta directly impacted the wording of the Declaration of Independence and structure of the United States Constitution. That is how powerful the concept of freedom is, to those who are not free and to those who seek rights to life, liberty, and the pursuit of happiness.

The Magna Carta was signed June 15, 1512. The Declaration of Independence was given birth on July 4, 1776. Two hundred, sixty-four years, nineteen days later.

These things take a verra long time. But they are worth it!

This vision is what drove the story. Enjoy!

The vision for

JOURNEY

ENABLE a better world of

Joy,

Trust,

Love,

and

Hope

Where we Forever trek to the **edge**, and explore **next**

The **power plans** of the few are the prison of the many

Open minds *and* hearts

Build **community**,

Family,

Dreams,

and

Aspiration

In place of being right, **foster** *curiosity*

Engaged Freedom is the end of tyranny,

Purpose is the PROMISE for humanity!

79. Meanings - Characters & Places:

Several readers have cornered me with numerous insatiably profound questions about the Journey trilogy. It seems their interests in answers are quite, shall we say, not to be assuaged with a lighthearted response. It appears, I have plucked a heartstring or two. And that my dear friend, is all a weaver of such tales can hope for.

However, the strength of the quest to find solutions to the vexations haunting these dear readers was so strong, I am honoring their desire to 'know' what is going on. They told me that the symbolism in these books is very robust. Symbolism that makes us laugh, cry, grieve and celebrate. But we don't know why.

Tell us! So here goes…

Questions posed include:
1. What does it all mean?
2. What do the key words, and some names of the characters mean?
3. What or who is with the dragon and what is the meaning of being swallowed by a dragon and then escaping?
4. How come the gods made Dessa?
5. What is the true role of Quillan as the guide?

1. What does it all mean?

It's really quite simple, we as humans should be able to live our existence with "Life, Liberty, and the pursuit of Happiness." As I pondered the deeper meanings of Journey, it became apparent that nature also deserves to enjoy the treasure of Life, Liberty, and the pursuit of Happiness. So, I turned it around and the quest of the story became: nature wants all of us, including themselves, to live this way. And the only way nature can enjoy it, is to ensure humans are living it. Predominantly because humans have such a dramatic impact on the earth and all its inhabitants.

2. What do the key words and names of the characters mean?

Key words and their meanings:

The **Promise**

The **Promise** is simply to live as a free person. Freedom is something all people desire. Now, freedom does not eliminate responsibility, nor the simple fact that we need to be respectful and nice to each other. Part III explores how much a threat personal freedom is to established power structures. The other side of the equation is just how vital freedom is to the true nature of things.

Purpose

Without purpose, you just have life and death and the normal way of things. However, if love is to conquer, then pieces need to fall in place and be embraced (although sometimes messy). And the future we are supposed to create, shall be. We all sometimes need help to accept, embrace and live to our higher purpose; the purpose to which we are called. This is sometimes challenging work, and others don't always understand us. As we grow, our purpose can morph. And the world needs to accept our change. Marjie (aka nature), accepted the changes in Dessa and Torrin and flexed her might to change her plan and ultimately drive towards success.

Gift

The '**Gift**'. The gift is immortality as long as you stay truly in love with your partner. Now, it's really not such a preposterous thought when you understand we know many people who have shared their gift of caring with us, and they still live on in history, lore and in our hearts (Mother Teresa, John F Kennedy, Marie Curie, Mahatma Gandhi, Abraham Lincoln, Walt Disney to name a few). This tale takes the longevity of true love, gives it power, a bit of fire and longevity. And, its adds a bit of spice to the relationship of Dessa and Torrin, because without them loving each other and doing the right thing, they become just like you and me. However, true love, lives on.

Key characters' names and their meanings:

Torrin

As his name is pronounced, it is what you get. Just say it out loud 'Torrin,' it sounds like 'torn.' As described above, Torrin needed to be torn from his unconscious self to begin the trek of being the person that nature intended him to be. And to be all we can be, we must accept, embrace and learn to love our destiny if we are to leave a mark in the world that is more than a mere skid mark. Torrin's destiny is pretty heavy, you may have figured that out by now.

To love who we really are is not just a sign of maturity, it is a sign of graciousness and acceptance (also known as wisdom). When we are true to ourselves, we can offer the world the gifts we have been given to share. And only then can we add value.

Dessa

The vexation with Dessa is her beginning as described in Part I, 'The gods determined the land needed a beautiful, enchanting princess...' Dessa is of royal lineage, and as a teen was quite full of herself. Dessa needed to 'walk through the fire (remember her husband Darius, teacher Tallon and rapist Haphethus) and hit bottom to become the true person the world needs. However, being in our own power can sometimes be better with a true partner, hence the name Dessa, (think 'destiny') and with Torrin, together they can be complete. Remember what happened to sweet Gwendolyn? She pushed against her and Torrin's true destiny, and Moher Nature would have none of it. Learning to accept our destiny is a very strong lesson in life.

Quillan

Portrayed as the 'guide' in Part I. Quillan keeps folks on track, doing what he needs to do, being strong, smart and clever when folks need that sort of help to endure and stay true to the path nature intended. At some point in our lives, our guides leave, and we are on our own. Quillan has assumed the ruling position in Tarmon's kingdom which frees Dessa to pursue her own path (or she would have had to stay as the only heir and rule the kingdom as Tarmon got old and finally returns to dust as we all do someday). When Normadia came to Tarmon's kingdom to reclaim Quillan, his guiding was now focused on the kingdom and people he is responsible for. His guiding days for Dessa and Torrin are over.

Normadia

I had to give Quillan a true love, and Normadia was the character I created for the big red guy. Normadia is that person who really is the salt of the earth and someone you can count on, no matter what. And those types of people are just the best, and they often don't get treated well by those in power. Yeah, Normadia could be you. And that was the point of her character. Quillan is a big softy down deep, and for he and Normadia to be together, just warmed my heart.

Other names are entertaining, chosen for the character they are meant to portray. One of my favorites is **Garwen**. It's old Gaelic and sports the meaning of 'spear-friend.' Just the name alone is hard to say, let alone imagine and for me, immediately conjured up bad sentiments. Beating him at his own game toward the end of Part II was fun.

Marjie

Marjie the spryte's name comes from a dear friend of the same name who is as full of life, love, curiosity and energy as you might expect from our dear friend Marjie in Journey. I was looking for a name who represented all that is, and one evening, around a campfire, our friend Marjie was commenting on something she was very adamant about. The thought stuck, the name stuck and Marjie the spryte was born.

Zach

I need to mention **Zach**. He is a real person, building a very successful sustainable aquaponics farm in upstate New York. And the personal code he required Gustav to commit to memory is tattooed on his arm. He lives by those words and is an amazing gentleman. I am forever in his debt to have met him and have him share his brilliant code. He is an inspiration.

3. What or who is the dragon and what is the meaning of being swallowed by a dragon and then escaping?

The dragon, Sebastian, is one of my favorite characters. As you read, evil Garwen's crew, on a scouting expedition, stumbled across Torrin as he was hiking the path near his parent's castle. They waylaid him and tossed him, rather unceremoniously, into the stream. Sebastain was on a suicide mission and was ready for the unconscious Torrin to be transported to a point, near the Journey Inn.

The dragon is a metaphor though, to growing up and emerging from being unconscious in the world and now consciously thinking about what is going on around you. So many folks just walk and live in what seems to be a timeless daze. For Torrin, the emergence from the dark septic environment of the dragon was his beginning of being a conscious person.

In the work I am blessed to do with leaders, the development goal is to create mindful consciousness. It is not an easy task; it takes a lot of soul searching to begin to enter mindful consciousness. In Part III of Journey, you will experience both Torrin and Dessa entering a mindfully conscious state of being.

What is mindfully conscious? We define it as being objective (fully rational) about what is truly going on and being openly curious (suspending judgement) to understand the environment. This means not getting hijacked by emotions or getting sucked in. You may know people who are kind and gentle, even when the world seems to be on fire. Generally, these are mindfully conscious people. I shall not labor the point here, there is a whole internet you can explore if you like.

If you finished Part III, you know of Sebastian's sacrifice, and in the end, when we can sacrifice for good, our souls rest easily.

4. How come the gods made Dessa?

Well, this gets a bit deep, so hang with me here. In my mind, god, or God makes all of us. And I feel God is nature. So, to take the terseness of religion out of all this, I use nature as God. In my humble opinion, humans have sort of messed up the purity of religion and the love force it offers. So, using the forces of nature was much more interesting, and more generally acceptable to a wider audience. Also, I feel that looking at all we have around us as nature is really more powerful than a human described god (or God).

However, just as in Greek mythology, when a god speaks, or performs something, most people perk up their ears. So, I had the 'Gods' make Dessa. It made her a bit special. But, when you look at the actual science of it, the gods made all of us (or, nature made all of us).

5. What is the true role of Quillan as the guide?

I had to create Quillan as a buffer to Torrin at Journey when Dessa arrived. Of course, you knew that Torrin and Dessa would get together, however, it had to have some drama, and not be too easy for either of them. Adding the brother, and his attributes was interesting, and of course, Quillan could not fall for Dessa, she was family. And I am a bit of a romantic, so the lovely lass Normadia had to end up with Quillan in such a way that was just wonderful for her (she is the salt of the earth kind of person and deserves life, love and laughter).

As far as being the guide, Quillan just kept things sane while hormones ran amok in the stream and the waterfall.

Location: It's pretty clear by the end that the story takes place in the northern part of Sweden. My ancestors from one side of the family emigrated to the US from Smålandsstenar, Sweden (pronounced smolen-stainer, stands for 'small land.'). Part of honoring my ancestral heritage are Bartoly and Rebecca. Steel goods manufacturing as well as other fine crafted items are a big part of the economy in Smålandsstenar.

There is lore in that area of the "Smålland Spirit," or "Gnosjöandan." This embodies the region's unique blend of resourcefulness, frugality, and community-driven entrepreneurship. Hence, the culture within the valley of the Journey Inn.

Hard living seemed the norm, long ago. My great-great grandparents are said to have raised eight children in a one-room cabin. I can understand the desire to emigrate to America. They settled in the northern center of Pennsylvania. My grandfather grew up and became George Eastman's office boy and then worked nights to gain his masters in pipe-fitting. His team, through purpose and dedication built one of the world's largest industrial complexes in upstate NY.

Double Walled Habitats: Both the hunting lodge in Part I and the Spirit Center in Part III have vestiges of ancient Viking, or Norse architecture. Double walled habitats were discovered at the northern tip of Newfoundland, Canada in a place called L'Anse aux Meadows, near St. Anthony. The buildings were designed to keep heat in, weather and

critters out. They are an amazing structures, built over 1000 years ago.
If you can go visit, it's worth the drive.

And of note, through gene mapping, there is pretty conclusive
evidence part of me is related to Leif Erikson. Uncle Leif, he helped settle
L'Anse aux Meadows in Newfoundland over 1,000 years ago.

The Viking people were not completely free, they had kings and
nobles, these were somewhat figureheads. In the middle of the social
structure, they had 'Freemen.' This group included farmers, warriors, and
skilled artisans. They elected officials who had most of the social power
in the towns and villages. So, they were edging toward a democracy.

We don't know much about the Vikings though. These hardy and
substantial folks did not write much about anything until about the 13th
century. Around that time, they delivered The Saga of Erik the Red. That
is an interesting read and harkens back to a complete range of different
views on the human condition, as well as relationships.

80. The Original Journey Inn

The original Journey Inn that was lost to fire near the end of Part II was an incredibly robust, log cabin style inn located in the middle of a huge deep forest way north of most any civilization. The place, at the time, was very remote and the people there had little to do with the modern world, until Garwen was conquered. Journey was nestled at the base of a large valley. The Inn was often visited by many a traveling stranger, peddler or a resident of the valley on some sort of adventure.

The place itself is monstrously old. Some of the stairways are worn to a smooth finish and the steps sport valleys in their centers where so many feet have trod.

Over time, rooms, additions, changes and variations happened. In some parts, Journey is two stories tall with a few special rooms upstairs (some not open to the public, especially the proprietor's bedroom). The antics and experiences in those rooms filled us with love, fright and some questions.

The horses and animals appreciated the attached stables, especially during the long, cold, snow filled winters. An enormous woodshed full of dried timber to heat the Inn during the angry winters that befall the area iwas attached to the stables. It is the requirement of all visitors to assist in the hard labor of firewood collection. Many storms kept everyone inside for days at a time.

During those days of captivity when the weather flexes its might, the great room is where much of the life of the Journey Inn takes place. This great room sports a huge stone hearth and fireplace (part of the lore of Journey in Part I) for heat and the constant drying of wet clothes. The great room is full of large tables and many folks sleep there in the winter on the tables to stay off the cold floor. Dances are held in the great room and it's a cozy place for many people to congregate. For your mind to form a picture, figure the room large enough to seat 50 people at the tables. There are many old artifacts on the walls of the great room and the ceiling is fairly high due to the pitched roof required to deal with the large amounts of snow.

To one side of the great room is a very innovative and large kitchen that produces enormous quantities of food and treats. Karina runs the place like a well-tuned clock (Normadia took over running the kitchen after Karina left with Harold). The kitchen is adorned with a fruit cellar, graviry fed running water, a large stove and baking hearth. You discovered much more about the magic of the kitchen and how it holds a dear many treasures and surprises for everyone in Part II.

The Journey Inn is the center of the world for all the people of the valley. They meet there, have their festivals there in its broad clearings and find refuge from life's storms amongst their friends who live there.

Just down the path is a modest creek and waterfall for summer enjoyment and washing up. Some folks have been known to have fun at the waterfall. The soft falling water, warm rocks and solitude of the place often inspire intimacy and romantic diversion.

Higher up in the valley are fields where various crops are grown, supplying the great kitchen of the Journey Inn. Most everyone helps with the farming process. It's a short growing season, and all efforts are expended to bring in a good crop.

When you need a place to go, Journey has always been there. Consider the inn as the heart and soul of the valley. The inn is the people's symbol of their culture, the desires and their freedom.

Alas, at the end of Part II, the original Journey Inn succumbed to a raging inferno. However, as you would expect from sturdy, hardworking people who love their land, the people of the valley and from Garwen's kingdom had already begun rebuilding before Torrin and Dessa left on the trail to head south and spread the idea that everyone should live as a free person.

As is with history when you study it, free people always endure.

It just takes a verra long time.

81. Acknowledgements

Peg, oh my gosh; what's to say? Your never-ending support and gentle prodding to continue was the force that kept the whole story moving forward.

Erin, your art speaks life and breathes joy into our vision.

Bruce, your purpose and the wisdom of your truth, wrapped up the end of the story nicely.

Marjie, thanks for your unbridled enthusiasm and your note that inspired your character! I cried when you first appeared during that trying time!

Cheryl, your thoughtful and consistent drive to free leaders from the cages that trap them has inspired me to take some different turns.

Herb, your ancestral research helped to form character linkages and family stories. Our folks are alive within the people you meet.

Barb, it's a great word, and delivers thoughtful twittering's.

Ross Quinn, you continue to haunt my reality with truth. A truth so powerful it lay across 900 pages of honesty!

Kim, your favorite curmudgeon, found his soul in more ways than he knew possible, thanks for the idea.

Grant, your idea of using a bear was a great one and many people who were hungry, thank you.

Zach, the blacksmith, your deed now lives forever!

Denise, how can I thank you for the professional touches you added, and it so sorely needed?

And to you, Dear Reader... without you, there is no Journey, and remember, you are verra much part of the story...

Tis time to trod forth to new adventures.

Thanks for coming along!

About the Author...

Catlan Samuels was born and raised in upstate New York. He currently lives near Lake Ontario in the Finger Lakes wine region, nestled on the edge of a forest where the steady flow of Mill Creek empties into the lake.

Having raised two very successful and happily married sons. Peg, a very supportive and adventurous partner, adds a personal, heartwarming layer to Catlan's narrative. Catlan and Peg's love for travel, combined with strong family bonds, plays a significant role both in their lives of exploration and the energetic tales woven through the Journey trilogy.

Catlan's life, just as the lives of his characters has been a bit of an adventurous journey! Traveling across all the countries of North America several times and wandering internationally contributes greatly to the inspiration behind his stories. Journey Part III of III, being a sequel to the previous parts, suggests there's a continuing, evolving narrative that ties all these adventures together.

The themes of love and adventure unfold throughout the trilogy. Hidden elements from all kinds of travel stand out the most in these stories. Hiking with mountain goats, walking on glaciers, traveling up to the northernmost tip of the island of Newfoundland to an archaeological site of a Norse settlement, all offer rich and varied experiences. These awe-inspiring locations provided a deep sense of adventure and wonder, perfectly fitting for a story about love and discovery.

When you climb into these stories, you climb into hours of adventure, romance and the myriad details of something bigger than life. It's a journey you will enjoy; and his Aunt Jeri said, 'It's the only book I ever read where I could taste the sweat and the dirt.'

email: CatlanSamuels@gmail.com

www.ingramcontent.com/pod-product-compliance
Lightning Source LLC
Chambersburg PA
CBHW071859020726
47502CB00003B/818